"What are we going to do?" he asked

"I don't know," she replied.

"We can't keep pretending we're just friends. I knew I was feeling more a long time ago, but I thought you wanted to be best buddies—nothing more. Is that what you want, Kit?"

It was what she had been asking herself for the past two weeks. She could no longer hold up the fiction that he was like her brother. That didn't explain the heightened awareness she felt in his presence, the way each reaction underlined the fact that he was male to her female. Protests to the contrary aside, she had been inexorably drawn to him since the moment she'd stepped off the plane. There was nothing casual about it.

Looking into those familiar blue eyes, her skin felt flushed and warm. "I want you to kiss and touch me. I want it all."

ABOUT THE AUTHOR

Julie Kistler calls herself "a hardheaded realist with the soul of a romantic." She started writing romances on the side to defuse a pressure-filled career as a lawyer. She ended up enjoying her sideline so much she turned it into her full-time profession!

Christmas in July introduces the unique Wentworth sisters, who will be featured in two more upcoming books.

Julie makes her home in St. Paul, Minnesota, with her husband.

Books by Julie Kistler

HARLEQUIN AMERICAN ROMANCE
158—THE VAN RENN LEGACY

Christmas in July
Julie Kistler

Harlequin Books

TORONTO • NEW YORK • LONDON
AMSTERDAM • PARIS • SYDNEY • HAMBURG
STOCKHOLM • ATHENS • TOKYO • MILAN

Dedicated to Scott,
who works so hard to make it easy for me.
Thanks for sharing my life since
Mrs. Aydt's class in tenth grade.

Published July 1987

First printing May 1987

ISBN 0-373-16207-3

Chapter One

Kit Wentworth was furious. Livid, to be exact. How dare he! After four years of complete silence, Riley Cooper had the unmitigated gall to fire off a letter like this. It was insufferable.

The funny thing was that his letter sounded too hot-tempered to be from the Riley she remembered. In the old days, when Kit was often flying into fits of fury, Riley acted as the calming influence. In all the years they'd known each other, she'd seen him completely lose his cool twice, and both times had involved defending Kit against an outsider. Riley had never directed his temper at her. Never. Maybe that was why the tone of this letter was so surprising. And so upsetting.

She blew pale blond bangs off her forehead and tried to calm down. Okay, when one considered the situation rationally, dispassionately, Riley had a right to be mad. She'd waltzed out of his life without so much as a good-bye, even though they'd been closer than brother and sister since kindergarten.

Waffling in her intention to be furious, she sank into the chair opposite her desk, tapping the letter against the chair's side with a rapid, regular beat. She frowned. What if he and his scurrilous letter were right? What if she had been behaving like a chicken and a coward? What if she would never be free to go forward in life because she had left her past as unfinished business?

Kit shook her head and sat up straighter. She was doing just fine. However badly she'd handled the situation four years ago, Riley still had no right to dash off poison pen letters at this late date. If he thought he was going to get away with it, well, he was sadly mistaken. Kit Wentworth could tell him a thing or two about how to treat long-lost friends.

Kit set her lips in a grim line. Standing abruptly, she leaned over her desk, and in the process, knocked a file full of notes on a new peanut butter account into the waste-basket. Ignoring the chaos, she pressed a button on her intercom decisively.

"You rang?" a low, throaty voice asked from behind her.

Kit jumped. Her heart leaped into her throat as she spun around. What was he doing here?

But it was only Didi, her secretary, no doubt growling in an attempt to practice her newest sultry and seductive routine. Didi was wearing a chartreuse minidress and plastic boots, with earrings that looked suspiciously like Tootsie Roll Pops. In other words, she was about as far from Riley as a person could get.

What an imagination. He was safely ensconced in St. Paul, she was safely hidden in an ad agency on the forty-fifth floor of a New York City skyscraper, and there was no immediate danger of the twain meeting.

"Why did you sneak up on me like that?" she asked, trying to steady herself. In Kit's mind, one's secretary should not appear out of nowhere like a ghoul. It was un-nerving.

Without waiting for an explanation, which from Didi wouldn't have helped much anyway, Kit announced firmly, "I've decided to go on a little trip."

Didi's eyes widened as she took a step back, clutching her steno pad to her chest. "What did you say? Are you implying what I think you're implying? Not the dreaded... vacation?"

"There's no need to get all melodramatic on me, Didi." She should have known her secretary would leap at the chance to say "I told you so." Didi had been trying to get Kit to take a vacation for at least three years.

"Come on, Kit, what gives? Isn't this kind of a drastic step for you?"

Kit frowned as she regarded her secretary over her desk. Maybe Didi was unknowingly right; maybe this was a drastic, impulsive step. Carelessly pushing aside a pile of pink phone messages, she made a place for the letter on her desk and smoothed it into a semblance of its former self. "I could use another opinion," she decided. "Read it and see what you think. Maybe I'm overreacting."

With curiosity lighting her face, Didi snaked forward to take the sheet of paper from her boss. She scanned the lines quickly.

"Who is this guy?" she asked after a moment. She fanned herself with the offending document. "I can feel steam rising off the paper!"

"Phoo." Snatching the note back, Kit considered it again. "He's a little out of sorts, that's all."

"You call 'acting like an irresponsible child' a little out of sorts?" Didi asked, retrieving the letter and quoting from it precisely. "What about 'purposely letting down everyone who loves you'?" Kit winced as the insults carried across the room, and Didi watched her slyly. "You never did say who he was. Old beau? Childhood sweet-heart?''

"No, of course not." Flustered, Kit bent to retrieve the peanut butter memos from the wastebasket. Her voice was muffled when she said, "He used to be my best friend."

"With friends like that, who needs enemies, hmm?"

"No, really, he was the best friend a person could ask for." The memos were left forgotten in her hand as Kit felt herself go all soft and misty, conjuring up Riley's face and smile. "Riley was the sweetest, nicest guy I knew."

Didi punctured the reverie sharply. "Yuck. I suppose he's thrifty, brave and cheerful, too. The kind of guy you take home to Mother." Peering out from under the jet-black China doll bangs she was sporting this week, Didi grimaced. "He sounds like a Boy Scout. I hate Boy Scouts."

"Riley?" Kit laughed. "No way. He's too dangerous for that. I mean, he'd risk anything as long as he had the angles figured first. And as for being the kind of man you take home to Mother, well, not to my mother. She never did like him." Kit lowered her voice dramatically, and her eyes sparkled with mischief. "Mother said you could see the devil in his eyes."

"Oooh," Didi said with a shiver, "that I like. He sounds like that guy who played Dracula on Broadway." Didi's eyes widened. "Don't tell me he's tall, dark and hand-some? Maybe with a scar on his cheek?"

"Heavens, no!"

"Oh, well," Didi sighed. "No one's perfect."

"Well," Kit continued, irritated for some unknown reason that Didi no longer thought Riley was perfect, "he is good-looking in his own way. Not because of his looks so much, but because of his attitude." She shook her head, remembering with annoyance the flocks of girls who'd always tried to get close to Riley, not in spite of but because of the careless indifference he gave them back. "Women seem to love that take-it-or-leave-it attitude."

Didi nodded emphatically. "I saw a survey about that in *Playgirl*. Take-it-or-leave-it is the number one hunk type right now. You know, like the guy on *Miami Vice*."

"Well, I suppose that's closer than Dracula."

Licking her lip, Didi watched Kit with avid curiosity. "The way you describe him, it sounds like you think of him as more than just a friend."

"Maybe I do." Raising her hand in front of her, Kit regarded the tips on her fingers thoughtfully. "We were blood brothers, you know."

Didi giggled. "Blood brothers with Count Dracula? This I've got to hear."

"He's nothing like Dracula! Anyway, there isn't much to tell. When we were in about second grade, we pricked our fingers, smeared the blood together and swore we'd be friends forever."

"Blood brothers... Isn't that cute? But I'll bet he was a real basket case when you walked out of his life forever," Didi said knowingly. "The article in *Playgirl* said that the take-it-or-leave-it guys are the very ones who fall apart the worst when they get dumped."

"I didn't dump him," Kit protested. "And besides, Riley knew that I would always be there for him if he needed me. No matter what happened."

Didi ignored Kit, tapping her fuchsia lips with a matching polished fingernail. Her eyes were narrowed with concentration as she became lost in yet another cloud of magazine-induced pop psychology. "You know, you never have peeped a word of what really did happen. If you and this guy Riley were such great pals, why'd you run out on him, anyway?"

"I didn't run out on him." Kit's answer held a certain amount of self-righteousness. She began to pace in front of her desk. "I left of my own free will because they were driving me crazy. Well, not Riley exactly, but at the end, he...oh, never mind." What had happened with Riley was not something she liked to discuss with herself, let alone other people. She put it out of her mind immediately, as she always did when the subject arose. "It was mostly my family. I've told you about my family. They're impossible! They don't like the way I look, or what I think, or even what I do for a living..." Kit lifted the end of the blond braid that had slid over her shoulder and gazed down at the short yellow skirt she was wearing with a matching cardigan and bright turquoise-blue top. The outfit was a perfect example—not crisp or professional, not stunning, not even very flattering. She sighed. "I'm not their type, and they make sure I know it. Could you live in a situation like that?"

Didi raised her hands in surrender. "If they're half as pushy, nutty, and, worst of all, as great-looking as you describe them, I wouldn't want to be within a hundred miles. Who needs it?"

"Not me," Kit returned vehemently.

"Okay, so we've figured out you don't particularly want to see our pal Riley or your family. But what's that got to do with taking a vacation? Wait, don't tell me," Didi volunteered with a gleam in her eye. "He's made you so mad you're running off to Club Med to forget about the whole thing, to find someone who is tall, dark and handsome, and has a scar."

"Ha!" Retreating behind her desk, Kit sat and hitched her chair closer to the edge. She began to studiously rearrange the paper clips in a Plexiglas cup. "No, I'm going back to give our pal Riley a piece of my mind."

"Back, as in St. Paul? You can't do that!"

"Why in the world not?"

"Because you hate everyone there," Didi replied patiently. "Didn't we just discuss this? And this Riley guy sounds like as much of a steamroller as the rest of them."

"He's the worst of the bunch." Kit's voice was gloomy. "It's just that his tactics are different. My mother and my sisters put a gun to your head until you do what they want. Riley makes you think it was your idea in the first place."

"And you're walking right back into his clutches. You're crazy, Kit." Didi crossed her arms over her chest. "Personally, I think you should write him off."

Kit shook her head stubbornly. "I could never do that."

"You already did. You've been gone for four years."

Kit had to admit Didi had a point. "But I always intended to go back and patch things up. Riley is a part of me. Even if we haven't seen each other for years, the ties are still there."

"Nice sentiment, but, Kit, come on, get serious here. Going back is just what he wants you to do. If you go," Didi warned, wagging one hot-pink-polished finger for emphasis, "he'll think he's won."

"He can think anything he likes for the time being." Tilting forward, Kit smacked her palm down on the desk, sending three phone messages and a proof version of a magazine ad flying. "He's not going to win. I'm going to make him admit I made the right decision when I left."

"I think it's a trap. He just wants to get you back into his clutches."

"What is it with you and his clutches?"

"You know, his clutches. Like Fu Manchu."

Kit's voice was tinged with humor when she said, "He doesn't even have a mustache."

"He doesn't need a mustache," Didi responded with an unnatural gleam in her eye. "He just needs a lair, so he can lure you there and do his evil deeds."

"You've been reading too much *Cosmopolitan* again," Kit scoffed. "Why in the world would he do any of that?"

Didi shook her head sagely. "Ego. You'll see. Mr. Take-it-or-leave-it got left, didn't he? He's obviously been dwelling on it for years. If you ask me, he wants revenge."

"That's silly."

Didi persisted. "Once you're there, he'll convince you of the error of your ways. Before you know it, you'll be on your knees, begging forgiveness for dumping him four years ago." She finished up triumphantly, "He'll have broken the spirit of the one woman who escaped him, and that will be his revenge."

"You're bananas, Didi." Twisting the long pale braid on her shoulder, Kit continued with determination. "I'm not a kid anymore, and I can stand up to anyone's challenges, including Riley. I can look Riley in the eye, I can live in the bosom of my family for a month, and I can survive it in good humor."

Didi's mouth dropped open. "Did you say a month? Now I know you've lost your marbles!"

"I have more than enough vacation time, and besides, once I'm there, I won't have a choice." Kit sighed, contemplating returning to the overwhelming Wentworth household. "If I'm there within a few weeks of Christmas in July and don't stick around for the big event itself, my mother will truly barbecue me."

"What are you talking about?"

"Christmas in July," Kit explained with yet another sigh. "It's my mother's personally created holiday. She decided that December was no time to ask relatives to come to Minnesota, so she forces everyone to celebrate on July 25, complete with a tree and tinsel and presents, the whole shebang. If there was any way at all, she'd commandeer snow and Santa Claus and reindeer on the roof." Kit raised her hands palms up, as if in surrender to the General Patton of a mother who was still a thousand miles away. "What can I do? I can't avoid the biggest, most elaborate family gathering in twelve states if I'm anywhere near it."

"I suppose," Didi said with evident doubt. "You know," she ventured hopefully, "it's not too late to change your mind about Club Med."

"Not a chance. As a matter of fact, I think I'm going to enjoy this. I have no doubt I'll make it through unscathed. I can't, however, say the same for Riley. After I strangle him," she said sweetly, "he's going to apologize to me for a few weeks. If he's very, very nice, I might even forgive him." She shifted her weight to the back of her chair and gazed into the distance with a small, smug smile. "Riley Cooper has got a lot of explaining to do."

RILEY'S FIRST THOUGHT was that she hadn't changed at all. If he didn't know better, he'd have sworn the past four years had never existed.

He watched her clear the jetway exit, even though her path to him was blocked by a crowd of other departing passengers. Scanning her face hungrily, he waited for the moment when she would see him and wondered what her reaction would be. Would she take one look at him and discern the feelings he had hidden so carefully all those years? Would the distance of four years help her see right through him, right to the reasons he wanted her back here?

He smiled wryly, realizing that his well-hidden romantic side had surfaced again. It had a habit of doing that around Kit.

And what was he doing worrying about such nonsense when he had won? She was back, wasn't she? He smiled triumphantly, crossing his arms over his chest and leaning back on the railing that marked the edge of Gate 41. No matter what the consequences, he'd gotten her back here, and he deserved to savor that victory for a few minutes.

Kit's first thought was that he didn't look at all the way she remembered. Oh, she remembered those mischievous blue eyes all right and the way they crinkled at the outside corners, and even those straight, dark brows that contrasted with his light brown hair. She could see how the features she had once known had gotten a bit more sculptured in the past four years, and his body, too, seemed leaner and harder. But those weren't what accounted for the change.

As she and a host of other people cooled their heels behind a man on crutches at the front of the line, she fidgeted impatiently, keeping her eyes on Riley. Why did he seem so changed? Maybe she wanted him to look different, so that he wouldn't remind her of the mistakes she had made before she'd left this town. Or maybe it was a simple matter of maturity. In the old days, he'd exuded equal parts mischief and arrogance, with both parts running constantly at high speed. Now it seemed as though his body and mind had caught up with each other and had liked what they'd found—he seemed serene.

It was not a word she would ever have imagined occupying the same space as Riley.

He was leaning casually against the back railing of the airport waiting area, wearing a loose T-shirt and faded blue jeans that had long ago forgotten any shape but his. Informal, relaxed attire, holding a man who looked as if nothing short of an alien invasion would faze him.

No matter what wonderful arguments she'd cooked up to toss in his face, she began to panic, seeing him like this. She suddenly remembered Didi's remarks about Dracula and Fu Manchu, and the whole idea was so ludicrous she had to laugh.

"Hi!" she said, and waved, even though she had barely moved off the jetway. The excruciatingly slow person was still holding up the departure process.

He waved back, feeling silly that he was so damned glad to see her. God, but she looked beautiful. Thank goodness she hadn't messed with her appearance, dying or cutting the pale silver-blond hair he remembered so well, or resorting to makeup to hide her delicate, pretty features. He'd always teased her about looking like the pastel illustration of a princess in a fairy tale. But he knew better than to be taken in by that misleading appearance. Nothing in her face suggested the bullheadedness that was a tradition on her mother's side of the family, passed down from generation to generation like the china tea cups in Mrs. Wentworth's living room.

It was the same bullheadedness that had sent her flying from St. Paul and away from him without a backward glance four years ago. Those four slow years had definitely taken their toll on his psyche, leaving him wondering what he could have done differently that last night before she'd left, or how he could have salvaged anything of the mess they'd made.

He knew himself well enough to know that he was not made for waiting games. Even after four years he still woke up in the morning thinking of tricks to make her laugh, he still blinked when he saw sunlight shine on hair that was her shade, and he still felt the frustration of conversations where every comment he made had to be explained. It wasn't their fault if these new women didn't understand in-jokes or witty references. But why did they give him blank stares when he suggested taking the day off to see the new *Star Trek* movie, or braving twenty below and huge crowds to watch a life-sized Ice Palace get knocked down? Kit would have understood, Kit would have made the outings fun, and Kit was nowhere in sight.

Could he help it if he'd finally gotten fed up with waiting and taken matters into his own hands? So he'd written her that carefully calculated letter, full of snotty comments he had concocted just to irritate her. It was the only tactic he could think of that was guaranteed to get her home. Riley smiled in secret amusement as he imagined the state of her temper when she'd read the letter. Now that she was here he'd better remember to protect his face if he didn't want to celebrate her first day home with a bloody nose. Kit was capable of that and a whole lot worse.

Kit caught the smile, and her own lips curved into an irrepressible answer. He looked wonderful. Seeing him after all this time was about the best thing she could imagine.

She had intended to be angry with him and take him severely to task, really she had. But, heavens, who could be angry at a time like this? Before she could stop herself, she had squeezed past the people in her way and plowed up to him until she was standing right in front of him and looking up into eyes that were bluer than seemed humanly possible. He made it so easy to want to forget the past, to go back in time, back to when they were the best of pals, before she had let misunderstandings and hurt feelings separate them.

Impulsively she held out her arms and asked, "How about a welcome-home hug for an old friend?"

She was enveloped in a hard, heady embrace that took her breath away. He said, "Gorgeous, you are a sight for sore eyes." And then he picked her up off the ground as if it were the most natural thing in the world and twirled her around above his head.

"Put me down, you lunatic," she managed. "We're causing a scene." When she asked for a hug, she hadn't imagined anything on this scale. She'd wanted to share a bit of comfortable, old home friendship. But this, this was like taking part in a Pepsi commercial.

At her meager protest, he tightened his arms around her waist and threatened to toss her higher in the air, until she was forced to hug him back. His arms felt warm and strong and terrific around her, she had to admit. She felt terrific inside them. All of her nerve endings zinged into life, and she felt like laughing and crying and telling him how much he meant to her. All of this from one welcome-home hug? How could she ever have left? She looked down into his sparkling eyes and flashing grin, and she laughed out loud at his impudence and silliness.

Finally, as she knew he would eventually, he gave in, loosened his hold and let her slide back down to the ground. But the process of disentangling herself, of sliding down his hard, muscled body, caused Kit to feel a little too warm and perhaps even light-headed. She looked up, startled, and pulled away the fingers she had lightly balanced against his chest.

Touching Riley didn't feel at all the way it used to.

Her stomach began to flutter, and she was suddenly jumpy and on edge under the warmth of his gaze. She took a deep breath and forced the odd sensations to go away as quickly as they had arrived, and she told herself it was all part of her general homecoming anxiety. Any other explanation would have been too weird for words.

A passerby interrupted that thought by jostling her, bringing Kit the realization that they were standing in the middle of a bustling airport and people were going to knock them down soon if they didn't move. Riley seemed to catch himself, as if he'd had the same thought, and he guided her over to one side of the concourse and under a sign extolling the virtues of Las Vegas.

Nervously she managed a smile, and Riley put his hands to her shoulders, holding her at arm's length.

"Let me look at you," he said simply.

She stood, rather obediently she thought, while he took in her appearance. Hoping to score a few points for displaying a calm, collected demeanor, Kit had worn the protective coloring of her work wardrobe. The concept of a work wardrobe might mean blue suits and blouses with bows to other people, but not to her. She generally showed up in comfortable, slouchy clothes in primary colors, often a bit disheveled, with wispy bangs slipping over her forehead. But no one cared at the office, where she was considered a successful, creative whirlwind.

She felt proud and strong at work, and she wanted to bring part of that with her when she came home, to make a clear statement about how much she had accomplished since anyone in St. Paul had last seen her. To that end, she'd chosen a striped sweater and cotton pants in a vivid shade of green. In the way she'd do for work, she'd French-braided her hair and put on big, colorful earrings and a bright yellow Swatch watch, the kind all of the kids were wearing these days. It might not be dressing for success, but it suited her just fine.

"I can't believe how little you've changed." He shook his head and grinned at her.

"I can't say the same for you. It's like night and day."

Again she noticed the subtle but pervasive changes. Even his trademark shaggy hair had been updated. Now it was layered and pushed away from his face on the sides, edging past his collar in the back. Without thinking, she reached up a hand to smooth a stray piece at his temple, and her fingers stayed there for a beat longer than necessary.

She wondered why it annoyed her that he had grown so damnably good-looking while she was away. Retracting her hand quickly, she covered her nervousness by commenting, "You never had trendy haircuts before. Are you dating a hairdresser or something? You always did have a fondness for women who worked with their hands."

He only smiled, ignoring her snide remark. But when a burly woman toting a huge suitcase crashed into him from behind and then told him in no uncertain terms to "move it or lose it," he winced and took Kit's arm, pulling her and her carry-on bag rapidly down the concourse.

She'd been laughing so hard at the expression on his face when he'd been upbraided by the woman that she almost didn't notice how fast he was dragging her along. They had already cleared the baggage pickup area when he paused long enough for Kit to take a breath.

"Is this a race?" she asked, digging in her heels. "And you didn't answer my question, either."

"What question?"

"The hairdresser. You're not really dating a hairdresser, are you?"

"Of course not." The look he gave her was deadpan, with just a hint of sarcasm around the edges. "Satisfied?" He held open the door to the outside of the airport and waited as she passed through. Would she care, he wondered, that he was currently unattached? "Actually,

I'm not dating a hairdresser or anyone else at the moment.''

"You're kidding. That's got to be a first."

Relief and curiosity washed over her face, and Riley was gratified. So it did matter to her. "After you left," he said, turning full face to her and using a tone that fairly sang with sincerity, "I discovered that no other woman compared."

"Right. And I'm the tooth fairy." Regardless of his pretty speeches, she wasn't going to just stand there and melt, even if his blue eyes did glow at her and make her feel as if she were the most important person in the universe. He pretended to be hurt by her mocking remark, and she shook her head in amusement. "You can really lay it on with a trowel, can't you? Yet I somehow find myself believing you, anyway. And as much as I want to, as much as you deserve it after all the nasty things you said in your letter, I can't stay mad at you. Darn you, anyway. You always did know how to get around me."

He grinned. "I know."

"You rat fink!" She laughed then and landed a mock blow on his arm. "Mr. Modesty, aren't you?"

He shrugged easily. "Why should I deny it? I must be able to get to you. I mean, your family has been barraging you with 'come home' messages for four years. I write one tiny note and—" he snapped his fingers "—you're here."

"Oooh, you are a fink." Pretending to be outraged, Kit narrowed her eyes and made a fist. "You know why I really came home, don't you?"

With a wide smile, Riley put up his hands as if to ward off blows to the face.

"And the only reason I haven't smacked you yet, as you so richly deserve, is because I haven't had a chance." Hands on hips, she glared at him. "You hustled me through the airport as if it were on fire. Good heavens, I just realized we zipped right past the baggage area, and you didn't even stop to ask me if I'd checked any luggage!''

"I knew you didn't," he returned calmly. "You're not the type. Besides, you'd have screamed bloody murder if you needed to stop."

"You can be so smug, Riley Cooper. It's downright disgusting." She paused, taking a breath while she decided how best to stop his master-of-the-universe act before it went too far. "Okay, look. You may have gotten lucky and guessed right about my luggage preferences, and I may have let you get away with provoking me into coming home and even with racing me through the airport at a record pace, but this is where I draw the line. You're on notice, okay?" She fixed him with a serious gaze. "The new Kit is her own woman and will not be pushed or manipulated into anything, got it?"

He feigned innocence. "I'm sorry, but I have no idea what you're talking about."

"I know you well enough to know that dragging me through the airport is only the beginning. If you're thinking you can con me into coming home for good and joining Mother's company, forget it right now. It's out of the question."

"I don't recall mentioning the subject," he said evenly.

"You didn't need to. I've been getting cards, letters and phone calls about it from every member of my family ever since I left." It was her family's much-repeated belief that Kit's destiny was to come home and go to work at Grand Affairs, her mother's party-planning company, with her sisters. "If you're sharing their pipe dream, you can kiss it goodbye."

He spread his hands out in front of him guilelessly, even though he had no intention of giving in on this issue. Once he considered a question and made up his mind, he rarely changed it. In his opinion, it was for Kit's own good that she stay home and become a full-fledged member of her family. Given time, he had no doubt she would see things his way. "You don't see me doing any pushing, do you?" he asked, neatly avoiding the issue once again.

"I'm not fooled, Cooper, so don't get too complacent." She raised her chin and found his eyes defiantly. "No doubt you've got some scheme up your sleeve to show me the error of my ways. I can see the wheels clicking from here."

"Come on, Kit," he said gently, changing tactics. He didn't want to discuss the wheels that were indeed clicking. "There's a perfectly good reason why I wanted you to come back, and it has nothing underhanded about it whatsoever."

"What's that?" she asked suspiciously.

His eyes were warm and caressing. "I missed you."

"Oh." No witty rejoinder or snappy comeback occurred to her. Riley had missed her. She was more touched than she wanted to be.

"How about you? Miss me?" He wished he could feel as casual about the question as his voice sounded.

"Maybe." She regarded him thoughtfully, feeling vulnerable and unsure. Yes, she had missed him. And she considered now whether it might be possible to resurrect their crazy old friendship. She threw out a test balloon. "Maybe I missed having piggy banks appear out of the blue."

"Oh, that's right." He said the words slowly, as if he were surprised. "I forgot about the piggy bank."

"Sure you did." In a tone that suggested she was not at all fooled by his innocent attitude, Kit continued, "And you forgot about the pennies in your mailbox, and the time I took all the labels off your canned goods, and the alarm clock you left in my high school locker, and all the rest, right?" She laughed, amazed at the depth of their silliness in the old days. The piggy bank tricks had occurred in the later stages of their battle of wits.

When they were young, they were content to see who could race around the lake and get back to the Wentworth house without knocking down any pedestrians or running into any trees. And then they would fuss for hours about who'd really won.

As they had grown a bit older, they had turned into pranksters extraordinaire, plotting tricks against each other that sometimes took years to pull off. After Riley had entered her name and a hideous picture in the college Homecoming Queen contest, she had retaliated by filling his apartment mailbox with hundreds of pennies, ready to pour out when he opened the little door. From that point on they had passed a glass piggy bank full of pennies back and forth for years without ever acknowledging what was going on. Kit could never be quite sure when or where that blasted pig would pop up.

She wondered now if Riley still had it somewhere. Maybe his letter had been meant to lure her back to St. Paul at any cost, so he could sneak the penny-filled piggy bank into her possession?

Her eyes narrowed with suspicion, and she glanced over at him. From all outward evidence he was innocence personified.

"I don't know if I'm going to be able to take this for a whole month," she muttered, mostly to herself.

Riley's ears pricked up. A month, huh? That might actually give him time to worm his way under her skin, to make her see that they needed each other as best friends. And maybe, if he were lucky, he could try for something more than the brother-sister relationship they'd had in the past.

For a man who prided himself on meticulously planning his projects down to the last detail, he had let this one stay woefully up in the air. Oh, he loved taking risks, but only when he could analyze and understand every angle first. He wasn't keen on jumping off cliffs, but that was exactly what faced him in the next four weeks. There was the potential to fulfill his wildest dreams, to have Kit trembling in his arms with love and desire. There was also the potential to see the whole thing blow up in his face, to watch helplessly as Kit slapped his face and told him she never wanted to hear his name spoken in her hemisphere. So cliff-jumping it would be. He only hoped he got an inspiration soon on how to accomplish this.

"What's this?" she asked dryly as they stopped next to a low-slung shiny black car. "A new toy? I didn't think you were the type for conspicuous consumption. And don't tell me a junior engineer's salary allows for trinkets like this?"

"It's not a trinket. It's a Ferrari," he pointed out politely, and unlocked the passenger door.

"Okay, okay, but where did you get the car?"

"From the Ferrari dealer."

Losing her patience, Kit glared at him pointedly. "Give me a break. Did you uncover oil under the Cooper house or what?"

"Not the last time I checked." He had been silly, teasing her because it reminded him of the old days. But with a sudden flash he saw that a little mystery about his lifestyle might help him out. There wasn't much excitement there; he had a few scattered investments including own-ing a piece of Grand Affairs, her mother's catering com-pany. And then there was his one big business concern—he happened to own the chocolate chip cookie concession for most of St. Paul. No, he had no claims to being a rock star or a tightrope walker, or even a Mafia hit man. He was in plain old business, but Kit had no way of knowing that. He had already planned to keep his connection with Grand Affairs under wraps. It was a minor investment, anyway, and if Kit found out about it, she was guaranteed to blow a gasket. She detested the place and any reference to its existence. So what if, instead of predictable old Riley, he became an enigma? He smiled to himself as he tossed her tote bag in the Ferrari's trunk. Not knowing where he got his money was going to drive her crazy. This could be fun.

"So?" Kit stood with her door open, unwilling to get in until she had an answer that made sense. "Did you, A, steal this snazzy little thing, B, win on *The Price Is Right*, or C, find engineering profitable beyond your wildest dreams?"

"D, none of the above. I don't believe in stealing, I've never even seen *The Price Is Right*, and I am no longer working as an engineer. I quit."

"And?"

"And I entered a new profession, which made play-things like this snazzy little car possible."

"And?" she said again. "What new profession is that?"

He took the edge of her door and ushered her in with amusement. He even had the gall to wink at her as he closed the door. "What fun is it if I tell you?"

"What fun is it if you keep it a secret?"

A mischievous light began to dance in his eyes. "I have an idea. I'll give you one month to figure it out. But if you can't figure it out before July 25, you have to take me to a restaurant of my choice and buy me anything my little heart desires.''

"And vice versa if I do figure it out?"

"Exactly."

"With my mother's Christmas in July brouhaha as the end date, right?"

"Right."

She considered a moment. "Okay, you're on. This ought to be a cinch."

Chapter Two

Her head was spinning with possible occupations as she settled into the car and pointedly fastened her seat belt. Riley drove like a demon even on a bicycle, and this little monster of a car would no doubt add to the problem.

As they left the airport behind them, Riley did indeed drive fast, with breakneck skill and fierce control. Kit was trying to concentrate on figuring out his mysterious job, but she gave up for the time being and held on tight to her armrest. The subject of Riley's occupation seemed minor compared to her personal safety.

The road to St. Paul was cut out through a hill, and planes and angles of sharp rock flashed by before she had a chance to really take them in, or bring their image back from her memory. She caught snatches of green trees and blue water whizzing past her as they headed toward the city.

She wished he would slow down, and her reasons encompassed more than his reckless driving. This was all happening too quickly. She hadn't really had time to get used to resuming her friendship with Riley yet, and it now occurred to her that she would be facing her family en masse in a matter of minutes.

When she had decided to come home, she had conveniently shut the door marked "family" in her mind, thinking no farther ahead than putting Riley in his place. That hadn't worked too well, had it? Aside from Riley, there had been definite problems living in the Wentworth household once upon a time. What would it be like now?

The "fabulous Wentworths," a nickname started by a smitten high school boy, were a high-handed, imperious bunch at their best. Kit smiled ruefully at the thought of keeping her head when once more planted in their midst. In the old days, she would have run out the door if they had put on too much pressure. And headed straight for Riley. She hoped that she had acquired enough polish and fortitude in her years of dealing with irate clients to be able to tolerate her family a little better now.

But it wouldn't be easy. She didn't look like the others, with their curvy bodies and flaming red hair, and she'd never really felt that she fit in among them. She had defied her mother's expectations and set off to be her own person. Small wonder that, coming back now, she was feeling more than a hint of trepidation.

As if he'd read the path of her thoughts, Riley asked, "Aren't you going to ask me how your mother and the girls are?"

"No," she said curtly, slouching in her smooth leather seat. "You'll just tell me they're all gorgeous and wonderful, and I'll get crankier than I already am."

"You're going to have to see them in a little while anyway," he offered softly.

"I know," she said with a sigh. She lapsed into silence for a few seconds, imagining the reception committee at home. It was easy to want to avoid the whole thing. "I don't suppose we could bypass my mother's house and go to yours instead?"

"You want to stay with me?" Riley's dark eyebrows shot up in the center as he turned toward her. His hands began to grip the wheel more tightly than he intended. She couldn't be serious. He shook his head and refocused on the road. What a nightmare that would be—her sleeping on his couch, or worse yet, in his bed, while he took up permanent residence under a cold shower, trying not to think up new versions of the erotic scenarios that had plagued him since long before she'd left. Under the same roof, it would only be a matter of minutes before Kit discovered how deep his feelings went. "No way." He shook his head briskly. "You staying with me is not a good idea at all."

Kit looked up, surprised at his sharp tone. What in the world had gotten into him? "I was only kidding. You know how my mother would react if I was in town and not staying at home. People have died for less." She watched him for a moment, still confused. Why, Riley had acted as if she was a hot potato or something. What was his problem?

When Riley skillfully passed three trucks and then zipped back into the right lane in time to take an off-ramp, her thoughts took a different turn.

"Don't tell me," she groaned. "Your new job is filming car chases for cop shows."

Glad she had abandoned the idea of torturing him in his own apartment, he responded cheerfully, "Nope. Not even close."

It was obvious that he was enjoying the guessing game about his job. He was probably just doing it to be aggravating. In which case, the only solution was to dispose of the game as quickly as possible. "Let's see. You don't work during the day, because you came to pick me up at three-thirty in the afternoon. Unless you work a very early shift, or took a day off. Either of those?"

"Nope."

"Call in sick?"

"Nope. There's no one to call in sick to."

"Ahhh." That was intriguing. "I would say you're unemployed, but what do we make of the Ferrari?"

"Exactly."

"And you're certainly not disabled." One look at his healthy body made that clear. "So that would seem to indicate that you are your own boss. Right so far?"

"Yes," he said, in exactly the voice the mystery guests always used after they "signed in please."

Kit laughed and leaned back against the headrest. "Whoever thought I'd come a thousand miles to play *What's My Line* with a lunatic?"

There was no answer from Riley as he speculated how long it would take her to get close to the real thing. Maybe a million years? He smiled with satisfaction. Not even Kit would guess that he was the Grandma Cooper behind the Twin Cities' chocolate chip cookie stores of the same name.

Although, once she knew the answer, she might see that it fit the pattern of his life. It was a risk, a departure from the norm, and everyone agreed that he had been crazy to try it. That was, of course, why it had appealed to him.

They'd all thought he was crazy when he'd taken his first engineering courses, too. Riley Cooper, an engineer? The same Riley Cooper who had gotten mediocre grades in the classes he'd sat still for and nonchalantly flunked the ones he'd skipped entirely? He was as surprised as anyone when it had suited the analytical part of his brain, and he had actually liked the elaborate problem-solving his classes had undertaken. He'd done it because he'd known he was smart, even if no one else had. And he'd known he could do it. That it had shocked the pants off everyone he knew hadn't hurt. Except for Kit, of course. Kit had always believed in him. When he had told her he was going to choose the toughest major at the U of M, she had said, "Great," without skipping a beat.

The problem was that he had found he hadn't really wanted to buy into the nine-to-five existence his fellow graduates inhabited. He was restless and wound up. All he could think of was launching something different and fun, something of his own.

It was amazing that it had turned out to be cookies. He didn't even cook. But he had been looking for a project, something to fuel his fire after the mediocre successes of the recording studio in his basement, the campus copy shop and a combination bookstore and coffee house hadn't quite made it. He'd eaten an inferior cookie from a popular bakery and instinctively known he could do better. From there it was a matter of trying every recipe he could get his hands on, mixing a little of this and a little of that—just like high school chemistry—and not taking no for an answer until Grandma Cooper's Cookies was off the ground. He was not given to false modesty, and he knew that the success of his operation was due to his own tenacity and the taking of a few well-planned risks, which suited him to a T.

He slowed the car enough to downshift and whip neatly around the corner onto her mother's street, still feeling smug over the game he had begun with Kit. Never in a million years would she guess the truth.

Their pace had become more leisurely in this residential area, and Kit began to catch signs of familiar sights outside her window. It was a century removed from the concrete world she called home in New York.

Even inside the car she could hear birds chirping happily in the summer air. She saw elms standing tall next to various sorts of trees that shaded the street, and a squirrel scampering down the sidewalk and up the trunk of a large oak near the roadside.

She hadn't realized she would feel such emotion for a mere place. And she had forgotten how lovely this neighborhood was, with its pretty clapboard houses and immaculate lawns and gardens edging the park. The lake that formed the park's centerpiece was visible over a grassy knoll, mixing the peaceful blues and greens that typified Minnesota. Everything here spoke of calm and tranquillity.

But as they pulled into her mother's driveway, Kit felt anything but calm. She forced her gaze up to the front of the rambling white house, with its eccentric turret and enough gingerbread to perhaps classify as Victorian. Her room had been on the second floor, in the front, with a double window that brushed up against the branches of the silver maple in the front yard. She and Jo had shared that room, and on occasion had used the maple to climb out without Mother's knowledge. Now, in a stiff breeze, the tree's leaves fluttered silver and green, dappling the front of the house.

It was the same old place, with its crumbling foundation and overgrown lilac bushes. She and Riley had always joked about this house and its perpetual state of benign disrepair. But now it looked, well, beautiful. Even the missing bricks in the foundation gave it character.

Kit stared at the house as Riley switched off the car's engine. "Well?" He turned to her, running a hand through his light brown hair. His hair looked as if he usually styled it that way, by dashing his hands through it, and forcing it away from his face. Lucky for him, the style held its own even for a man with impatient hands. "Ready to go in?"

She sighed. "I guess so."

Leaning over, he squeezed her hand. "Don't worry. You'll be fine."

"Yes," she said with resolution, "I'll be fine."

Riley grabbed her canvas tote bag out of the trunk and led the way quickly up to the front porch. As he moved to the door and raised his hand to clang the brass knocker, Kit felt a flurry of anxiety. She wished that Riley would take her hand again, but she didn't want to ask. There wasn't time to worry about it; the door was opening.

Jo, second youngest of the Wentworth sisters, and the family's peacemaker, looked at the two of them and tipped her head, spilling red-gold waves to one side. "Are you going to stand on the porch all day?" she inquired pleasantly.

Caught in the doorway, Kit reached out to hug her sister, and Jo reciprocated easily. Feeling that a gap had been bridged, Kit relaxed somewhat. One member of the family had been met without incident. That only left four to go.

Kit drew back to look at her younger, smaller sister. The pretty, gentle face was the one she remembered, with a frank, wide smile, and a small nose liberally sprinkled with freckles. Jo was wearing a lace-edged full cotton skirt and peasant blouse in a tiny floral print. With no jewelry and bare feet, she was fresh and natural and very real.

"You look wonderful!" Kit reached out to touch her sister's cheek. It was probably because she had lumped all four of her sisters together in her mind, but Jo's hair was not the brazen red she remembered. Instead, it was a soft strawberry blond, with strands of copper and ginger mingled throughout the shoulder-length waves. Strands of her bangs tipped over her forehead and into her eyes. Not exactly the voluptuous vamp Kit remembered, but instead a petite woman whose honest hazel eyes were too large for her face.

"You're so skinny!" Kit exclaimed. "I don't know why, but I thought you were..." Her hands formed a curvy shape in the air.

Jo backed into the house, laughing out loud. "Me? Never! I'm the shrimp, remember? You're confusing me with Alex. She's always been the curvy one, like Mother. I guess you've been away too long, Kit."

"You're probably right." Kit shook her head and held the door open carefully as Riley came through with her bag.

He placed it on the hardwood floor next to a bentwood rocker. "Hiya, sweetheart," he announced casually, crossing back to Jo. He bent to drop a kiss on her cheek and give her a quick hug.

Surprised, Kit watched as Riley turned the hug into a mock headlock. He messed up Jo's hair playfully with one hand and pinched her cheek with the other.

Isn't that just too cute for words? Kit tried vainly not to be so mean-spirited. In her book, anything that cutesy ought to be terminal, or at the very least illegal. It wasn't that she thought there was anything syrupy or romantic going on between her sister and Riley. She didn't. She just thought they could behave themselves more like adults if they tried. Of course, she herself had not been acting like an adult since she'd gotten off the plane and run headlong into Riley's arms, but that had been a momentary aberration. This babycakes stuff between Jo and Riley looked like standard operating procedure. How utterly appalling.

Kit cleared her throat, to pull the others' attention away from their little game. "Where is everyone?" she asked politely. Tiny Jo was hardly the overwhelming reception committee she'd anticipated.

"Oh, they're around," Jo said brightly. "They'll be out in a sec."

On her way into the living room, Jo edged her way carefully around the tiny tables holding their mother's collection of knickknacks. Motioning that Kit should follow, she sat on a dark velvet sofa, the same one that had graced the living room since well before Kit's time.

Patting the cushion next to her, Jo asked, "Why don't you sit and talk with me for a few minutes? We've got a lot of catching up to do."

"Yes, we do." *Here it comes,* Kit thought, *the deluge.*

"Look," Riley interrupted from behind them. "I'll leave you two to each other, okay?"

Jo nodded and rose to escort him to the door, linking her arm through his. "Thanks for picking up the prodigal, Riley. We appreciate it."

"No biggie."

Kit wasn't sure she appreciated being "no biggie." And she'd assumed that, out of loyalty, he'd stick around while the reunions were in progress. How long had he stayed? Maybe five minutes?

Riley and Jo whispered conspiratorially at the door for a few seconds, and then Riley slipped out. Watching them, Kit felt the new sensation of knowing that Riley was sharing secrets with someone else.

After waving to Riley from the door, Jo came back to the sofa. She sat down and tucked her bare legs underneath her full skirt. Her wide eyes regarded Kit steadily, and she seemed to be waiting for Kit to make the first move. Before Kit could think of anything pithy to say, a large and complicated clatter resounded from the area of the kitchen, followed by a ringing exclamation that sounded suspiciously like, "Bloody hell." They both knew it was their mother and that she must have dropped something pretty awful to resort to swearing. They exchanged amused glances, and then both began to laugh.

"Oh, Kit," Jo said, "I'm so glad you're back. This is going to be wonderful, with all of us together again. The five Wentworth sisters on the same team. Isn't it terrific?"

Kit thought perhaps her sister was overstating the case, but she didn't want to put a damper on things. "Sure, Jo. Terrific."

"I want to hear everything you've done since I saw you last. Absolutely everything."

"I don't know," Kit responded self-consciously. "Most of it's pretty dull."

"Oh, come on!"

"No, really. I mean, I've been working really hard at the agency, and I like it a lot, but other than that . . . I haven't had any great adventures. I'm sure there's been much more excitement here."

"That's for sure." Jo settled back on the sofa, hugging her knees. Her eyes danced as she related an anecdote or two about the flamboyant family and their activities. It was easy to see that Jo hadn't lost her enthusiasm for life, or her sense of humor.

If Kit had been there when oldest sister Alexandra had had three dates backed up at the front door, expecting someone else to let them down gently, she would have been furious. Jo had found it amusing.

If Kit had been there at the governor's inauguration when their mother had bodily removed youngest sister Eliza from the premises for wearing a skimpy dress, she would have died of embarrassment. Jo had thought it was hilarious.

Kit had never felt less a member of the family than at that moment. It was all so foreign to her now. She rose from the sofa and moved quietly to the fireplace, to the collection of family pictures that graced the mantle. Fingering a framed photo of the five girls, taken when they were young enough to wear matching full-skirted party dresses, Kit frowned and bit her lip absently. Four adorable redheads and one sulky blonde. Odd that she didn't remember them ever having matching dresses.

Jo's soft voice brought her attention away from the mantle. "What is it, Kit?"

When Kit didn't answer, Jo stood up and came to her sister's side. Even though she was the smaller sister by several inches, she draped her arm around Kit's shoulders. "Look," she said sympathetically. "It's bound to be a little strange at first. But don't worry. In a few months, it'll be like you never left."

Kit was so touched by Jo's sweet gesture that she almost didn't catch the words. Puzzled, she turned to Jo. "What do you mean? I won't be here in a few months."

"What? You're not serious!"

"Of course I'm serious. How long did you think I was staying?"

"Well, I thought…I mean, we all thought you were here for good." Jo's hazel eyes were round with surprise.

"Good heavens! Why would you think that?"

"Well, Riley told me—"

"Riley told you I was coming home to stay?" Talk about high-handed. "Whatever he said, it isn't true. Believe me, Jo, I would never do a crazy thing like that."

"Living with us is 'a crazy thing like that'? You make it sound awful!"

That didn't sound like the younger sister she remembered, who looked for the best in everything. "I didn't mean it like that, Jo, but you know as well as I do that I don't belong here."

"Well, you certainly don't belong in New York. You're part of this family, and you should be here."

"Why can't I be part of the family and be there?"

It was Jo's turn to stand before the mantle. An outsider could have entered the room and known immediately that the two women were related, although their coloring and builds were little alike. But when Jo bit into her lower lip thoughtfully and frowned, gazing at a picture on the mantle, it echoed exactly the movements Kit had made a few moments ago. She said firmly, "The family belongs together here, where there's so much history behind us."

Jo was right on that count. Wentworth history was all around them, from the Columbian Exposition teacups to the photographs on every table and wall. In this room Wentworth history was stifling, exactly what Kit wanted to avoid. "I know the family is important to you, but it isn't that way for me. I like depending on myself and living by myself."

"But why do that when you don't have to?" Shaking her head, Jo crossed to point to the large portrait of Great-Grandmother Fitzgerald that dominated one wall. "You can try, but I don't believe you can back away from your heritage. Family and friends aren't things you should take lightly."

Kit remembered too late that Jo rarely took anything lightly. It was no secret that this Wentworth sister was a believer, fiercely committed to causes from wildlife to clean air. Apparently Jo saw the family as one more cause.

"I happen to believe that involvement with people and issues is what makes life worthwhile." Jo had slipped into her persuasive mode, the one she used to coax extra pennies out of reluctant donors to her favorite funds. "When it comes to the people who love you, you're connected whether you like it or not. You get loyalty and support, and all you have to give is a little bit of yourself." Leaning over the back of the bentwood rocker, Jo sent Kit her best beseeching look. "Doesn't it ever bother you to come home to an empty apartment? Or to know that we're all here, laughing and talking, on the *real* Christmas, when you're alone?"

No one ever said Jo wasn't effective. That's how she was so successful at fund-raising for her causes. But pride stiffened Kit's spine. "Jo, don't start with me, because I'm not coming back here."

"If you're not here for good," Jo responded softly, "I'm not sure you should've come at all."

That hurt. "How can you say that to your own sister?"

Wilting, Jo didn't meet her eyes. "I'm sorry," she sighed. "I shouldn't have said it. But there's more to this situation than just us." As if playing a trump card, Jo sped up and threw in, "Don't forget about Riley!"

"What about him?"

"Does he know yet that you're not planning to stay?"

Kit looked up sharply, narrowing her eyes. "What do you mean? Of course he knows. He's the one who demanded that I come home for a visit! He told me if I didn't show up it would prove I was cowardly, childish, lily-livered and a whole lot of other unflattering things."

Running her hands through her hair, Jo turned away from her sister. When she swung back, it was only halfway. "I... Oh, I never should have said anything. I didn't know Riley wrote such awful things to you. You know of course he didn't mean them." She added gently, "He adores you.

I'm sure he was only trying to get you mad enough to come back and face him."

"I know." It annoyed Kit that Jo was able to discern Riley's motives so easily.

"And now that you are back, well, there's the potential to really hurt him badly. It's just that he's my friend now, and I'd hate to see him unhappy again."

"I see." But she didn't see at all. "You and Riley are such good buddies that you have to protect him from me? Or is it that you're afraid I'll take your place in his affections now that I'm back? After all, he was my friend first."

"But he's my friend now." Jo rose to her full height, a few inches over five feet.

Kit was verging on real anger. Imagine Jo insinuating that Kit would somehow scar Riley just by being back. As if it were any of Jo's business! As if self-assured Riley couldn't take care of himself! Holding on to her temper, she asked quietly, "Jo, Riley was my best friend for eighteen years. Why should my coming home make him unhappy?"

"It's not the coming home. It's the running away again."

"I'm not running away again!"

"It doesn't matter what you call it. If you leave again, it will have the same effect. I don't want you to hurt Riley again, that's all." Jo spun toward the dining room and swatted the wall in frustration. "Oh, forget it. Look, I have to see what's keeping everyone. They should have been in here with the tea things ages ago. Just try to be careful with Riley, will you?"

Kit brought her hands up in front of her, not understanding. "I'll try..." Her hands dropped to her sides. "But I don't see what I can do. He invited me! He obviously knew what he was doing, and he wanted me here, even if only for a visit."

"You could change your mind and come home for good," Jo suggested hopefully.

Unconvinced, Kit drew her pale brows together. "Don't start that again. I have a job. I have a life. I'm not coming back just because of some vague worries about Riley."

"Okay, okay." Jo swished her full skirt as she moved to go into the dining room. Before leaving, she announced, "I really am sorry, Kit. I didn't plan to argue with you on your first day home. But you have to admit, it isn't easy to pick up threads that have been unwound for four years. That's a very long time."

"Yes," Kit replied flatly. "I know."

As Jo left the room, Kit let herself sink to a short stool near the fireplace, and she sighed unhappily.

The pressure had begun. She didn't know why she'd hoped they would have changed, and learned to be more receptive to other people's choices.

She wanted to feel that the people who knew her the best, like Riley and her family, respected her, and thought fondly of her when she came to mind. Where was it written that it had to be black and white—accepting a whole family crowded into one another's pockets, or having her pride, but existing like a hermit? Why couldn't there be a choice in between?

A muffled crunch sounded behind her as the front door opened and closed. Still on the stool, Kit turned toward the door, and the pleasure of knowing she was not all alone filled her. It was Riley. He might be Jo's friend, but Kit knew there were years and memories tipping the balance in her favor. Hadn't they been blood brothers since the second grade? When push came to shove, Riley would be her ally.

He saw the strained expression on her face immediately, and he felt responsible. He was the one who coerced her into coming here, and it had made her unhappy. "What is it?" he asked softly.

Seeing Riley standing there, exuding health and strength, made her even less willing to accept Jo's odd warnings about hurting him. She said carefully, "I'm not sure I should stay." Her tongue edged her lip surreptitiously. "Jo seemed to think it wasn't a good idea, that it wasn't fair to you if I was here and then left again. What do you say?"

Damn Jo anyway for her good intentions. When he found his voice, he made sure it was casual and easy. "You can't leave yet, Kit. You haven't figured out what I do for a living, and you're going to owe me a dinner."

Smiling at him, she rose from the stool and moved quickly in his direction. When she was close enough to touch, she seemed to lean into him, and Riley felt his arms go around her of their own volition.

"Thank you for being here for me," she said simply. "I know that I shouldn't have expected to find unquestioning loyalty from you after all this time, but it's wonderful to know you're still here, and the friendship hasn't disappeared."

His hold tightened, bringing her under his chin, and he grazed his cheek against the fine blond hair that swept back into her braid. Above her head, he could smell the slight lemony fragrance of her hair, and he held himself very still, trying not to feel all the things he was feeling. He wished it could be as uncomplicated as she thought. Friendship, loyalty, being there when someone needed you—all those things the two of them had once taken for granted. But things were different now. As her words continued, he realized how different.

"Jo gave me such a hard time about belonging here. How can she not understand? I really don't want to live here or work here. Why is that so hard to understand?"

He didn't know what to say. His instinct was to reassure her, to tell her anything she wanted to hear. But in his heart he knew that wasn't the truth. He wanted more from Kit than a casual long-distance friendship.

"Be patient," he managed to say in a reasonably calm voice. "Maybe we can work on a compromise."

Kit shook her head and spoke in a clear, strong voice. "There are some things in my life that are not subject to negotiation. I'm willing to control my temper for a few weeks in the interest of peace, but I won't give up my career or my identity to do it. It would be like giving in to my mother and her demands if I came back here. She'd start running my life again, and I'd hate it. Don't you see that, Riley? I can't just give in at the drop of a hat."

"It's okay, Kit. They'll understand." He kept his voice soothing, although he knew he was lying. He had discussed this issue too often with her family not to know how they all felt. Damn it, what was all this "they" stuff? He was one of "them." More than anyone, Riley himself had decided that she would have to see the light and come home to St. Paul. But given the obvious strength of her feelings, how was he ever going to convince her?

He wanted to shout that she belonged here, and why couldn't she see that? Or that now that he had her back, he was never going to let her leave again.

He reminded himself that one did not allow Kit to do things. The very idea was guaranteed to send her running in the opposite direction.

He set his jaw, biting the bullet. The important thing was that she was here now, and that he would have her for a month. Sometime in that month a plan would occur to him, he would carry it out, the scales would drop from her eyes, and she would understand. But he had to make sure he had his month within which to try. No more of this "Should I leave now?" stuff every time someone got under her skin. "Promise me one thing, Kit," he said slowly. He rubbed the edge of his jaw against her hair unconsciously, gazing into space over her head. "Promise me you'll stay the whole time. No matter what, promise me you'll be here until Christmas in July."

She leaned back enough to look into blue eyes that had suddenly become unfathomable. "Okay, I promise," she said lightly.

She sighed with contentment and shut her eyes tightly, settling closer against the soft cotton of his T-shirt. Accidentally, inevitably, her breasts brushed the three layers of fabric between them, and her body began to tingle and come alive. She told herself it was a natural reaction, that it meant nothing.

But as she pressed against him, there was a sharp intake of breath above her head, and Kit looked up quickly, confused. She saw a light she hadn't anticipated in Riley's eyes, and she caught her own breath. It was clear he had felt the longing, too, and something more complicated than comfort was passing between them.

Kit fixed on his face, not sure she could believe what her eyes told her she saw.

Desire.

Riley, her pal, with more on his mind than friendship? The tension of coming home and finding her family was giving her delusions.

Riley recognized his own symptoms, and he knew this was much too soon. He had to cement the friendship before he branched out into other things. She was already thinking of escaping to New York because of the pressures here. Promise or no promise, what would she do if he added his feelings to the burden?

Wheeling away, he rummaged in his jacket pocket for a pack of cigarettes. The nasty habit he'd supposedly quit was reasserting itself with a vengeance.

Kit saw that he was fiddling with his pocket, and the source of his search surprised her. It didn't matter. She would gladly have leaped to Attila the Hun as a topic of conversation at that point, if only to take her mind off the second when she thought she saw desire in his eyes. "Since when do you smoke?" she asked quietly.

"I don't." She raised an eyebrow at the pack in his hand, and he relented. "Okay, so I quit. And I guess I've started again."

With feigned horror, she demanded, "You're not thinking of starting again in my mother's house, are you?"

They—as well as much of the city of St. Paul—had heard the whole argument way back when Alexandra had decided to take up smoking black Russian cigarettes at the age of eighteen. Their mother had hit the roof, warning all of her daughters that such behavior would not be tolerated in her home.

He didn't light the cigarette, letting it dangle between his fingers. With a challenge in his eyes, he said, "Lilah lets me smoke in her house all the time."

"I don't believe it," Kit responded, giving him a pooh-poohing wave of her hand. "Not my mother. For one thing, she never did like you all that much. She thought you were a bad influence on me."

"That was a long time ago." A mocking smile danced around his narrow lips. "Why, I've been told I have a real touch with mothers."

"I'll just bet," she retorted. There was no doubt his blue eyes and pretty smiles could con many a mother. "But even if you've got her wrapped around your little finger, I don't believe she lets you smoke in her house." Remembering her mother's imperious tone, Kit drew herself up and intoned, in an exaggerated and richly modulated voice, "Why, the smell of smoking hangs in Irish lace curtains for months, haven't you heard? Not to mention the fact that you could burn a hole in the sofa that Great-Grandmother Fitzgerald sent west from New York in Queen Victoria's time!"

"At least my daughter learned something from all her years in my household," an exaggerated and richly modulated voice called from the doorway. "Riley, put away your foul weeds this instant. You know better than to behave like that under my roof."

At another time Kit might have been gratified to be proved right so easily. It was an incontrovertible fact that Riley was not allowed to smoke here, just as she'd contended. Her victory, however, was small comfort at this particular moment.

In front of her, Riley grinned and did as he was told without a murmur. She knew there was only one person in the world an immovable object like Riley would obey so meekly.

She turned.

"Hello, Mother," she said softly.

Chapter Three

Lilah Fitzgerald Wentworth looked beautiful, but then she always had. She was a little larger than life, not quite real. The bright red of her hair and the emerald green of her slightly tilted eyes were almost too vivid to be believed at first glance. Her features were pretty, but not extraordinary; it was the vibrant personality underneath that made her linger in the thoughts of her admirers as a spectacular beauty. For Lilah, as she often repeated, beauty was a state of mind.

Everyone in St. Paul knew about Lilah, who'd married and then divorced the most eligible man in town. After nine fiery years of marriage and five lovely daughters, she had simply dismissed Alexander Wentworth from her life, unwilling or perhaps unable to accept his overpowering weaknesses. The only reminder that he had ever been there lay in the coloring of their middle child. Katharine Emily Wentworth, named after an ancient aunt but called Kit, bore the unmistakable stamp of her father's silky blond hair and gray-blue eyes.

Without her husband, Lilah had set out to make her way in the world. She had turned up her nose at the Wentworth money and had found little Fitzgerald money left to have. So, for the past twenty-odd years, Lilah had man-

aged by arranging soirees and celebrations for the cream
of society. She had had the connections and drive to pull
it off and had ended up with a thriving party business,
christened Grand Affairs when she'd set up her office on
historical old Grand Avenue in St. Paul. Being in trade and
catering to other people's whims weren't the sorts of things
Wentworth relations generally did, but Lilah got by. And
on her own terms.

When Kit looked at her mother, she saw the same spectacular woman she had left behind four years ago. Lilah's
hair was thick and styled full around her face, in a vivid
shade of copper-red that men found fascinating. She was
wearing a stylish, deep green dress in a fluid knit, with
some kind of cape tossed negligently over one shoulder.
Even though she was several inches shorter than Kit, Lilah's queenly carriage, commanding voice and direct gaze
held them spellbound as she made her entrance.

Sweeping over to Kit, she held out her arms and enfolded her daughter. "Katharine, my dear, it is marvelous
to have you back in my home."

"I'm happy to be here, Mother. You look lovely, as always."

"You don't, Katharine. In fact, you look dreadful."
Lilah frowned as she surveyed her middle daughter.
"You're much too thin, you haven't got a spot of color,
and what have you done to your hair?"

Riley interceded, taking Lilah's hand and pulling her
aside. After whispering in her ear for a few moments, he
released her with a pat and a smile.

Lilah raised her chin. Her eyes glittered a dangerous
shade of green. "Your young man says I'm not to provoke you. Well, daughter? Am I to pussyfoot around until you've recovered the gumption you were born with?"

"Lilah!" Riley complained, but the older woman raised her hand to forestall comments.

"You have always been very nice-looking, Katharine. You've been working too hard at that job of yours, haven't you? And obviously neglecting your heath and appearance. As if being a *shyster* were worth it!"

"I hate to interrupt, Lilah, but advertisers are called hucksters, not shysters," Riley tossed in helpfully.

Lilah glared at him, but otherwise paid him no heed. She paused for dramatic effect, drawing herself up before plunging onward in a regal tone. "When one chooses to live all alone, Katharine, one has only oneself to blame. There is no one to look after you, to make sure you eat properly or take care of yourself."

There was no one in the world who knew how to scratch below the surface like her mother. She had managed to insult Kit's profession and her looks , her two most sensitive areas, in one fell swoop. "You're right, Mother," she said in a studiously level tone. "I don't waste valuable time worrying about my appearance. It may not be glamorous, but it suits my job and my personality."

"Ha!" Lilah retorted. "None of my daughters has ever let her appearance go to pot. The Wentworth women know that one changes one's job in one's own image, not vice versa!"

"I can't believe you two haven't seen each other for four years and this is the best you can do."

"Stay out of this, Riley," Kit said heatedly. "It has nothing to do with you."

Lilah shot next. "I can't believe you ever saw anything in this daughter of mine. She is disrespectful and unkind. Truly a serpent's tooth."

Although she knew her mother's bluster meant nothing, Kit responded automatically. "Mother! Riley never had to see anything in me! We were and are friends, and that's all. First you call him my 'young man,' like something out of the stone age, and now you imply—''

But Lilah never got to hear just what Kit thought she was implying. A slow, amused voice from the direction of the dining room stopped the tirade.

"My, my, this is like old times, isn't it?" Alexandra asked in a rich, tickled voice. She sidled into the room, looking so like her mother it was uncanny, and smiled broadly at Kit. Only Alex would have dared pair long, curly red hair with a hot pink dress, but she pulled it off with gusto. "Darling, you are a sight for sore eyes. Now Maggie's right behind me, and Eliza's somewhere or other, and I know they're anxious to see you, too, so you and Mums will just have to take a time out between rounds to properly greet us."

Kit welcomed the opportunity to cease fire with her mother. The old patterns had reemerged so quickly she hadn't had a chance to squelch them. The diversion her oldest sister Alexandra was offering gave Kit time to step back, breathe slowly and assert a sense of control. It had suddenly become important, even more so with Riley watching the whole thing, to prove she could handle this family.

"Hi, Alex. You look super," Kit said, retreating to a safe statement of what was undeniably true.

Alexandra smiled and posed languidly against the curved archway of the dining room, looking for all the world like a pinup poster of a glamorous star. "Why, thank you. How kind of you to comment on it." Alex's tone was mocking but not self-deprecating. She was very comfortable with the way she looked, and she had stopped apologizing for it years ago. "And how are you, sweet sister? I see you've come home all bright and perky in your little green outfit—and such a charming hairdo. How do you do it?"

"Alexandra!" their mother warned, but the oldest Wentworth daughter ignored her.

Shaking an armful of gold bangles, Alex left her doorway for a closer look at her sister. "What have you been doing for the past four years, anyway? We've all been betting on the reasons for your hasty departure. Did you run away to join a man who was so sleazy you couldn't bear to tell us about him? That's my guess."

"Alexandra!" Lilah repeated in an even more ominous tone. "I won't stand for this sort of vulgar talk."

Alex shrugged. "It's no worse than the things you said, Mother. You called her a serpent's tooth. I only wanted to know about her love life."

"I beg your pardon! Is that any way to speak to me, young lady?"

"What's going on here?" Jo and Maggie asked in chorus as they entered from the kitchen. They were sharing the responsibility for carrying an ornate silver tea service and a tray of dainty china cups.

Seeing three of her sisters together helped fill the blanks in Kit's recollections. It only added to the confusion in her mind that they didn't look as much alike as she had thought. Jo was tiny and thin, Alex was medium and very curvy, and Maggie was slim and taller, quite close to Kit's size. Although their features and coloring were somewhat the same, and the fact that they were sisters was unmistakable, there were clearly differences, too.

There was Jo, pretty and delicate, without a hint of makeup, and Alex in the flashy pink dress, simply commanding attention. And then there was Maggie. Quiet, deep Maggie, every bit as beautiful as the others, but in a way you might not catch at first glance. She was the smart, practical Wentworth sister, who could always be counted on to look you straight in the eye and tell you the truth, whether you wanted to hear it or not. After all, someone sensible had to look out for the rest of the nutty clan. That someone was Maggie. The trademark Wentworth red hair was parted in the middle and calmly tucked behind her ears, revealing long gold earrings that brushed the collar of her plain black shirtdress. She looked like a redheaded Indian princess. Right now, Maggie was trying very hard to balance the tea tray without spilling anything, and a frown of concentration marked her brow.

"Mother and Kit were fighting, but I stepped in to break it up," Alex said loftily.

"Alexandra! I would hardly call your behavior that of a peacemaker!"

"Oh, come now, Mother! I had one little question about the reason behind her abrupt exodus, that's all."

Alex swung the flaming red waves of her hair over her shoulder and fixed curious eyes on Kit, who was wishing she could disappear for a while until the hubbub died down.

"So, dear sister, do tell. Did you run off with a man?"

"Alex!" Jo protested, while Maggie merely groaned quietly.

"I don't see what you're getting so upset about," Alex answered with a great show of innocence. "After all, Jo, if you ran away and lived in sin for four years, I'd certainly want to hear about it."

"I've been here, giving you free rein to ask anything you want. That's a lot different from coming home after being missing for four years."

"Stop arguing, you guys," Maggie said with resignation. "You really sound awfully childish."

Ignoring Maggie, Alex attempted to skewer Jo with an imperious stare. "Kit hasn't exactly been missing, now has she?"

Jo rolled her eyes. "That's not a fair way to argue. You haven't caught what I mean at all. You're arguing over semantics. Who cares whether she was missing or not? The important thing is that we should be nice to Kit so she won't run away again."

"Oh, come now!" Alex was not impressed. "First of all, anything's fair in an argument. And second, I don't see why we should be artificially nice to Kit. She's a member of the family, and we're not nice to one another, are we?"

"Children, children! Stop this disgraceful display immediately. Alexandra, please refrain from antagonizing your sisters. And Margaret, Josephine, put the tea things down before you drop them. All we need is to ruin the Persian rug Great-Grandmother Fitzgerald had sent from New York City in Queen Victoria's time!"

"Oh, Mother!" three Wentworth sisters complained in unison. But they did as she asked. Alex and Jo continued to fuss with each other while Maggie made comments disapproving of both, but eventually the tea things were laid out on a marble-topped side table. As they all knew, it, too, had been sent from New York in Queen Victoria's time.

It was all Kit could do to follow who was saying what to whom. She hadn't been around this much noise and confusion since she had personally supervised a television ad featuring fifteen first-graders. How could she have let herself wander helplessly back into the midst of this household?

"Kit!" Alex said testily. "Are you paying the slightest bit of attention to me?"

Abruptly Kit switched her focus to her oldest sister. "I'm sorry, Alex. What were you saying?"

Smiling like the cat with the proverbial canary firmly between its teeth, Alex perched on the arm of the sofa. She crossed her arms, jangling her bracelets. "You have so far successfully dodged my question, but I don't give up easily, little sister. Now come on, tell all! Who is he and what does he do for a living?"

Kit's gaze made the rounds from one blank face to another. "Who is who?"

"Him! The one you ran away with four years ago. Was he married? Did he go back to his wife? Has a tragedy sent you back to your family's bosom, Kit dear?"

If Alex was expecting a tragedy, then why were her green eyes sparkling so wickedly? "I'm sorry to disappoint you, Alex, but there isn't and wasn't any man or any tragedy."

Riley had felt fairly certain there was no man in Kit's life, but it did him a world of good to hear it from her own lips. He mentally thanked Alex for being such a tenacious little beast. At least he didn't have to worry that Kit would hurry back to the arms of some creep in New York.

Kit continued. "I left when I was ready, and I came back when I was ready. People in other families do that all the time. Nothing dramatic."

She looked up at Riley then, where he stood casually in the back of the room. Flashing him a smile, she wanted to tell him that she was proud of herself for fielding the question without losing her temper or threatening to leave the room. As Riley well knew, she had not always been so temperate.

Before she'd left, she had often found herself unable to maintain a cool head when the others had dug a bit too deeply. It had infuriated her even more when it had seemed she was the only one who couldn't deal with her temper, and she had always ended up storming out of the room and sulking by herself, or pouring out her troubles to Riley.

Now, all these years later, it was a moral victory to submit to Alex's best effort to provoke her and escape unscathed, with temper intact. Feeling reckless, she winked at Riley, and was gratified when he winked back with only the slyest flicker of his eyelid. It felt as if she and her old best friend were on the same wavelength again.

"Ah, well," Alex announced, "I suppose we'll take you anyway, even without a dramatic entrance." Stepping prettily over to Kit, she made a kissing motion in the general area of her sister's cheek. With her hands still on Kit's shoulders, Alex leaned back and grimaced. "But we're going to have to do something about your hair. What do you think, Maggie? Jo?" She moved elegant hands to frame Kit's face. "Chin-length bob? Sleek and simple?"

"I think you ought to sit down and stop acting like a ninny," Maggie interjected with calm precision.

"Girls, please!" their mother commanded. "Sit down, Katharine, and have some tea. You look about ready to faint away from lack of nourishment."

Kit smiled. "I don't think it's that serious, Mother." She wondered when tea had become synonymous with nourishment, but didn't voice her objection.

As she sat in the flowered chintz wing chair, the seat of honor in this house, Kit carefully balanced her saucer and teacup. It was one more bit of behavior she'd learned here and not used since. But Mother had always said that every proper lady must know how to drink tea without looking indelicate. Even after four years there were some things you didn't forget.

She tried to ignore Alex's continued comments about possible hairstyles. She might not be the neatest French-braider in the world, and her hair was really too fine to stay in place, but she liked it that way, and that was all that counted. Alex could jolly well keep her paws off.

It wasn't long, but it seemed like forever before her mother announced that dinner was ready. "Welcome home!" Lilah intoned, using dramatic vibrato to underline the sentiment in her voice. She opened her arms wide, to indicate that her home was once more Kit's home, and flung open the door to the dining room. Pure Wentworth drama.

Maggie and Jo linked their arms through Kit's and walked with her into the dining room, while Riley escorted her mother. This was all too strange for words. A special family dinner, and yet Riley, a nonfamily member, of whom her mother had once strongly disapproved, had been invited. Not only that, but he was wearing blue jeans. What had the world come to, when Lilah Wentworth's dinner guests wore jeans? This wasn't just a knack for handling mothers; this was a miracle.

The dining room was small, and rather haphazardly decorated in Lilah's usual more-is-better style. The large dark walnut table and chairs were heavily carved Victorian, and they stretched the available space all by themselves. Against a sprigged wallpaper stood the china cabinet, displaying pieces from several sets of old Fitzgerald dinnerware and giving the room an even more crowded feel. The dishes seemed to lean down from the walls, and Kit remembered being fascinated with them as a child. She was sure that they would tumble down onto the table sooner or later, and she had always hoped it would be during dinner. Plates would rain down from heaven, and she wouldn't have to eat her peas.

As they sat down, Lilah tinkled a small bell, signaling the maid to begin serving. Even in the worst of times, Lilah Fitzgerald Wentworth insisted on maintaining the proper customs. Family dinners were one of those important events that required rules and regulations. That meant Kit would have to remember not to put her elbows on the table, and to be extremely careful not to spill anything on Great-Grandmother Fitzgerald's Irish linen tablecloth. Unless, of course, all the rules had been relaxed with the onset of blue jeans. Kit didn't think it was likely.

She grinned at Riley across the table; she was glad he'd been invited even if it wasn't de rigueur.

Just as the maid entered with the soup, the living room door opened and another Wentworth slipped in.

"Nice of you to join us, Eliza," Alex commented dryly.

Their youngest sister was dressed simply in a sweet yellow dress with puffed sleeves and a round lace collar. Above the demure dress, Eliza's curly red hair spilled to her shoulders, and petulance glimmered in her pretty green eyes. Kit saw the warning glances the others gave Eliza, and the sulky, resentful expression they got in return. What with fending off Alex, she hadn't noticed Eliza's absence up to this point, but the others must have.

"Hello, everyone." Eliza nodded to each of them in turn. "Mother, Alex, Maggie, Jo, Riley." As her eyes lit on Kit, Eliza stuck her nose in the air. "I don't believe we've met. You are . . . ?"

Kit's eyes were wide with surprise. It appeared her youngest sister planned to cut her dead. What had happened to the Little Miss Sunshine she remembered?

Her mother, however, was not about to see a homecoming dinner get out of control. She stood and stared down the length of the table. "Elizabeth, please! This is neither the time nor the place for your foolishness. Sit down and behave yourself, or you will find yourself eating on the street."

Everyone heaved a sigh of relief when Eliza conde-
scended to lump herself into the chair at the foot of the
table. Although Kit was on her left, Eliza devoted herself
completely to Riley, on her right. As the meal progressed,
she made it clear she was not acknowledging Kit's presence. Kit was irritated that Riley went along with Eliza,
letting her whisper in his ear and make private jokes while
other conversations proceeded around them.

Riley was a bit embarrassed by Eliza's attentions, and he
would have liked to paddle her behind for acting so rudely
to Kit. He'd been holding his breath during the reconcili-
ation scenes with the rest of the family, hoping Kit would
be all right. He'd actually let himself relax until Eliza
showed up, but he couldn't for the life of him figure out
what her problem was. Was she resentful that Kit had returned home and become the focus of attention, perhaps?
But that was an awfully slim grudge to hang this spoiled-
brat performance on. In the interests of peace, he did not
paddle her behind, but instead made an effort to listen
politely so she wouldn't cause any more scenes at Kit's expense.

As dinner proceeded, it became a showcase for Alex to
relate anecdotes about her life as the main spokesperson
for Grand Affairs. Listening to Alex, one would think she
ran the place single-handedly. Kit found herself alter-
nately entertained and outraged by Alex's exaggerated view
of herself, which was surely what Alex intended. The others retorted good-naturedly, laughing, shouting and enjoying themselves immensely. If Kit had had comments to
make, there wouldn't have been a place for them. The
conversations moved too swiftly, with a rhythm that ran
right past her.

She was afraid to jump in for fear it would stop the talk dead. All eyes would turn to her, and she would have absolutely nothing to say.

No, it was far wiser to let the babbling brook of her sisters' chatter flow around her. Even Eliza's sullen face didn't put a pall on things.

Dinner in the Wentworth household always dragged on for hours, and tonight was no exception. Kit was beginning to feel a bit bedraggled by the effort of listening to so much high spirits. In the old days she had despised these everlasting affairs around the table, anxious to escape and be outside with Riley, no matter what the weather.

Raising her gaze, she watched him curiously. Did he remember those days as vividly as she did? Of course, he wouldn't know how they had begun from her perspective. But it had been like this, idling at her mother's table, fidgeting and sighing until she was finally, blessedly, excused. Then she would race upstairs to change her clothes and sneak out before her mother could catch her or yell, "Meeting that hooligan again, Katharine?"

More often than not, as if by telepathy, he would be halfway to her house when they met. It didn't matter where they went or what they did, because they simply enjoyed being together. Whatever they found to do, they laughed and teased and ran around until Kit absolutely had to go home.

Watching him across the table, she was reminded of so many small moments. They had shared a lifetime of autumn leaves, snowball fights and spring showers, and the memories were threatening to overwhelm her. Kit felt as if she and Riley were alone at the bustling table. He had the strangest look on his face, and again, she found herself wondering if he knew what she was thinking.

All he knew was that Kit was watching him with a soft, hopeful expression, and he was mesmerized. At first he had been merely curious, but her eyes were so intent that funny things were beginning to happen in the pit of his stomach.

His mouth went dry. There were five other people in the room, five noisy, demanding people, and all he could think about was smashing his arm across the table and throwing dishes and flowers and glasses and food to the four winds. He didn't care. All he wanted was to clear a space so that he could make love to Kit on the dining room table.

God, he had it bad.

Kit tipped her head, unable to fathom that curious, hot spark in Riley's eyes. It made her feel very nervous.

Finally Eliza broke the spell. She rapped his elbow hard, and he had to react fast to catch his water glass before it toppled.

"Riley, I was talking to you!" Eliza interrupted in a peevish tone.

Kit shook her head, trying to get herself back to the present. Still flustered, she stood and tried to clear her mind. She found she was exhausted; all these memories were too much for one day.

"I hope it's not impolite to run off right after dinner, but I'm afraid I'm awfully tired. I think I might go up to my room now."

"Um, I don't think you should do that." Jo's voice sounded a little peculiar. "I'm afraid things have changed since you were here last."

"Changed? How?"

"You're not going to be in your room, Kit," Alex returned with an extravagant wave of her hand. "I've moved out. Did you know that? I'm living in the house on Grand

Avenue now, above Grand Affairs. So you can have my old room."

"Oh, that's okay," Kit assured her. "I'd rather be with Jo in our room. It will be like old times."

Kit was mystified. Her sisters and her mother were all sending significant glances at one another, and Maggie was chewing the end of her fingernail. When implacable Maggie resorted to nervous habits, it was a bad sign.

What could it be? Were they afraid that Eliza had booby-trapped her room, and they wanted to send in the bomb squad first?

"Oh, come on," Eliza snapped. "Tell her she doesn't have a room here anymore. Tell her you didn't leave her old place a shrine like she expects."

Kit noted the guilty expression on the faces around her, including Riley's. "I think you'd better tell me what she's talking about," she said quietly.

"Don't get upset, Kit." Riley moved to her side. He and the others had discussed how to break this news to her once they'd found out she was coming home. Riley, more than the others, felt guilty about it, because the whole thing had been his idea from the start. They had no idea whether she would be furious, mildly upset, or not care at all. In the absence of knowledge, they all knew only to proceed cautiously, because Kit's temper could be awesome when unleashed. He lifted his arm as if he were going to touch her but dropped it back into place instead. He offered softly, "It's no big deal."

"Don't patronize me, Riley." Her words were deadly calm. After feeling so close to him during her reverie at the dinner table, the fact that he knew what the others were talking about and she didn't wounded her deeply. "If it's no big deal, why is everyone acting like this?"

"Come on, Kit, that's not fair. Don't blame Riley."

It did not escape Kit that Jo had jumped to Riley's defense yet again.

"Tell me," she demanded.

"I'll tell her," Maggie said at last. "We've split up the old room, Kit. It was always too big for one room, anyway, and to be blunt about it, we needed the extra space. Jo's still in half of it, but the other part—your half—is an office now. So you see, you'll really be more comfortable in Alex's room."

"I—I see." But she didn't see at all. So they had turned her room into an office. Did they think that the news would make her run from the room in tears or temper or what? All of them, including Riley, thought they had to pussyfoot around because she couldn't handle the fact that her old room was gone. She'd show them how ridiculous it was to keep secrets from her, and to treat her like a child. If any thought of resenting the loss of her room surfaced, she repressed it.

Her sisters chorused enthusiastic good-nights, and Kit yawned deliberately, slinging her bag over her shoulder.

"Good night," she said softly, and met Riley's eyes. She wanted to say that she was disappointed in him for conspiring with her family to keep such a trifling secret. But his gaze was warm and compassionate, and she remembered melting under its spell at the airport. It was so easy to feel like they were two halves of the same whole, best friends forever. But she just wasn't sure that was true anymore. He seemed to fit into her family now—clowning around with Jo, whispering to her mother, occupying Eliza at dinner and now siding with all of them in keeping the news about her room from her. Such small things, but such a departure. As she took the stairs up to Alex's room, she wondered where he stood, and wished she didn't have to wonder.

Alex's old room was on the third floor, tucked into the back, with a charming, sloping ceiling and dormer windows. Like the rest of the house, it was decorated in a fussy, feminine style, with lots of tiny prints and lace. Kit's initials were still where she'd carved them long ago into one of the tall bedposts, and Alex's Homecoming Queen tiara was even now gracing the chest of drawers. Some things never changed.

The thing that had changed was the ceiling. Right over her head, a skylight had been cut into the roof, spilling moonlight onto the eyelet-trimmed coverlet. It was lovely, very romantic, to have moonlight in her room. But it didn't fit her image of her mother's house to have a hole cut in the ceiling. Kit felt a certain fondness for whoever had convinced her mother to go ahead with the skylight. It was a nice touch. Nothing major. Just a touch.

It appeared that someone was making changes all over the place, what with the skylight and the office down on the second floor. She wanted to see this new office for herself, to see if it looked at all like her old room.

She told herself she didn't care that her room was gone. She hadn't given that room a thought in four years.

So where was this melancholy feeling coming from?

In the old days, in her old room, she might have climbed out on the maple tree and tiptoed over to Riley's house, to see what he thought of the situation. That was very close to what she'd done the night before she'd left, the night when she had made such a hash of things. No, tripping over to Riley's place in the middle of the night was not a good idea. It was, in fact, downright impossible.

Chapter Four

For the next two weeks she didn't have time to turn around. The Wentworth household was like a whirlwind, everyone running every which way at top speed at all times. Somehow they made sure there was always someone to drag Kit around, to show her what was new and exciting in the Twin Cities. Her sisters—with the exception of Eliza, who avoided her—were always sweet, never too pushy, but the comments they dropped were clear enough. Wonderful, marvelous, fun-filled Grand Affairs. She didn't know what she was missing by not working there, too. No matter how much they talked it up, she politely refused all invitations to attend Grand Affairs' actual functions. She wanted to make it clear that their little schemes were going nowhere.

When Riley was her "custodian," he was equally nice and faultlessly easy to be with. Their topics of conversation ranged from the people they went to high school with, many of whom still seemed to be Riley's pals, to the weather, but nothing more serious than that. He seemed to be available to chauffeur her around at all hours, and never complained of job obligations or other responsibilities. After two weeks, Kit didn't have a clue about what he did or how he did it without ever appearing to work.

He, too, would nonchalantly remind her that the Cities were a great place to live, or that Grand Affairs was certainly doing well. Never more than casual chitchat, never anything overt enough to complain about.

Kit was ready to scream. But she was determined to last it out, to prove how even-tempered and calm she could be.

She was also exhausted. She wasn't used to this kind of social life. In fact, she wasn't used to any social life at all. She felt like a Ping-Pong ball, ricocheting back and forth from person to person. There appeared to be no rhyme or reason to any of their schedules, and Kit couldn't figure out how they stayed alive at this constant, hectic pace. She finally put down her foot and announced that she was going to sleep late the next day, that she wanted to relax and not do anything for at least a few hours.

On the morning of her one day to sleep late, she was forced awake by an incessant pounding. At first she dreamed there was a giant woodpecker right outside her window, trying to hammer through the wall and into her bedroom. Half-conscious, she pulled the sheet around her more closely and slid her pillow over her head as a shield against the pesky bird in her dream. It didn't help. As the pounding continued, she came awake, realizing slowly that the sound wasn't being caused by a bird, no matter how big.

It sounded too close to be road construction or telephone repair. No, this was definitely from inside the Wentworth house. Kit couldn't picture her mother or sisters standing around hammering. As far as she knew, none of them would be caught dead with a tool in her manicured hand. But it appeared the skylight was only the beginning as far as improvements to the Wentworth house were concerned. The hammerer might not be related, but he or she was definitely down there, working away like a busy little beaver and bringing Kit out of her slumber with a bang.

What time was it anyway? she wondered, managing to locate her plastic watch after a hasty search. Ten o'clock— how had she slept so long?

Grumbling, she pulled a robe out of the closet and wrapped it over her T-shirt. The robe was made of deep rose silk and smelled faintly of exotic perfume. Alex's, without a doubt, Kit thought, and sneezed when the scent hit her nose. Nonetheless, she couldn't go investigating in a T-shirt that barely hit her thighs. And she refused to get dressed until she had coffee first and a shower second, so Alex's slinky robe would have to do.

The banging noise reverberated through the house, jarring Kit's sleep-cloudy brain and giving her the stirrings of a headache.

"What in the world is going on?" she demanded of no one in particular. Without even combing her hair, she padded downstairs in search of coffee and an end to the clatter. She determined quickly that the pounding was coming from the second floor, but she didn't feel capable of confronting its source until she had some caffeine in her blood.

Rummaging in her mother's old white cabinets turned up nine or ten varieties of tea, but no coffee. Kit gave up and put the kettle on to boil, although her cranky mood was getting worse at the prospect of making do with tea when her body craved coffee. It wasn't like her to frown at the sun, but she pulled the lilac-flowered curtains closed over the kitchen window rather than face the bright light.

After waking up groggy in a soft bed made with fussy, lacy sheets, encasing herself in a perfumed robe and facing the prospect of a morning without coffee, she felt like she was lost in the wrong century.

When the kettle began to sing, she hustled to turn it down. One more set of noises and she would pack and go to a hotel. Kit made a pot of tea and slumped gratefully onto a chair at the kitchen table, letting the steam from the cup unglue her eyelids. After a few seconds, the hammer's annoying clanging also stopped, and she smiled, enjoying the bliss of silence. She barely heard the kitchen door swing open behind her.

"Good morning," a low masculine voice volunteered.

Realizing immediately that it must be the workman from the second floor, she whirled, hastily pulling Alex's robe together.

"Oh, it's only you," she said in relief.

Riley quirked an eyebrow. "I'm not sure I like being 'only you.'"

Now that she was past her initial surprise, she regarded him more closely. In fact, her gaze raked him up and down. "Why in the world do you look like that?" she demanded.

"Like what?" He swung his arms out at his sides, giving her free rein to look at whatever she pleased.

Kit's first thought was that she wasn't ready for this without coffee. Riley didn't look like Riley; he looked like a TV construction worker she would cast to throw back a brew or two with his buddies in a beer commercial. All he needed was a hard hat and some kind of shirt. Even as a construction worker, she couldn't put him on TV half-naked.

Wearing faded, patched jeans, he was bare to the waist, with an empty tool belt hung around his hips. From the top of his head to his belt loops, he was covered with a fine sheen of sweat sprinkled lightly with plaster and sawdust.

The debris streaked the tawny brown strands of his hair, making it almost white in places. With one hand on his hip, staring at her coolly with eyes the dazzling blue of a Minnesota lake, Riley was dirty, unshaven and very masculine. He seemed about as out of place as a person could get in her mother's demure lavender-and-white kitchen.

"Tea?" she asked weakly.

His brows drew together in confusion. "I look like tea?"

"No, of course not." Kit opened her eyes wide on purpose and met his gaze. At a time like this, she needed her wits about her. "I wondered if you wanted some tea. I made a pot."

"Oh, no thanks." Crossing to the cabinet over the sink, Riley opened the door and took out a large metal canister that said Flour on the side. After prying off the lid, he whisked out a small jar of instant coffee. "Forget the tea—I need some coffee. I was up early this morning, unlike some people I could mention."

Her disagreeable mood wasn't improved when she saw the coffee. "How in the world did you know where the coffee was?"

"I've needed it a lot since I started working here. Somebody showed me where it was a long time ago." He cracked a smile. "You know me. I help myself."

His familiarity with everything in this house was creepy. She had felt it necessary to appropriate her sister's robe just to come downstairs, while Riley was perfectly at ease wandering around her house bare-chested and filthy!

Bare-chested and filthy? And didn't he say something about working here? Finally, things began to fall into place. "That wasn't you upstairs?"

"Yeah, it was me. I'm redoing the room upstairs, making it into an office." He yawned and ran a hand through his hair as he poked into the refrigerator. Watching plaster particles scatter in a shower from his head, he scowled and straightened. "I'm a mess."

"I don't believe this," Kit declared.

"Why not?" His blue eyes were all innocence as he poured himself a glass of orange juice. "You helped me turn the basement of my house on campus into a recording studio, and you were there when I remodeled the old massage parlor into a copy shop. You know I'm good at this kind of thing."

"That's not what I mean. I know you're capable of doing it." She shook her head. "But how could you? To my old room?"

"You said that didn't bother you."

"Well, why, that is—it doesn't," she sputtered. "But you could have told me. Besides, I think it's awful that my mother is taking advantage of your friendship. Even if you are your own boss, you shouldn't have to use your free time slaving away for my mother."

The self-righteous look on her face amused him. So Kit disapproved of him doing favors for her mother. "Don't worry," he remarked calmly. "How do you think I got the Ferrari? Your mother's paying me very well for my efforts."

"That's even worse!"

Her mother was paying him, but with dinners, not money. And he knew he was misleading her, making it seem as if being a handyman was his job. Pulling one over on Kit made him feel like the old days, when they'd constantly tried to con each other just for fun. Back then, Kit would have known immediately that he was teasing her. But now, from the way her jaw dropped open, he'd say she was going for it, hook, line and sinker.

"No, don't tell me!" she gasped. "This can't be your new career? A handyman for my mother? Have you no self-respect at all?"

Riley took in the wide-eyed incredulity on her face, and he laughed out loud. "What's wrong with a little physical labor?" he asked, mischief lighting his eyes. He downed the glass of orange juice in one swallow. "It keeps me in shape."

"Yeah, I can tell," Kit muttered.

"What was that?"

She expelled air in a rush. "Nothing, nothing." The water was boiling for a second time, and Kit rose from the table to take advantage of the instant coffee he'd produced. "I suppose you did the skylight, too," she muttered, feeling inexplicably annoyed that he had created something that pleased her.

After fixing two cups and handing her one, Riley regarded her shrewdly. He leaned against the cabinets, stretching his long legs in front of him. "Come on, Kit. Go ahead and say it. I can tell you're sulking about something."

"I am not sulking." Folding the robe more protectively around her, Kit lifted her chin and tried to stare him down. "It's just that I think this job is beneath you. You have a good education. I mean, my goodness, you were supposed to be an engineer."

He shrugged. "Didn't like it."

"So you prefer to go from house to house half-naked and covered with dust?"

A grin lit his face, revealing white teeth and a deep dimple on one side of his mouth. "Half-naked, huh?"

"Well, you know what I mean!"

She hadn't taken the time to stop her runaway mouth, and she hadn't realized his bare torso was bothering her so much. It must be that his appearance reminded her of the one night she had blocked out of her mind for so long. It was the night she had made a mess of things, and she never thought about that night.

But today, like then, he was half-dressed and rumpled, and watching her with eyes so blue that, like a laser beam, they cut a hole right through her.

If he got rid of the sawdust and undid the top button on his jeans, he'd be a dead ringer for the Riley she'd left behind four years ago. Her eyes flew to the top of his jeans. No, they were securely fastened.

But where had that thought come from? Until this moment, she didn't remember noticing the condition of the top of his pants on that night four years ago. She didn't think she remembered much of anything about that night. It had been buried somewhere in her memory, waiting to come out and bop her on the head when she saw Riley in jeans and no shirt. She felt her face suffuse with warmth, and she knew she was blushing. Good grief, what next? Kit was not a blusher by nature, as Riley surely knew.

"What are you looking at?" he asked bluntly.

"Nothing," she said again. She lifted the full length of her hair in one hand and turned away from Riley and the memories stirred up each time she glanced at him. She gulped down scalding coffee and, almost choking, dropped her cup abruptly on the table. Moving to the far window, she shoved back the ruffled curtains and stared out into the backyard.

Riley stood stock-still, analyzing in his mind what he had just seen. He hadn't missed the high color in her face, and he smiled when he decided he knew its source. Kit had noticed his body. His smile widened. Things were going better than he had a right to hope. He'd been so careful to take it easy, to anticipate that gently resurrecting their friendship would get her to trust him, and that he could then take her one step at a time closer to seeing him in a different light. It was getting harder and harder to hold back and leave it on such a light and easy level, but it looked as if he was doing the right thing. If she had discovered he was a man as well as a friend, then in no time at all he could show her he was only too aware she was a woman.

He stuck his right hand in his pocket and waited for her to get tired of avoiding his eyes.

"Nice outfit," he said finally.

She spun around, startled. "The robe, you mean?" What was wrong with it? Looking down, she saw that the robe gapped below the tie belt, revealing several inches of thigh as she walked. It made sense that it wouldn't fit properly. She and Alex had little similarity in the area of measurements. She pursed her lips and grabbed the sides together, trying to think of an insult to hurl at him to put them on a more even footing.

Riley had tossed out the comment about her bathrobe without thinking, noticing only that the sleek lingerie didn't fit her style and didn't go with the wrinkled T-shirt underneath it. Thoughts of the robe vanished as soon as she turned and her hair spiraled out and slid over her shoulder. It was pale yellow, the color of corn silk, and it lay in a tangle down one side.

Just when he'd been congratulating himself on his steely self-control, it all went out the window. He had an overpowering desire to touch her hair and let it spill through his fingers.

He caught himself before his hand moved from his side. Rubbing his fingers against one another absently, he speculated on how long it could be before he could broach the subject of their being more than friends. Was he going to die of sublimated lust first?

She was looking at him expectantly, and he realized he must have missed something. With determination, he focused on her eyes, keeping his gaze away from her hair and her robe and her earlobes... Damn, but it was hard to find a place that didn't appeal to him. "I'm sorry," he said, "I wasn't paying attention."

Irritation leaped inside her. She didn't want to pick fights with Riley, but he was making it tough to stay cool. The fact that he was working for her mother was enough by itself to annoy her, and adding in the crack about her robe and his lack of attention—well, she was way past the provocation point. "I asked if it bothers you to be a...a..."

A corner of his mouth curved upward. "A common laborer, you mean?"

She nodded reluctantly. He didn't appear to feel too insulted.

"Nah, it doesn't bother me at all. In fact, I kind of like it." He smiled, refusing to rise to annoyance. "What is it you don't like about manual labor?"

"You doing it."

"Well, that says it all, doesn't it?" Laughing, he set down his coffee cup and rested one thigh against the countertop. "And what, in your humble opinion, should I be doing?"

"Oh, I don't know. There are any number of choices that wouldn't be so beneath you." She waved her hand in the air as she walked toward him, halting to lean forcefully over the kitchen table. "I just find it hard to believe you don't care about money or power or position. I mean, achievement and ambition are very important. Don't you ever want to be somebody?"

He didn't like what he was hearing. The Kit he knew from childhood had never cared about money or power. "I'm surprised, Kit. You didn't used to be such a snob."

"A snob? I am not!"

"Then what's all this stuff about ambition and money and position? After all your arguments with your mother over your right to choose your own profession, I would've thought you'd be a little more tolerant of other people's choices. So you think being a handyman is beneath the likes of you and me, huh? What if I told you I really enjoyed it?"

"I happen to believe that people should live up to their potential, that's all. You're so smart, Riley, and good at so many things. You could do anything you want. Why settle?"

Shaking his head, Riley slid off the counter and advanced on her, stopping when the kitchen table was all that separated them. He laid his hands flat on the table and leaned over, meeting her eyes steadily.

Under his stare, feeling the warmth of his bare skin radiate out and touch her, Kit backed off and took the opposite chair. She crossed her arms over her chest, absently rubbing the silk sleeves of her robe. Her temples were pounding, and she was angry with him for arguing with her when he was half-dressed. It was distracting, and not at all fair.

He responded matter-of-factly, "I don't consider it 'settling' when I do something I like."

Kit narrowed her eyes, trying not to be cowed. "And this handyman stuff is really enough for you? I don't believe it."

He saw that they had moved to the point where he should straighten things out before they went any farther. "Kit," he said gently. "I do the handyman stuff for fun.

It's not my job, okay? But I like it. It relaxes me and lets me actually create things. That appeals to me.''

She sat up straighter. "Are you trying to tell me you've let me go on thinking this is your job when it isn't?"

"Sort of."

"And this handyman business is like entertainment for you?"

"Yeah," he said slowly. "But if it were my real job, I would think you'd accept it because I do. I was very serious about that part of what I said."

Letting out a long breath, Kit regarded him steadily. "You can be a real moron sometimes, you know that? I mean, here we are, arguing over a nonexistent situation. Maybe I'm more of a Wentworth than I thought."

"I think we were arguing over something real, whether the handyman job is real or not." He raked his hand through his hair, and plaster dust fell on the table. "I mean, some of what I said is true. I really do believe that no job, no matter the title or the money, is worth it unless you like it."

"Okay," she returned softly, "I'll buy that. But when did you get so philosophical about such things? The Riley I used to know was always trying out some get-rich-quick scheme or other. That Riley never had time to think about whether he liked a job or not, just how much he could make off it."

"As it concerns the working world, I guess I figured out I wanted more than nine-to-five when I was stuck in the middle of it. I did work as an engineer for a while, you know. But it wasn't any fun, and I wanted more." He stopped and watched Kit for a long moment. Shifting a bit, he inclined a thumb toward the window over the sink. "Do you remember the lilac bushes in the backyard?"

"Sure," she answered, mystified. "But it's way too late for lilacs to be in bloom now."

He nodded. "They've long since come and gone for this year. But I was thinking of how they were when we were in high school. They came in really full one year, do you remember?"

"Vaguely." She couldn't for the life of her figure out where all this was leading.

"You decided you wanted to fill up your room with lilacs, and you made me help you cut down about half the bush. I was giving you a hard time, so you gathered them up and ran back to the house. You were laughing at me and trying to carry a truckload of lilacs all by yourself."

When Riley wanted to capture her attention, he slowed his voice down to a snail's pace. She hung on each lazy, trailed word, as he must know she would. Once again she felt manipulated. "I don't remember any of this."

"About halfway up the lawn, you tripped. It wasn't surprising because you were running, and you couldn't see anything over all the flowers. You tripped and fell and lilacs went everywhere. You didn't move, and I ran up to see if you were okay." A smile began to lift the corners of his lips. "You were fine, but you were laughing so hard you couldn't stand up. I started to laugh, too, and we both ended up lying in those lilacs, laughing so hard we cried."

"Okay, so I was a klutz when I was sixteen." She colored slightly and twisted the end of a strand of hair. "What does that have to do with your job or my job or your view of the world?"

"It has everything to do with it." Riley began to lose a bit of patience, and his voice speeded up accordingly. "It's been more than ten years, and I still remember everything about that day—exactly how you looked with your hair every which way, with little purple flowers stuck in it, and tears running down your face from laughing so hard.''

"How complimentary," she said dryly.

"It was beautiful, Kit. The sun was shining, the lilacs smelled so strongly, and it hit me that I was really happy."

"You're a sentimental fool, old pal," she chided softly. "I never would've guessed. You hide it very well."

"Nope." He grinned, teeth white against golden brown skin. "I'm a realist. You don't get too many moments as fine as that one. I realized that life is made up of small moments, like us laughing in the lilacs. No money in the world can buy that." His eyes were blue and tranquil, as gentle as his voice. "Here, living the life I choose, watching the trees grow and feeding the ducks, I have those moments whenever I want. That's more important to me than anything."

"It's a pretty picture, Riley," Kit responded impatiently. "I admit that. And even a pretty idea, this bit about small moments. But it's also naive and unrealistic. The big picture is what counts—the sum of what you achieve and what mountains you climb." She was frankly surprised by Riley's attitude, and she didn't like the way his remarks made her feel. She'd never thought of herself as materialistic or petty, but she'd never thought watching ducks on the lake was her mission in life, either.

"I'd like to think I count my achievements in terms of people, not things." Rising, he picked up both coffee cups and set them in the sink.

"Right," Kit commented sardonically. "That's why you drive a Ferrari, right?"

Grinning, he retreated to the kitchen door. "Nobody's perfect."

It was only after he'd left that she realized she still didn't know what he really did for a living. But he wasn't a handyman, and he didn't do anything normal, that was for sure.

SHE HAD LONG SINCE SHOWERED, rebraided her hair and changed into a bright blue jumpsuit with a yellow T-shirt under it, when the hammering and drilling stopped, and she could assume that Riley had left for the day. Coming down the stairs, she found Jo, sitting in the middle of the living room floor, surrounded by stacks of cards, envelopes, stamps and a few sponges.

"Hi," Kit ventured. "What are you working on?"

Jo looked up with a vague expression. "Oh, hi, Kit. I volunteered to send out invitations for the Minnesota FoodShare benefit." Her arm swept the mess around her. "I was trying to get a head start, but once you get into these things, it's hard to stop."

Kit bent and retrieved an invitation. It was on nice quality paper stock, a creamy vellum, with the words "Minnesota FoodShare Ball" in black print across the front of the card. Inside, a plain typeface told her when, where and how much. The bare details. "Imaginative," she murmured.

"Oh, I know it's nothing exciting," Jo responded with a good-natured smile. "But no one seems to care. We always get money."

Kit was unimpressed. "But just think how much you could get with a really good campaign. You could include a classy brochure about what they get for their money, with details of what this benefit is. With such a good cause, you could've done a heartbreaker of a flyer about the hunger problem. They would've been giving till it hurt."

"Sure, sure." Jo waved her hand airily. "Maybe next time. At least this way, I get the invitations out on time."

"Do you need some help?" Kit asked. She had gotten carried away for a moment by the marketing possibilities of Jo's benefit. She had to remind herself that it was none of her business.

"Actually, I'm going to have to call it quits here anyway. We're doing a party for Puff Blaisdell tonight. Do you remember the name? One of the department store Blaisdells, and we're going all out for her fortieth birthday party. Costumes, decorations, food—you name it, it's all beach party motif." Jo grinned. "Wait till you see it—you'll throw up. Alex got a little carried away, if you ask me. Anyway, I've got to go pick up the flowers and arrange the sand. Do you want to come?"

"Sand? Did you say something about sand?"

"Sure did." Jo stood and brushed out the wrinkles in her peasant skirt. "This is going to be a sloppy one. We hired some guys to lay plastic over one entire side of the ballroom floor at the Blaisdell house. Then we're dumping sand over it, right next to the chaise longue and the beach umbrellas. We're back-projecting slides of the ocean against one whole wall, with appropriate tide noises." Her smile grew wider. "I told you, Kit, you're going to love this."

Kit decided quickly to accompany her sister rather than sit in the empty house. It sounded as if all of the Wentworths were involved in Puff Blaisdell's birthday party, and she would be the lone holdout if she chose not to go. In the old days she would have refused and sought Riley for refuge. At this moment, however, remembering that he had called her a snob, she made up her mind to go ahead and go behind the scenes of Grand Affairs and see what its parties were all about. She'd give Grand Affairs all the chances any of them could ask for, and show them that it didn't make any difference.

She found herself following Jo out the front door and down to the unattached garage. Kit stopped to read "Call Grand Affairs for your total party experience" with the company's phone number, all painted in a swirling dark purple script against the side of a lavender van that took up most of the garage. She couldn't recall ever having been in a lavender van. Not that she'd ever wanted to, of course.

Joining Jo, she saw that the vehicle was half full of beach balls. Jo sighed and stared at the load of bright-colored plastic.

"What's wrong?" Kit asked.

"Oh, Eliza was supposed to take the beach balls." Jo started the van and began to back out of the garage. "Now I'm not sure the flowers will fit. And the Blaisdells live way out in Minnetonka, so I can't make two trips." She gritted her teeth. "We may end up deflating all these dumb balls. Oh well. *C'est la vie.*"

Beach balls bounced around in the back as Jo chattered cheerfully about the hunger benefit and steered them to the florist. Kit helped her as they patiently undid the plugs on every single ball and then squashed them into one corner of the van. Two young boys from the florist shop loaded the van with boxes and boxes of flowers.

After today, Kit thought, she would certainly have her fill of beach balls. Oh, well, at least they were in bright colors. After her mother's house and the lavender van, Kit had had quite enough of pastels.

The lavender van brought to mind Riley's crazy story about the lilacs in the backyard. Looking over at her sister, Kit wondered what Jo would have made of that conversation and all its strange talk of flowers and ducks and small moments. "Jo, how friendly are you and Riley?" she began, not sure of where she was headed with the conversation.

A touch of humor lit Jo's eyes. "Is that your way of asking if we're romantically involved? Because we're not."

"Oh, I know that." Kit had dismissed that thought ages ago. "But I saw him this morning, and he was very odd."

"How so?"

"It was the first time since I've been home that we discussed anything serious. And his opinions were so different from what I expected." She shook her head. "He's changed, Jo. He seemed disapproving—like he expected more of me than I was giving. I mean, he actually called me a snob. He was always so sympathetic when we were young. I'm not sure I even know him anymore."

"Some things haven't changed, Kit." Jo's hazel eyes were luminous and soft. "He still cares about you more than anything in the world."

"Do you really think so?"

"Yes, I do. But don't take my word for it." She pulled the van up in front of a rather ugly brown house on a side street near the university campus. "Ask him yourself."

Kit recognized the place immediately. It was the home Riley had lived in while they were in school. It appeared he still lived there, because he was coming out the front door even as they stopped, with what looked like every intention of joining them in the van.

"He's helping us at the Blaisdell party," Jo offered matter-of-factly. "Move over and make room."

Chapter Five

Crowded next to him in the front seat, Kit felt very uneasy. It was one thing to discuss him with her sister when he wasn't there, but it was quite another to sit next to him, with his elbow at her ribs, and ponder the extent of his feelings.

How could she ask him what he was thinking or feeling, not just about her, but about everything? Could she turn to him and casually inquire, "So, Riley, what besides lilacs and woodwork turns you on?" She blushed in spite of herself. "Turning on" had been an unfortunate choice, even in her own thoughts. She really didn't care to know what or who turned him on.

Luckily he and Jo were perfectly capable of carrying on a meaningless conversation around her, and she let them. But she couldn't ignore the warm feeling of his long, hard thigh pressed so close, or the soft puffs of his breath on her cheek when he turned her way to talk. It was a tangible relief when they got to the Blaisdells' rambling mansion and Riley took off to help the workmen create the fake beach and ocean along one wall of the ballroom. Kit stood in the doorway, unsure of what was required of her.

Within a moment or two, Maggie crossed to her, carrying a clipboard and chewing on the end of a pencil.

"Hmm," she murmured. "Let's see where we can use you."

It appeared seniority had no place here. Even though Maggie was younger than Alex, and younger than most of the male workers busy pouring sand and setting up tables under striped beach umbrellas, Maggie was clearly in charge. As she stood in front of Kit, several people came over to verify what happened next and where it happened. Calm and collected, Maggie was the eye in a hurricane of activity.

"I'm sorry, Kit," she said after a moment, "but I don't have anything very exciting left to do. What would you like to do? Arrange flowers or sculpt sand castles, maybe?"

At Kit's dubious expression, Maggie tried, "We could really use someone to blow up beach balls."

Kit couldn't deny it was something she could handle, so there she was, crouched in a corner of the bustling ballroom, huffing and puffing and staying out of the way. She spared several mean looks for Riley, who was helping with the sound equipment for the wall-sized screen that would impersonate the ocean at the party. He was laughing and joking with the audiovisual technicians, and every once in a while, playfully kicking sand at Eliza or Jo, who were raking the stuff.

Silly people with silly parties, Kit told herself. What had she expected? She'd known for a long time that Grand Affairs was not her cup of tea. Well, they were all mistaken if they thought she'd jump at the chance to be the fifth Wentworth wheel, whose most important function in life was to blow up beach balls. Why didn't they ask her to boil a product down to features and benefits, or convince a thrifty client to spend lots of money on a TV ad? Those things she was good at. And those things had absolutely nothing to do with Grand Affairs, just as she'd contended all along.

Scanning the work around her, she was amazed to realize that a transformation had taken place. A rather stodgy ballroom had turned into *Beach Blanket Bingo* right before her eyes.

Her cheeks and lungs were ready to give out from excessive puffing, and Kit stood up, dusting off her pants. As Alex, stunning in a hot pink and black jumpsuit, flew past with a ceramic half of a beach ball, filled with bright tropical blooms, Kit called out, "Anything I can do to help?"

"No, no, nothing. If Maggie put you here, you'd better stay."

"Kit," Maggie called out sweetly behind her, "are the beach balls finished?"

Gritting her teeth, Kit managed a semicivil, "No."

Maggie reversed direction and lifted a hand to cup her mouth, to help carry her voice to where the youngest Wentworth sister was artfully sticking red and yellow plastic pails in the newly created sand piles.

"Eliza, Kit needs help with the beach balls. Have you got a minute?"

Nodding, Eliza abandoned her sand buckets for the time being, flouncing carelessly toward beach ball central. "All out of hot air?" she asked saucily.

"Don't start with me, little sister," Kit warned. "I've been blowing up these stupid balls long enough to have lost most of my temper. Besides, I'm not going to be in town that long, so why don't we call a moratorium on your Dennis the Menace routine for the duration?"

Wearing pink-flowered shorts, a matching cropped top and little pink sandals, and with strawberry curls dipping gently over her shoulders, Eliza was the picture of sweetness and light. She even had a bow in her hair. "All right," she sighed. Her wide green eyes seemed guileless enough. She asked softly, "What did you mean when you said you wouldn't be in town that long?"

"Exactly that." She didn't think it required amplification. Besides, even though she and Eliza had done a good job of avoiding each other, she assumed the others would have passed on the information to Eliza by now.

"Well, how long, then?"

Kit's gaze came up sharply. "Does it matter?"

"I—I guess not." Chewing her lower lip, Eliza shifted her weight from one foot to the other. "It's just, well, I wondered if Riley knew you were planning on leaving so soon."

"Of course he knows," Kit said impatiently. "He's the one who demanded I come home in the first place. We hashed it out the second I was off the plane that I would be here through Mother's Christmas in July festivities, and that's it."

Surprisingly Eliza took in the information, nodded sagely and then plopped down to blow up a beach ball.

"Well?" Kit demanded. "Is that it? As long as I'm leaving and Riley knows, you're happy?"

"Yes, that's right."

"But why?"

Eliza's fair cheeks took on a pink tinge. "Well, I don't know. That is, I mean, well..." Eliza blew her strawberry-blond bangs off her forehead and looked decidedly uncomfortable. Pursing her lips, she continued defiantly, "I just didn't want you dancing back in here and monopolizing Riley again. Unlike you, other people really care about him!"

An idea of what was really going on here occurred to Kit. "Eliza, do you by any chance have a bit of a crush on Riley?"

Deep rose stained Eliza's cheeks, and Kit had her answer. It went a long way toward explaining Eliza's juvenile behavior ever since Kit had come home. Funny thing she hadn't thought of that possibility before.

In the past Eliza had always had a mad crush on someone; it fit her rather goofy outlook on life to swoon over fantasy lovers. It was common in the old days for Eliza to fixate on one of the other's boyfriends, since Alex especially had tended to date good-looking, exciting boys, exactly the right kind to secretly worship from afar. No one had ever taken Eliza's crushes seriously, as far as Kit knew, not even Eliza herself. But this new unrequited love for Riley might make Eliza difficult to handle. Eliza obviously preferred that Kit stay on the other side of the universe just so there was an open field with Riley.

Whew! It was tough work untangling relationships with people as complicated as Riley and her sisters. Her prideful resolve to come home and coexist in their world looked like stuff and nonsense when the realities of Riley and her sisters raised their beautiful heads.

"You know, Eliza, I don't mean to sound pessimistic," Kit said carefully, "but Riley really isn't your type anyway. Why waste time mooning over someone who's wrong for you?" This was a new hat to wear—that of the wise elder sister. All of the Wentworth sisters left that role to Maggie, who was quite good at it.

"Why is Riley bad for me?" Eliza demanded.

"Don't take this the wrong way, but, well, there's no other way to say it. You're too young. Not in years really, but in attitude. I think you'd do better with a guy who's less settled than Riley, maybe a little less sure of himself."

Eliza protested immediately. "You make him sound like an old fogey. He's not like that at all! He's crazy and funny, and he likes a lot of the same things I do."

Kit gazed into space and pictured the ever-present light of mischief in Riley's blue eyes. "No one knows his good points better than I do," she murmured. She narrowed her eyes. "But he's also stubborn and opinionated, and he can be a real jerk when the mood strikes him. He's so smug about his priorities, so clear and straight on where his life is going. You're only twenty-one, Lizzie." She hadn't called Eliza that since grade school. "Your life is still up in the air."

"I don't believe you," Eliza contended stubbornly. "You don't really think he's wrong for me—you just want him for yourself! It's written all over your face!"

Kit batted a ball a little too hard, and the whole stack began to wobble. Grabbing for them as they teetered, she smashed the pyramid of beach balls back into shape.

"You can't even face me!" Eliza reached for Kit's arm to try to pull her around the other way. "That's why you're here, isn't it? You never came to Grand Affairs parties before. You only came today to chase after Riley, didn't you? Didn't you?"

"Lower your voice," Kit commanded. She looked around quickly to see if anyone had noticed the shouting over here. All she needed was for Riley to overhear this lovely conversation. "Do you realize how ridiculous you sound? Why in the world would I expect Riley to be here today?"

Eliza's whole face was pink now, and she stepped back, crossing her arms peevishly over her chest. "All of the owners are here, or haven't you noticed?"

"Owners?" Kit's voice lowered ominously, and her fierce glare skewered Eliza as a terrible, rotten idea took shape in her mind. "Riley is an owner of Grand Affairs?"

"Well, yeah," Eliza managed nervously. The whole family knew the extent of Kit's temper when unleashed. It was an awesome, fearsome thing. "I thought you knew."

"Knew? Knew?" Kit was beyond making sense. Still dangling a beach ball in one hand, she wheeled and strode across the ballroom under a full head of steam. "Riley Cooper, you mealymouthed slime—how dare you?" she shouted.

From the top of a ladder, amid a sea of heads turned their way, Riley gazed down at her calmly. "How dare I what?"

Eyes narrowed, she spit out, "How dare you own a part of my mother's company!" She advanced on his ladder, staring straight up at him with fire in her eyes. "How dare you cheat, lie and act like, like..." She supplied with a flourish, "Like pond scum!"

Eyeing her hands on the bottom rung, he said gingerly, "I think we'd better discuss this when I am in a less precarious position."

"We're not discussing anything."

"Oh, yes we are." He jumped neatly off the ladder from several feet off the floor and took her elbow, planning to usher her to a less conspicuous place to conduct an argument.

"Don't touch me, pond scum," she muttered, and reached around with her beach ball to bop his hand where it rested on her elbow. Even with all of her effort, it did no real harm, but it did make a nice, resounding smack, and she couldn't help a tiny smile as Riley removed his offending hand posthaste.

"Excuse me," Maggie murmured, quietly approaching them from one side. She positioned herself so that she blocked many of the interested glances from around the ballroom. Although Kit could tell Maggie was trying to be stern and disinterested, a glimmer of amusement was discernible in the depths of her dark green eyes. "Why don't you take my car and go somewhere where you can discuss this a little more privately?"

"Good idea," Riley answered lightly. He pried the beach ball out of Kit's fingers and, with nothing more than a sardonic lift to his eyebrows to suggest how he felt about that would-be weapon, exchanged it for Maggie's keys.

He didn't say anything to Kit as he led her outside and walked up to a navy blue Toyota. As he fitted the key in the passenger door, Kit exploded. "This is so typical. You even know all of their lousy cars!"

Sighing, he asked, "What are you talking about?"

"It wasn't enough that you conspired with them to destroy my old room—"

"There was no conspiracy, and you said the room business didn't bother you," he protested.

"What was I supposed to say?" she retorted. Without giving him a chance to interrupt again, she raced on. "But my room was only the beginning! After that, you really got rolling. First you got to be best friends with one of my sisters, and then you conned another one into thinking she'd fallen in love with you. Next you took odd jobs from my mother, practically laying yourself prostrate at the old dictator's feet, and for your finale, you even bought into her cruddy company! You're like some disgusting clinging vine, wrapped in a death grip around the bosom of my family!"

One corner of his mouth lifted. "Interesting image."

"Don't you dare smile at me, Riley, or I'll knock it off your face, I swear."

"I'm sorry," he said penitently.

"No, you're not. You think this whole situation is a scream. Well, I don't find your being in bed with my family particularly amusing."

"In bed with?"

"You know what I mean!"

"Kit, get in the car, and I'll take you home." His tone was firm. "We can talk about this on the way."

Rather than stand in the middle of the Blaisdells' driveway, she got in, but she wasn't pleased about it. "Take me home, did you say? That's a laugh. It's a lot more your home than mine. Remember this morning? You knew where they hid the coffee, not me! Why haven't you moved in yet, anyway? You can have Jo as your best friend, and maybe marry Eliza eventually. She'd like that. Or maybe my mother will adopt you and save you the trouble of marrying in."

"Oh, so Eliza is the one I supposedly conned into falling in love with me. I wondered about that."

He started the car and pulled away from the Blaisdell house without a backward glance. Although she was carefully not looking at him, Kit saw him chew his lip thoughtfully as he gazed out the windshield.

"I want to clarify a few things," he said finally. "First, about Grand Affairs. I own a small share because I put in some cash a few years ago when they wanted to expand the business. The extent of my involvement is going to an occasional board meeting and, once in a blue moon, lending a hand with a hammer. Okay?" He glanced over her way. "I want it clear that Grand Affairs is not of major concern to me." He grinned then, flashing a mischievous smile at her. "By the way, Grand Affairs does not qualify as my occupation, or entitle you to dinner at my expense."

Kit shook her head. It was so easy for him to turn everything into a joke. "Do you really think I would eat dinner with you? I'm furious with you."

"Okay, so you're furious." He noticed that she had calmed down considerably, and he hoped the emotional storm was about over. He had always been able to defuse her wrath when they were kids, but he was badly out of practice. He really ought to have found a way to break all of this to her when she'd first come home. But he had been afraid of losing her trust before he had a chance to... A chance to what? To convince her that he loved her and wanted her? To convince her to love and want him? He hadn't done so well with any of it yet. Well, he ought to be able to get rid of a few misconceptions, anyway. "Kit, you have to know that I didn't do anything to encourage Eliza. She's sort of goofy about that kind of thing. And, as for Jo, she's a friend, but she's not my best friend. Not by a long shot." His gaze once again held her, caressed her. "You will always be that to me. And no one will ever take your place."

She ducked her head, annoyed with herself for believing him so easily. Yet she did believe him, because she knew what he'd said held true for her, too. No one else could ever take his place. As usual with her temper, the initial burst had faded rapidly, leaving her feeling guilty and unreasonable for losing control. But even without the excuse of her anger, one item needed to be cleared up. "Riley, why in the world are you so tight with my family?"

"Because I missed you." He was telling the complete, unadulterated truth, without taking the time to think about the consequences. He was scared to death. "If I hung around them, I was connected to you."

She didn't know what to say. She was so confused.

"You think I'm disloyal because I get along with your family, don't you?"

"Yes," she admitted, "I guess I do."

"I'm sorry, Kit." A small smile again curved his lips. "But I like your mother and your sisters because they're so much like you."

"They are not like me. Not in the least."

He only shook his head, grimly pondering the ironies of fate. Although she was the only non-redhead of the Wentworth women, she had the fiercest temper of them all. She was also the most pigheaded, and the least likely to back away from conflict. Where was the justice that he should fall in love with this one?

As they arrived at the Wentworth house, Riley leaned across to open Kit's door. She flinched as his arm brushed her and realized she had no idea how she should treat him. She'd been furious, but he had apologized awfully nicely. In a rush of words, she said, "I don't want to see you for a few days. I need to clear my mind and decide what to do about you."

"No," he said flatly.

"No?"

"No." He had had about enough of Kit's screwy behavior. He'd let her rant and rave at him and had even said he was sorry when the occasion had called for it. But upsetting plans that were already made and allowing her to sulk in her room for a few days was just plain ridiculous. "You'll see me tomorrow."

"Come on, Riley. Don't be so stubborn. I only want a few days to sort things out."

He was immovable. "It's too late. I already signed you up. We're canoeing tomorrow as part of Jo's Mississippi River cleanup project."

"Well, you can just unsign me! I'm not going in some dumb canoe with you!"

"Oh yes you are. It's a very worthy cause, and Jo has her heart set on this thing being a success. I'm not going to let her down."

"Signing me up without my knowledge," she muttered. "Is there anything else you're planning on springing on me within the next few days?" She sighed, wishing she could scrape up a particle of the anger she'd felt before. It might have come in handy and gotten her out of the dumb canoe trip. All she could think of was what it would be like—sun, water and sharing a tiny canoe with Riley.

There would be just the two of them.

Riley's torso would glisten golden brown in the sunlight, and the muscles in his arms would bunch and flex as he dipped the paddle in the water with even strokes.

The vision was so real she could almost touch the drops of perspiration on his brow.

She shivered unexpectedly, remembering Eliza's suspicions about her feelings. Didi had said the same thing weeks ago, and Kit was getting tired of denying it, especially since it was becoming quite clear that Didi and Eliza were right.

She spared Riley a quick glance, biting her lip as she watched him watch her. What would he do if she told him that her feelings had begun to change in the past week or so, that she might love him *that* way, the way that wasn't supposed to happen to old friends like them?

SHE DIDN'T KNOW WHY she was going on the blasted canoe trip, only that she couldn't stay away.

At ten o'clock in the morning, the designated pickup time, she descended the stairs in a determinedly pleasant, if wary, mood, dressed in red sweat suit and sneakers and carrying a cheerful yellow-striped canvas bag. No sign of Riley yet. Jo, however, came careening into the living room, balancing a box of garbage bags, masking tape, markers and several butterfly nets.

"Ready for canoeing?" she asked brightly, and Kit almost turned around and went back upstairs.

"Ready as I'll ever be. Any sign of Riley yet?"

"Not that I know of," Jo offered vaguely. She tried to hitch up her unwieldy box by raising one knee. "Oh, dear," she lamented as the cuckoo clock in the parlor loudly struck ten. "I've been so tied up with last-minute crises, and I was supposed to be down at the Water Works festival an hour ago to talk to reporters. Oh, by the way, do I look okay? I think I'm going to be on the six o'clock news. But first I have to get down there, don't I? And before that, I have to find the permits. Heavens, what did I do with the permits?" Jo shook her wayward waves and grinned at Kit, obviously loving every particle of the confusion and uproar. "Well, I guess I'll see you down at the river. This is going to be such fun—we're hoping to raise tons of money for the clean water fund. Isn't it exciting?"

Kit didn't have a chance to answer, because Jo had whirled out the front door with her box of junk. Shrugging her shoulders, Kit turned toward the living room, intending to sit and twiddle her thumbs or something equally amusing until Riley arrived. As she planted herself on the sofa, Maggie entered briskly, wearing a cool blue silk dress and a straw picture hat, and looking quite lovely.

"You look very posh. Business or pleasure?" Kit asked.

"Business. We're doing a wedding this morning. Believe me," she said with a laugh, "I do not wear silk on my own time. I mean, the stuff is so impractical. But Alex wanted us to wear matching dresses to this wedding, and I gave in." She smiled, the enigmatic, wry smile that put

Maggie as close to Mona Lisa as the Wentworth sisters got. "A wise sister gives in on the dumb things and then pulls in her markers for important concessions."

"I'll remember that," Kit replied with a smile of her own. It amused her that Maggie was offering advice on getting along in the family. Unfortunately her emotions were always too close to the surface to sit back and decide which arguments were most important to her. No, Kit would probably have to leave the calm and collected approach in Maggie's expert hands.

A quick glance at the cuckoo clock told her that Riley was now ten minutes late, which was very unlike him. She frowned and slumped on the sofa.

Maggie leaned over the back of a wing chair and gave Kit a grave, thoughtful expression. "I know it's none of my business, Kit, and you can tell me to butt out if you want to, but what's going on between the two of you, anyway? Eliza was mad enough to spit last night. She swears you and Riley are carrying on some sort of..." Maggie coughed discreetly.

"Affair? Ha!" Kit scoffed, sitting up straight. "Eliza has about as much sense as a doorknob."

"Quite true," Maggie responded with a twinkle in her eyes, "but something is making you and Riley act awfully silly to each other. Why don't you talk it over?"

Kit sighed, remembering calling Riley names. That probably didn't qualify as talking it over. "I don't know," she said dubiously. She had the idea she didn't want to be too overwhelmingly honest with Riley. What if she bared her soul, and he rejected her? Something close to that had happened once before and had sent her racing out of St. Paul as fast as a DC-10 could carry her. What would it solve to embarrass herself again?

"Well, you ought to do something," Maggie said sensibly. "It's crazy for two people as attached to each other as you and Riley to be fussing all the time."

"Quite true," Kit answered softly, echoing Maggie's words of a few moments before.

"Good. I hope that's settled then." Maggie swept briskly toward the kitchen. Not quite there, she frowned, and regarded Kit over her shoulder. "I can't imagine why I forgot, but I was supposed to pass on a phone message for you."

Kit thought immediately that Riley was going to cancel the canoe trip, and much as she'd been dreading it, she felt a real pang of dejection that she wouldn't be able to go. "From Riley?"

"Yes, as a matter of fact." Maggie narrowed her eyes and then pronounced clearly, as if quoting, "Riley had a softball game this morning and called to say he would be unable to pick you up. So he asked that you walk down to the field on Lexington, south of the park, and meet him at his game. Do you know where that is?"

"I think so. Good thing I wore my tennies." Gratified to be in action, Kit said a rushed goodbye to Maggie and raced off to find Riley's softball game.

As she approached the field Maggie had specified, Kit thought she must have heard wrong or that Maggie had screwed up the instructions. But that wasn't really possible, not with Maggie. So this must be Riley's team. But instead of the postcollege weekend jocks she expected, she saw two squads of skinny little girls who couldn't have been more than eight, wearing bright colored T-shirts that hung just short of their knees. A bit closer, she could make out the words on the front of the batting team's purple shirts. Riley's Raiders. Kit smiled to herself and picked up her pace.

She would have liked to have scooped up this moment and taken it back a few years in time, when Riley Cooper wouldn't have been caught dead coaching a little girls' softball team. She could have had a field day teasing him about being a softy. Now she had a feeling he wouldn't have cared if she razzed him all day about it. She hung back, behind the other team's bench, waiting for a good opportunity to announce her presence.

Wearing a matching purple T-shirt and standing on the first base line, he was carefully instructing a kid who sported pale pink sunglasses and had a one-inch ponytail that stuck straight up.

"Now, listen, Tory, don't run unless I tell you, okay?" The girl nodded. "If it's hit in the air and they catch it, you can't run, okay?" The girl nodded. At that moment, the batter tipped the ball with a swing, which resembled golf more than baseball, and it soared in a graceful loop toward the pitcher. The girl Riley had called Tory took off in a lazy saunter for second base, with Riley shouting at her, "You weren't supposed to run!" The pitcher circled under the ball, squeezed her eyes shut tight and thrust her mitt in the air.

The ball plopped into the mitt, and the pitcher's mouth fell open. "I caught it!" she screamed, and Riley rubbed a hand over his brow. Kit heard Riley mutter, "The first miracle of the year." The other coach screamed for the pitcher to throw the ball to first, and Riley shouted at Tory to get back before the ball got there. Tory stood at second, ignoring everything and doing a tap dance around the bag as the ball wobbled over to first.

"Batter's out, and runner's out at first," the umpire called. "That makes three."

With a gloomy sigh, Riley walked back toward his bench. He picked up a clipboard from the dirt near his players. "Okay," he announced loudly, "Jenny L. is pitching this inning, Jenny A. goes to the outfield and Sara comes to first base. Everybody else stays the same."

It was as if his words were a signal to his team. A dozen little girls began to whine and moan and scuff their toes in the dirt.

"But, Riiiiley," one said, dragging his name out to about six syllables, "Jenny pitched last game, and I never get to pitch."

"Riley, Riley, Riley," another one interrupted, jumping up and down, "I hate the outfield, and Sara hates first base, and can't we just trade? Please, please, please?"

"Come on, Riley, let me be somewhere else. Nothing ever happens at third base!"

"Can I be on the bench this inning? I don't like to play."

He dealt with each one in turn, applying logic and patience to girls who were obviously testing his limits. Kit was amazed at how seriously he took them; it seemed to her that he was letting himself get taken advantage of by a gang of third-graders. Finally, with every little whine disposed of, he shooed his players out to the field and sat on the bench. Kit came up behind him, shaking her head and clicking her tongue.

"Those girls have got you hoodwinked."

He looked up and grinned. "Hi. Welcome to the worst team in the history of the universe."

Crossing her arms over her chest, Kit walked around the edge of the bench and sat beside him. "You are in sore need of some discipline, pal. They don't listen to you at all. I mean, they call you Riley. What ever happened to Mr. Cooper? And that one girl paid absolutely no attention when you told her to stay at first base. And it was the third out. That's terrible."

"What do you suggest I do, beat them?"

"You could at least yell at them a little. They're never going to win this way." Trying to make her point, she called out loudly to the outfield, "Wake up out there!" A girl who was spinning like a ballerina stopped in her tracks and peered at Kit, wondering where this mysterious complaint was coming from.

"Aw, come on," he said, "they're only little kids. This is the first team most of them have been on, and they have zip in the way of skills. I'm just trying to make it fun for them and let everybody get a chance to play. They have plenty of time to get into winning."

"Okay, it's your team." The gleam in her eye belied her words. "But give me those girls for about six weeks, and I'd whip them into shape."

"Yeah," Riley responded, reaching over to playfully tap the tip of her nose. "Before I knew it, you'd have them doing marine push-ups and rolling baseballs around the field with their noses."

She nodded, as if considering his suggestion. "That might do it."

He laughed and poked her in the side, threatening to tickle her, and they joked together over exactly what constituted suitable punishment for eight-year-olds who did ballet in the outfield and ignored their coach's instructions.

The rest of the inning was mercifully short, as it appeared the other team was every bit as bad as Riley's, and that signaled the end of the game. The little girls drifted back to the bench.

"Is that your wife?" a chubby brunette asked. Her eyes were round with curiosity.

"Naah," a second furnished. "Who'd marry Riley?"

And then they all giggled and giggled and giggled.

Riley rolled his eyes above their heads and introduced them to Kit, again displaying endless patience with them. As the girls opened up a cooler with soda pop in it, Kit whispered, "They haven't even asked if you lost."

"We always lose. They've stopped asking."

"Hey, Riley!" a hearty voice called out from a station wagon parked near the field. "Don't forget the game Thursday night. We need you."

Turning toward the voice, Riley answered, "I don't know, Bob. We'll have to wait and see."

Bob got out of the station wagon and trundled over in their direction. "Come on, Riley, give us a break. We want to win this one."

"Game for the big guys," Riley said as an aside to Kit. "Do you remember Bob Powers? He was a year ahead of us in school."

"Oh, sure." Kit was surprised. This man was paunchy and losing his hair and only barely resembled the high school athlete in her memory.

"Bob, this is Kit Wentworth. I'm sure you remember Kit."

"Oh, you bet. Haven't changed a bit." Bob smiled good-naturedly. "You're the one with all the sisters."

"Right." Her return smile was wan, but she put out a hand to shake as a gesture of goodwill. "You married Sally Hansen, right?"

"Yeah." Bob laughed and pumped her hand self-consciously. "Got three kids now. The oldest is Tory on Riley's team."

Ah, yes, Kit thought, *Tory of the pink sunglasses who made the third out.* It seemed ludicrous that someone only a little older than her had that large a child.

"Bob's the one who conned me into coaching the Raiders," Riley explained. "I can't imagine how I let myself get talked into this."

"Aw, quit beefing. You know you love it." To Kit, Bob offered, "He's great with the kids."

Kit smiled. "Yes, I know. We were discussing that."

"So, Kit, you back in town for good?"

"Nope. Just visiting."

"Too bad." Bob grinned. "Riley here could use a good influence."

Cocking an eyebrow at Riley, Kit asked, "Oh, yeah? You been causing trouble again, Cooper?"

"Not me. I'm clean as a whistle."

"Hey, Kit, why don't you talk Riley into playing for my team this Thursday? You can be a cheerleader."

"A cheerleader?" Now Kit raised both eyebrows. "You mean I couldn't play?"

"See you later, Bob," Riley said hurriedly, picking up a bulging bag full of bases and bats and taking Kit's arm to pull her toward his car. "Come on, Kit," he muttered under his breath. "It's not fair to pick fights when you're only visiting."

"Poo," she retorted.

As Riley dumped the bag in the trunk, Kit caught his arm. "Wait a second," she said slowly. "Wasn't it Bob Powers whose nose you punched in fifth grade when he wouldn't let me play baseball with the boys?"

A smile threatened to break through Riley's grim demeanor. "Yes, it was."

"Some guys never learn, do they?" Kit threw an arm around his waist and mischievously gazed up at him. "Are you going to punch his nose for me again?"

"Uh, no." He adjusted to cross his arm over hers, then pulled her closer against him.

The distance between them was now very slim, and Riley watched as the mischief died in Kit's eyes. He looked down into those soft grey-blue depths, and his mind went completely blank. The air seemed thick and still, and Kit's face was so close, so approachable. Inclining his head a fraction nearer, he heard an indistinct intake of breath and saw Kit scan his eyes for a reassurance he hoped she'd find.

He knew he was getting very close to the edge of a cliff, and he was just about to jump right over. "The hell with it," he mumbled, and he bent his face to find her lips.

She felt her body stiffen and freeze to the spot, anticipating the pressure of his mouth on hers. His warm breath mingled with hers, and she let out a small moan, hating this agony of indecision. And then . . .

Honk. Honk, honk.

Chapter Six

They jumped apart and whirled. A station wagon squealed to a stop a few feet away, and Bob Powers leaned out of the driver's window. "Don't forget Thursday," he yelled, and then blasted his station wagon down the street.

"That man is a menace," Kit declared. "No wonder his daughter didn't pay attention." She glanced quickly at Riley, wondering if he wanted an end to this uncomfortable moment as much as she did. "I really think you oughta punch old Bob again."

"Yeah." Riley's answer was a bit gruff, and he reached inside the car for a package of cigarettes. Lighting one, he said softly, "Get in. We're late for the canoe trip."

Trying to lighten the mood, she commented, "I hate to be picky, but we don't have a canoe. Is that a problem?"

He rewarded her departure from the previous mood with a smile, and it took Kit's breath away. It was a lovely smile that created long grooves in his tanned cheeks, where there used to be dimples when he was young. Once again he was unshaven, and the light growth of beard was a golden brown shadow on his jaw. She wondered idly what it felt like to touch it. She wished that he had kissed her, that he had given in to the impulse and just done it. But he had known her too long, and treated her too carefully all that time, to act on impulse now, and they both knew it. If they were going to experiment with kisses, it wouldn't be in the parking lot after a kids' baseball game.

She got in.

Riley crushed his unsmoked cigarette in the car's ashtray. "We're picking up the canoe at my house. I want to change my clothes, too."

"Okay." Kit settled back for the short trip to the house on campus where Jo had picked him up yesterday. After a moment, she said, "Are you really friends with Bob Powers? He's kind of a jerk, isn't he?"

"He's not so bad." He grinned at her. "You seem to bring out the worst in him."

"A cheerleader, did you hear that?"

"I think he was kidding."

"Right," she returned cynically. "And I suppose if I showed up Thursday, he'd let me play."

"If he didn't, I'd punch him in the nose."

Kit laughed. "My hero."

He gave her a sideways glance. "I don't think I'd mind being your hero."

Turning slightly in her seat, Kit reached over and took his hand between both of hers and held it gently. She had always thought that Riley had nice hands, with those long, slim fingers, slightly square at the ends. Not hands to play piano or craft violins, but hands that were clever and strong and did very well at tasks like showing an eight-year-old how to hold a bat, or smacking a bully in the nose.

Smiling at him, she squeezed his hand and then released it. "I told my secretary you were the nicest, sweetest guy I knew. That's still true."

He sighed. He had never wanted to be the nicest guy she knew. "I would've settled for the best-looking."

She shook her head. "But if I told you that, it might spoil you."

He brought the car up into the driveway next to his ugly brown house and waited for her before walking to the door. She stood up on tiptoe and placed a very small kiss on his cheek.

"Thank you for punching out Bob Powers in the fifth grade. You always were a hero to me."

"Don't get carried away here," he said, but he was smiling, too, as he unlocked the door and let her in.

In college he had rented the first floor of the house while someone else with an entrance in the back had the upstairs. It appeared that was still the case. "Good grief," Kit exclaimed. "This place hasn't changed at all! Same early garage sale decor, same cinder block bookshelves." She paused and surveyed the rather dismal surroundings. "I think it's even the same dust."

"I wouldn't doubt it." Heading for the back room, he said over his shoulder, "Sit down. I'll only be a minute."

After clearing a pile of books off the couch, Kit did sit down. With some interest, she scanned the titles. *Coaching for Children* sat cheek by jowl with *Small Business for Fun and Profit* and a Betty Crocker dessert cookbook. She stacked them neatly on the floor and began to drum her fingers on her knee.

"Riley?" she asked loudly. "Why are you still living here? I figured you'd have moved a long time ago."

His voice echoed from the back of the house. "It's not so bad. Besides, I'm never here. Who needs a great place to change clothes?"

"I suppose so." She couldn't imagine even doing that much here. Oh, well, if he was sloppy, at least he wasn't unhealthy. There were no dirty dishes or overflowing ashtrays, so she supposed it could have been worse.

"Anyway," he called out, "I do have another place. I just haven't moved in yet. It's kind of a reconstruction project. Should be ready pretty soon—I've been working on it a while."

"Oh? That sounds like fun. Can I see it?"

"Maybe," he said quietly as he came in from the bedroom. "If you don't mind being the first. It's been sort of a secret."

He was lounging against the doorframe, wearing slim khaki pants and a plain white T-shirt and filling the available space nicely. Light from behind dusted his hair a soft gold, providing him with a hint of a halo.

A halo? Riley? She wasn't sure if that was appropriate. As if he could read her thoughts, his eyes crinkled, and he winked at her. His lips curved into a smile, and he lifted one eyebrow rakishly. "Are you ready for deep water?"

It wasn't what he'd said, but the way he'd said it. She almost blushed at the underlying implication. "I'm always ready," she answered breathlessly. "Now let's hope you know what to do with your paddle, or else we'll both be up a creek."

"That idea has possibilities." The dimple in his cheek deepened into a long groove. "But it's a river, not a creek."

"Who cares?" she tossed out with bravado, and rose to stand by the doorway. She needed air. Suddenly Riley's half of a house had become stuffy and hot.

It appeared Riley's Ferrari was going to sit this trip out. Once outside, he eased up the garage door to reveal a borrowed station wagon packed with picnic gear and ponchos. A metal canoe was strapped securely to the top of the wagon, and Kit almost laughed. Yesterday's flashy playboy had given way to a suburban dad going fishing for the weekend. Suddenly their trip seemed innocuous enough.

They arrived at the river quickly, since it wasn't far from Riley's campus apartment. One of Jo's co-organizers, a thin man with wire-rimmed glasses that kept slipping down his nose, checked their names off on a sheet and assigned their canoe a number. He told them to get their canoe down to the launch site, even though the festivities wouldn't officially begin for a few minutes. The man's voice was hushed with awe when he informed them that everything had to wait for Jo Wentworth's speech. Did they know her? he asked eagerly. He thought she was wonderful. Only after she blessed the effort with her golden oratory could the canoeists push off with their garbage bags and butterfly nets to make mincemeat of floating trash.

"Should I tell him that the magnificent Jo Wentworth is my sister?" Kit whispered in Riley's ear. "Or would that be too much of a disillusionment?"

"Better keep it quiet for now. We wouldn't want to be swamped with autograph seekers."

She flashed him an okay sign. "Good thinking."

Local musicians were setting up to play socially relevant music for charity as other would-be canoeists mingled with them and the onlookers on the banks of the Mississippi near the University of Minnesota campus.

Although it was a warm end-of-June morning, the breeze off the river was cool, and Kit was glad she'd thrown warm-up pants and a sweatshirt over her shorts and T-shirt. She'd had sufficient memory of other boat trips to know that layers were the best bet in case of sudden bursts of sun, rain, clouds, wind or whatever.

Jo arrived while they were dragging Riley's silver canoe down to the bank, and Kit tried to catch her sister's eye across the crowd. After waving and sending them a quick smile, Jo got back to the business of chatting with supporters, handing out bags and nets and cheerfully directing people here and there.

"Funny, isn't it?" Kit mused. "Jo turned out so committed to her causes. None of the rest of us ever cared about politics or social issues, beyond the stage of writing checks, of course."

"You sound a little jealous."

She shrugged. "It might be nice to throw yourself wholeheartedly into an effort like Jo does. I guess I also find it surprising that the others let her devote her energies to benefits when she could be helping out with Grand Affairs."

"Why, Kit, are you only now discovering that there is room in your family for individuality?" One uplifted eyebrow gave his expression a certain sarcasm.

"No, of course not," she said earnestly. She didn't want to sound like she was putting down the company just to be negative. On the other hand, she did think her family's absorption with it bordered on the odd. "I'm amazed that such a big part of Jo's life is outside Grand Affairs, that's all. The company is so all-consuming to the others."

"I don't think that's true, Kit." He gave the canoe a shove into the mud and threw the paddles in after with a resounding smack.

"Oh, come on. They live, eat and breathe Grand Affairs. You can't deny how important Grand Affairs is to my family."

"I don't see anything wrong with it being important to them." Riley sighed and pushed his fingers through the short-cropped hair over his ears. His hair reflected tawny yellow streaks in the bright sun, blending with his golden skin and giving him a burnished, healthy look. A golden boy, bending over his canoe before he set off to undertake noble deeds. "It seems like you're bound and determined to characterize things as badly as possible. It's an okay place, that's all."

"Fine. Let it be an okay place. And quit lecturing me about it."

"I have never said one word about it."

She kicked at the tip of the canoe with the rubber toe of her sneaker. "I'm sick to death of all of you, thinking you can push me into working at that place. Every one of you has been trying to manipulate me, to oh-so-discreetly let it drop how charming Grand Affairs is, and how silly I am not to come back. The others I understand, because it validates their dumb company if I give in. But you—I don't know what you think you'll gain by it, except the satisfaction of pushing around the one person who slipped out of your grasp all those years ago."

"Come on," he said with a certain amount of irritation. "I don't behave like that."

"Ha!" Kit muttered, "My secretary tried to warn me about you. She said you'd be just like Fu Manchu."

"Fu Manchu?" He laughed in utter amazement. "I don't even have a mustache."

Someone in the vicinity cleared his throat discreetly, and they both switched focus abruptly to the intruder.

It was the same mild man with the wire-rimmed glasses who'd registered them earlier. "Sorry to interrupt," he ventured. "I forgot to tell you that you are required to have life jackets in the canoe before you can go. You don't have any."

"I must have left them in the car." Riley cocked his thumb back in the direction of the musicians and the milling crowd. "Kit, why don't you go and get them?"

He fished keys out of his pants pocket and flipped them to Kit with a challenge apparent in the firm line of his jaw.

Would she accede to a harmless request? Or would it represent being "pushed around" yet again?

Her blue-gray eyes sizzled with repressed fury, but she caught the keys neatly and stalked back up the incline to the car, with the registration man hustling to keep up.

A smile played around Riley's lips as he watched her move away from him with determination in every footfall. He liked her best when she was stubborn and impossible.

A new thought changed the hint of a smile into a wary scowl. What if she took his car keys and drove away without him? Damn. He wouldn't put it past her.

But she returned in her own good time, toting two glowing orange life jackets as she ambled back his way. "Your life preserver, captain, sir," she announced smartly.

"Thanks, mate." From his position crouched next to the canoe, he grinned up at her. "If I'm captain, do you have to do whatever I tell you?"

"Not on your life." But Kit couldn't keep her lips from turning up at the corners. After all, she wasn't really mad at Riley. It was just that same old nemesis that always raised red flags in her mind. Grand Affairs. Giving in. Being a good little girl while the others ordered her around. She casually tossed the jackets into the boat and then stepped gingerly into the mud at the river's edge. "Should I get in first?"

"By all means. Everyone knows the captain goes in the back."

"Right." Kit ignored him for the most part, hopping lightly into the canoe and up to the metal seat in front. She tried not to rock things too much. But after all, she hadn't been near a boat in years.

Riley got in behind her with practiced ease, barely moving the canoe, and stuck his paddle into the mud so he could push off from the shore.

What with cans of soda, fruit, sandwiches, plastic trash bags, a butterfly net and extra clothes in between the benches, this was one crowded canoe. She could almost feel his knees behind her, inches away from brushing her bottom. It reminded her that they were all alone, and no honking good old boy would interrupt if she spun around, put her arms around Riley's neck and pulled him down on top of her in the canoe. She would probably succeed in overturning the whole thing, but at least she'd kiss him and find out what she was missing.

Suddenly she was glad she was in the front and he couldn't see her face. Because she was blushing furiously.

Quickly she pulled a can of soda out of the cooler and gulped down about half of it. She saw now that Riley had brought enough provisions for a small army. Good. At this rate she would drink all of his pop before they got away from the shore.

"How are you going to shove off with all this weight?" she asked.

"I'll manage. I don't think you're that heavy."

After sending him a dirty look, Kit stared out the front of the boat and vigorously paddled away from the bank. She had no idea if her strokes combined well with Riley's; she only wanted to occupy herself and her lascivious thoughts.

Think about something, she commanded herself.

"Do we get a prize if we collect the most garbage?" she inquired suddenly, twisting slightly to look at Riley as they slid cleanly into the cool, blue-green water.

"We'll be lucky if we pick up any garbage."

"No, I'm serious. There should be a prize offered for finishing the fastest, or filling the most bags, or even for finding a special message hidden somewhere on the river."

He groaned out loud. "Leave it to you to be looking for prizes."

"But what a great promotion! Some company, or a radio or TV station, something like that, could donate the prize, and then you could advertise it like crazy all over the place." Kit's eyes shone with enthusiasm as her idea got rolling. "Just think—the river could be thick with canoes."

"And even thicker with the litter left behind by all those prize-seekers," Riley remarked dryly.

"You have no imagination," Kit complained. "Why, with the right kind of promotional campaign, we could turn Jo's river cleanup into a media sensation."

"A circus, you mean. I don't think Jo would stand still for that for a minute. Maybe we should forget the grand scheme for the time being and concentrate on picking up trash. What do you say?"

"Keep stroking," she grumbled, and trailed her paddle in the sparkling water.

The morning's light clouds had by now blown away, and the sun was beginning to feel intense on her head. Kit sent a glance over her shoulder to see what disturbing things her companion was up to now. Every time he leaned forward to deepen his stroke, she could feel him behind her, not quite touching her, and not quite *not* touching her. He was driving her crazy.

With very little help from her, he appeared to be steering them easily down the middle of the Mississippi and putting some distance between them and the other canoes. Fine, just what she needed was to be absolutely alone with him. Most everyone else had taken off immediately for banks and bushes near the registration site to pick up the nearest milk cartons and candy wrappers. But Riley seemed to want to stake out turf of his own, guiding them farther downstream.

At river level, there were only the two of them, an expanse of dark, cool river that smelled of fish and the rhythmic slap of Riley's paddle against the surface of the water.

As they slid smoothly down the river, Kit could feel his eyes on the back of her neck. No wonder it was feeling awfully warm back there. Although she'd wanted to sit in front so he would do most of the work, she would have preferred to be able to stare at him and make him all jumpy instead of vice versa.

Anticipating this trip, or perhaps dreading was a better word, she'd imagined his muscles and skin gleaming with sun and water and being forced to look at him, all healthy, glowing and self-satisfied, for hours on end. It was almost worse not to look, but to imagine and to know he had her firmly in his line of vision, like an animal caught in the cross hairs of a hunter's rifle. What a horrible image. Kit shuddered, and the boat mocked her by echoing the movement.

She determined to keep her eyes peeled for trash and to forget about the man in the back of the canoe. Her determination did very little good.

Kit closed her eyes as she sat stiffly on the metal seat, willing her body not to notice his presence, not to lean back nearer to him of its own accord.

Behind her, Riley was trying not to watch her every move. It was impossible. She was so close—almost sitting in his lap—a thought that made sweat break out on his forehead. He paddled harder.

Damn. Why was he so unsure of himself? She had seemed susceptible enough at the ballpark. Maybe if he pulled her back into his lap, she would be as eager as he was to shoot off a few sparks.

"Kit?" he asked roughly.

"Yes?" She turned sharply, breathlessly, wondering if he would ask, or maybe not ask, maybe just ... begin ...

He swallowed. She looked scared to death.

"Aren't you going to help paddle?" he asked abruptly.

She sighed. Trust him to think of the work load at a time like this. She pulled her paddle a tad too sharply on purpose, sending a few glistening drops back onto him. She smiled with malevolent satisfaction as she heard them hit the target. "Better?"

"Not really." He wiped away the moisture on his cheek and mumbled something about it being high time to pick up trash. He steered for the shore and then struggled to fasten a garbage bag to the side of the canoe. It took him three tries to do the simple task, and he was furious with himself.

Kit sank all her extra energy into retrieving a soggy newspaper stuck to a low-hanging branch and emptying a rubber boot of water. How did boots always get into rivers, anyway? Taking a deep breath, she realized she was wilting fast. It was difficult balancing herself while she leaned out of the canoe, pushed the net, pulled the junk and then stashed it in the bag, all at the same time.

She was overheating from the unexpected exertion and the refracted light from the metal canoe. A quick glance at Riley showed him beating the water with short, rapid strokes on both sides to steady them against the motion Kit was causing. She would have sworn he was staring at her bottom as she leaned over the edge of the boat, but his eyes skittered away when she tried to catch him at it. She bit her lip. He looked tanned, healthy, muscular and absolutely gorgeous. She sighed deeply, feeling heat and moisture cloud her vision.

My, she was hot.

Refusing to consider the implications of removing layers of clothing, she pulled her sweatshirt over her head, revealing a T-shirt the color of egg yolks. In flaming script across the back were the words "Hot Stuff!"

In the bright light, Riley saw a blaze of slim yellow and red curves. To his way of thinking, Kit was hot stuff indeed.

"Nice shirt," he mumbled.

"What?" All she knew was that she was dying of heat and that she had to get her sweatpants off under her bottom and over her long legs without leaning back too far, which would risk colliding with Riley, or jiggling up and down too much, which rocked the boat.

He raised his voice. "I said, nice shirt."

"Oh." With her pants scrunched around her knees, she surveyed the front of her shirt distractedly. From her side, it was only an advertisement for an old client. She inquired with surprise, "Are you a fan of Pepe Swanson's popcorn?"

As she half twisted to face him, he was able to read her front, which proclaimed the virtues of Pepe's Gourmet Hot Tamale Popcorn. Riley shuddered. Even with his libido in the shape it was in, that stuff made him lose all appetite. He appreciated junk food as much as the next guy, but Pepe's multitude of far-out popcorn flavors stunk. "No way," he said vehemently. "Don't tell me you like it?"

Her spine stiffened, and she looked down her small nose at him coolly. With her blood running hot and cold, she found things rather more irritating than normal. "As it happens, I'm quite fond of Pepe Swanson. He was my first real client at McCafferty and Sloan.''

Riley's patience was also short. "Just because he's your client doesn't mean you have to eat his terrible popcorn.''

"Riley!" she protested. "I wouldn't write ads extolling the virtues of a product I didn't belive in.''

His lip curled cynically. "Sure you would.''

Honesty prevailed upon her better judgment. "Well, maybe I would. And I'll agree that the hot tamale flavor is kind of strange. But, overall, Pepe's Popcorn is a very good product.'' She rallied to her cause, trying hard to ignore the way Riley was looking at her. "And I did a great campaign for it, too. When Pepe came to the agency, no one had ever heard of him or his crazy recipes.''

"I can believe that.''

Staring a hole in a point below his collarbone, she rambled on. "I talked him into sponsoring popcorn parties and giving away free T-shirts and Frisbees at every school in the country. Do you know that college kids eat more popcorn than anyone else in the country, per capita? And did you also know that Pepe's is now the number one selling popcorn on college campuses?''

Did she know that her T-shirt was slightly damp and molding her every curve like it was born there? Did she know that when she got huffy she sat up straight and her breasts pushed against the T-shirt? Riley groaned and said the first thing that came to mind. "Doesn't it ever bother you that you're stuffing awful popcorn down the throats of unsuspecting children?''

His eyes blazed a path between them, and she was only vaguely aware he was asking her something. "No," she answered hastily, hoping that was an appropriate answer. She practically shouted, "Leave me alone. There's nothing wrong with Pepe's popcorn.''

"Or his T-shirts, either," Riley said slowly.

Kit followed his ardent gaze. She hadn't realized this T-shirt had grown so snug. Suddenly her face felt flushed, and she was much warmer than when she had been in the sweatshirt. She could feel the inevitable wisps of hair falling down from her braid and sticking to her moist skin.

"Cut it out," she snapped in his direction, and bent to finish extricating herself from her pants.

Riley saw a flash of short red shorts and long, slender legs. He swallowed uncomfortably, even as he smiled at the sunshine-yellow anklets she wore with the shorts. When they were younger, she'd thought she was gangly and skinny. Now that gently curved body looked just fine.

He watched as she pulled her socks and shoes off and hoisted a leg over the side to dip her toes in the water. "Ahhh," she sighed. She leaned forward in the softly bobbing canoe and wiped sprinkles of river water across her forehead with the back of her hand.

He knew he couldn't just sit there, hanging on every tiny motion. His breathing was ragged and his pulse irregular, varying every time she bent one way, exposing a few more centimeters of skin at the thigh, or turned the other, pulling the fabric of her shorts tighter across her curves. He had been putting the adrenaline into his paddling, but they were already too far down the river as it was. "Taking time off already?" he muttered. "What ever happened to Miss Achievement and Ambition? We'll have the least garbage on the river at this rate."

"All right. All right." She sat up and stuck her paddle back over the edge. "If you're bound and determined to work me to death, let's jump to it. I vote we find a messier spot so we can fill our bag and get this over with."

"Why do you want to get it over with?" He paused, unable to resist the thoughts that were forming in his mind.

His voice was soft and suggestive when he said, "Is there something else you'd rather be doing?"

She didn't know what she wanted anymore, except to take a long, cool shower and get out of this stupid boat that was the size of a peanut.

And so she once again began to paddle like a demon, until her back and arms were straining with the unfamiliar effort. It seemed as if she and Riley ought to be halfway to New Orleans by now.

This combined canoeing and garbage pickup was sticky, unpleasant work, and she didn't care anymore if Riley yelled at her for loafing. Setting down her paddle, she stretched carefully and hunched forward in the canoe so she could splash water on her arms and legs again.

As her awkward movements began to rock them, Riley was fit to be tied. The way she was tipped over the edge, a great deal that he didn't want to see was revealed to him. "What are you doing?" he demanded.

"Nothing." She sat back down hastily, right onto the tip of her paddle. It was just like playing tiddledywinks. With pressure only on the end, the paddle flipped into the air, spinning prettily, with water droplets dancing behind it in a wide arc. It landed with a solid splash farther downstream, floating there and mocking her to come and get it.

"Oh, dear." Kit leaned in its direction, but she was much too far away. She was fresh out of patience at this point. "Damn the stupid thing anyway."

"No problem." With resignation, Riley stroked hard to catch up with the wayward paddle.

As they approached it, Kit got ready. It was so close, only inches until her fingers would close around it, and she prepared to jump at her chance.

In pursuit of the paddle, Riley steered the canoe every which way, not paying much attention to the depth of the water they were in. Unfortunately the back end veered close to a shallow spot, where a sandbar stretched for several feet.

Just at the moment Kit leaned forward hard to grab at the paddle, the back of the canoe scraped the sand. She was knocked off-balance while she was a good deal over the edge, and there was nothing to hold on to.

Legs and arms flailing, she ended up in three feet of river water, defiantly holding on to the missing paddle. "I got it!" she proclaimed, trying to stand up.

With only Riley in the boat, it came ungrounded immediately and swung around toward Kit. He took one look at her dripping hair and triumphant face, and the tension inside him released like a burst balloon. He started to howl with laughter.

When the wicked sound showed no signs of letting up, Kit squinted, trying to stare daggers at him. "You ran the thing aground on purpose, didn't you?"

"No, I swear," he managed weakly. "I was only trying to get closer to the paddle."

"And pigs can fly." She threw her paddle back in and reached out for the edge of the canoe, but it dipped away. "Stop fooling around and help me back in."

But Riley couldn't stop laughing long enough to steady the boat.

Anger began to rise from the mud squishing between her toes to the strands of hair plastered to her forehead. "Damn you, Riley Cooper." Without thinking she reached back and shoved her hand along the surface of the water, splashing the inside of the canoe and dousing his pants thoroughly.

"Not smart, Kit." A maniacal spark lit his eye, and he pulled the prow of the boat away just as she lunged for it.

The contest was on. The more water she splashed at him, the more delicately he engineered to keep her from climbing back into the canoe, using countersplashing as a diversion. The battle raged back and forth, with water spraying between the two of them like a broken fire hydrant. Choking and dripping, but mostly laughing, Kit could barely see him, and fatigue was setting in from fighting against the water and Riley at the same time. Finally, with one last lunge of desperation, she caught the edge of the canoe firmly in both hands.

"Aha!" she shouted in triumph. With her gaze firmly locked on his, almost in slow motion, she put all her weight onto her arms, purposely unbalancing the canoe.

It rocked heavily, once, twice, then overturned completely. Riley came pitching out sideways with a definite lack of grace. The rest of their belongings—life jackets, clothes, pop cans—spiraled out with him. After the ripples of the smaller articles receded, and Riley stood up, river water pouring from his clothes, Kit crowed with laughter.

Her victory was short-lived. From out of nowhere he grabbed her and slung her over his shoulder. Water streamed from both of them as he stalked from the river and dumped her unceremoniously on the grassy bank.

"What do you think you're doing?" she sputtered.

"Cleaning up the river," was his terse reply.

She expected him to go back for the rest of their things, still floating lazily in the water. But he didn't move. Braced on his elbows, with a knee on either side of her, he stayed there, like a rock, pinning her to the ground under the hard, wet length of his body.

Plink. Plink. Like Chinese water torture, single drops of water slowly slid from the ends of his hair, down his neck and off his shirt, spilling onto her T-shirt and pooling just around the second *p* in Popcorn. She watched the progress of the drips with wide eyes. "Come on, Riley," she managed in a husky voice, "I didn't mean to capsize the boat."

"You've gotten out of hand, old pal, and someone's got to teach you a lesson." As he uttered the words gruffly, he leaned forward an inch or two, bringing his eyes and lips even closer.

Licking her lips, she watched him get nearer. This was no good. Just more of his mastery games, like making her go back for the life jackets and exhorting her to keep up her end of the paddling. She'd be damned before she'd give in to that nonsense. With sparks of fire in her eyes, Kit met his gaze. "Teach me a lesson?" Her tone issued a challenge. "Did you say you were going to teach me a lesson?"

He smiled. "Yeah. What are you going to do about it?"

"Well, I'm not going to learn anything from you, that's for sure." She rolled to the left deftly, collapsing the barrier of his arm as she sneaked between it and his knee. When she was a few feet away, she scrambled to a standing position. "Gotcha," she taunted. Then she tore back down the river with Riley in hot pursuit.

Just at the edge, she screamed to a stop. She watched him try to stop, too, but fail, sliding past her, right back into the mud and the water, and she laughed so hard her sides ached.

"Think you're pretty smart, don't you?" he asked, rising from the waves like a wrathful sea god in a Greek myth.

"Uh-huh." She nodded, still stifling giggles.

So he reached around, hoisting her up in his arms and against his body. They stared into each other's eyes in silence for a long pause, and then he let her go, pitching her away from him with tremendous effort, and she splashed back into the river as if dropped from an airplane.

At that rate it took a long time to haul the canoe and the remainder of their possessions up to the bank.

"But you took the boat out," she remarked pointedly. "How are we going to get back to the car?"

"I don't know." His eyes were pensive. "We weren't supposed to come down this far. We should have gotten picked up by a canoe trailer about two miles ago and driven back to the registration area."

"But you must have known we were coming too far."

"Yeah." He grinned ruefully. "I did. I guess I figured something would occur to me later."

Here they were, dripping and uncomfortable, in the middle of nowhere, with no transportation back to Jo's festival headquarters. Kit felt that placing the burden squarely in Riley's hands was only fair. "You volunteered to be captain." She couldn't keep the mocking smile from her face. "What do you propose, fearless leader?"

"I propose we stash the canoe and most of our things here, and then we walk until we find someone who will give us a ride."

Kit was aghast. "But we've come miles too far! And my socks and shoes are soaking wet!"

"If you hadn't capsized the canoe," he pointed out, "your shoes and socks wouldn't be wet."

"If you hadn't run it aground," she returned, "I wouldn't have fallen out."

He advanced menacingly, showing every intention of picking her up again and throwing her back in the river.

"If you didn't sit on your paddle—" he began.

But Kit yelled, "Oh, no, you don't," and ran ahead of him away from the riverbank.

She shouted down the slope, "Face it, Cooper, you're a failure as a canoe captain. Let's see who wins at hitching rides."

Then she stuck her tongue out at him and scampered up toward the nearest road.

Chapter Seven

Luckily no one's prowess at hitching rides had to be tested. Apparently Jo had noticed they were missing and had sent one of her volunteers out to look for them. This volunteer, a muscular youth who didn't talk much, managed to mumble that he'd found them from the puddles they were creating as they walked. He was none too thrilled to let those puddles inside his car, but since Jo had asked him to find them and bring them back, he would endure it for her sake.

They dried out quickly inside, but their clothes stayed soggy. It was an uncomfortable ride back to Riley's station wagon, but they had managed to avoid walking the whole way and that was good enough for Kit.

She kept giggling every time she remembered Riley flipping through the air out of the canoe. Mr. Calm and Cool, with his pretty little haircut dripping and his T-shirt and khaki pants plastered to his body. It was a wonderful picture.

In more ways than one, she realized, swallowing air in midchuckle. Even with water running in rivulets out his ankles, Riley looked great. And with his clothes painting him like a second skin, Riley looked terrific.

She was getting used to thinking about him and his damned body in inappropriate ways, and just as used to closing her mind to such ideas the moment they arose. Now she clamped down firmly, determined to steer clear of these impossible emotions.

Managing to avoid looking at him too closely, she was relieved when their truculent driver dropped them at the station wagon. He informed them that Jo, whom Kit was starting to think of as Saint Jo what with all the awe and reverence in the air, expected to see them before they left. Kit demurred immediately.

"Riley, I don't want to hang around. I'm miserable in these wet clothes. Besides, I'm in no shape to appear in public." She swept an arm down her side, indicating the sorry state of her shorts. "I wouldn't want to disgrace the Wentworth family."

Riley's gaze grazed the length of her. "You're right. You're in no shape to appear in public."

Kit was surprised he agreed, until she followed the path of his gaze. It was the damned Hot Stuff T-shirt, clinging to her as closely as his clothes hung on him. She'd noticed his; why had the status of hers escaped her? And why did he feel so compelled to tease her about it? To Kit, looking like a reject from a wet T-shirt contest in front of Riley was no laughing matter, while it didn't seem to faze him a bit. Oh, he got a little stern, as if, like an older brother or something, he thought he should keep her from making a mockery of her family name. It was infuriating. Feeling a flush rise on her cheeks, she yanked open the door and jumped into his station wagon without delay.

They drove without comment back to the canoe, to pick up the belongings Riley had hidden when they'd left the river. It was a short route by car, and the job was quickly done.

As they stuck the last of their things in the wagon, Kit couldn't resist a few jibes about how funny he had looked when he and those same items had overturned.

"Such grace and charm, Riley. Really. I was impressed. What was that, a backflip with a one-and-a-half twist?" She did an exaggerated double take. "No, wait, that was the life jacket. You just fell out."

"Guffaw all you want. At least I didn't sit on my paddle."

She leaned back in her seat, laughing, and propped her knees against the dashboard. "It wasn't my fault. The darned thing crawled up underneath me."

"Kit's Amazing Stories."

"Why, Riley, are you saying you don't believe me?"

"Do I ever believe you?"

"No," she answered emphatically, "and I'm crushed. What did I do to deserve this?"

He arched an eyebrow, one of those disturbing eyebrows that were darker than the rest of his hair. "How about purposely capsizing the canoe with me in it? That'll do for starters."

"You're no fun. Really, Riley, I swear I had your best interests at heart." She regarded him solemnly. "You looked so hot and stuffy to me."

A crooked smile lifted one side of his mouth. "Just wait. Dumping a canoe is nothing compared to what I've got in store for you." With her face flushed and her eyes sparkling, she was infuriating, impossible, and captivating beyond belief. She had won by escaping him at the river, and somehow he vowed he would pay her back. If nothing else brilliant occurred to him, he supposed he could make do with one little item still in his possession. As a matter of fact, it was under his back seat, just awaiting an opportunity like this. Now all he had to do was get it into *her* possession. He grinned, thinking of the easiest way possible to pass the glass piggy bank full of pennies back to Kit. Child's play.

Pretending regret, he clicked his tongue. "I thought you knew better than to make me look bad. I don't have a choice now. I'm forced to respond with an equally foolish and meaningless gesture."

Kit had no doubt he would. She spent the rest of the trip to the Wentworth house trying to figure out what he was planning, but he denied every guess she made.

He did say she was giving him a lot of good ideas, and she responded by doubting that he had anything in mind at all. As they entered the house, they were playing the "remember when" game, rating the pranks they'd played on each other in the past. Contending heatedly that her past tricks had shown much more finesse and style than his, Kit almost forgot to be wary. It was so much fun to have someone to be silly with again.

"Hmmm," she said with surprise as they piled their damp things inside the front door. She peeked around the corner into the living room. "No one home."

Taking this moment while she had her back turned, Riley slipped the pig into her tote bag and then turned around quickly. Now all he had to do was think of a reason to stick around until she found it. "I don't feel right leaving you here alone," he improvised. "After all, I did have custody for the whole day."

"Custody?" she inquired dryly. "I'll let that pass this time. It just so happens I want to keep you where I can see you so you don't have a chance to run off and set up buckets of water over doorways or anything."

"Hey," he protested. "I've never done anything that obvious."

She narrowed her eyes. "Maybe not, but I still don't trust you. You stay right here. Don't even move till I change my clothes and come back."

Smiling serenely, knowing that her precautions were too little too late, Riley picked up a porcelain shepherdess sitting on a tiny table in the front hall. He hummed a cheery tune as he pretended to examine it, and Kit raced up the stairs, carrying the soaked clothes and yellow-striped tote bag she'd taken with her in the canoe.

Fooling around with Riley had put her in such a good mood that she moved speedily, taking the wet things into the bathroom near her room, intending to take a quick shower and clean up. But she didn't get very far.

Singing the Pepe's Popcorn jingle to herself, she unbraided and loosened her hair and began to look for her hairbrush. She was in the process of dumping everything from her tote bag into the sink, discarding soggy tissues and rescuing pens and hairpins, when she saw something that didn't belong.

It was wrapped in a white hand towel, but even swaddled and shapeless she knew instantly what it was. As Riley's promised practical joke, it would be a small glass pig with a stomach full of pennies. The same pig that she and Riley had made a career of sneaking into each other's possession for five or six years before she'd left. Unfolding the towel, she shook her head and thought she really ought to have known better.

Somehow, someway, Riley had managed to worm the ugly little piggy bank into her tote bag. And she'd been watching him so carefully! She couldn't help smiling, even as she cursed the name of Riley Cooper.

The pig felt cool and heavy in the palm of her hand, and she took it and ran out of the third-floor bathroom before she had a chance to stop herself. In all the years they'd passed the piggy bank back and forth, they had never acknowledged it. It was part of the joke to accomplish the switch silently.

But this time she was blinded to mundane considerations like how they had set up the rules of their silly piggy bank game ten years ago. He had called her bluff and pulled off the practical joke, and it was more than Kit could suffer in silence. Without thinking she was going to call him on it.

"Riley," she sang out as she hit the landing. He was still standing in the front hall lounging carelessly near the doorway to the living room. "When did you put this pig in my bag?"

"Me?" he asked, with a great show of innocence. "I don't know what you're talking about." His slow, crooked grin gave him away.

A wicked chuckle escaped Kit, and she took a few steps in his direction, brandishing the bank. "You do know you're going to take it back, don't you?"

"Who's going to make me?"

"Try and stop me, Riley." Advancing, keeping her gaze steady on his, she swung the pig back and forth between her hands. "Please, try and stop me."

It was as if a little steam had escaped from the pressure cooker of her emotions when she'd really let go with Riley. Now, as she faced his mocking challenge, there was enough steam to make a teakettle sing. Kit knew she had gone past the point of making sense. She was a mature adult with a responsible position in life, yet here she was behaving like a grade-schooler on a dare.

"Tell me when you did it, and I'll go easy on you," she tried.

Riley only laughed.

Her words became singsong, trailing as she slid two steps closer. "You're going to be sorry."

Their gazes locked and held for one, two, three beats.

Then she let go. In a rush, scrambling, she bridged the gap between them and tried to stuff the pig down his pants.

If she'd stopped to consider what she was doing, she probably would have been horrified. She hadn't even realized what she was going to do until she'd already tried it. It was as if she were on automatic pilot. He'd been so beastly, always knocking her off kilter just when she'd thought she had him pegged, that she was willing to attempt even the ridiculous to wipe that smirk off his face.

Riley was certainly shocked. "Kit," he said weakly, trying to catch her arms. "What are you doing?"

"Giving you back your piggy bank," she managed between gritted teeth.

Now that surprise was no longer a factor, her resources were limited. He was obviously stronger, and if he didn't want the pig in his pants, it wasn't going to get there. Near certainty of failing only made her more determined to succeed. She pressed on.

Riley was amused and still somewhat dazed by her choice of attack, and that slowed him down. He tried not to laugh, but whatever she was doing tickled and brushed against him. She was wiggling so much he could barely hold her wrists and keep her a few inches away. She had suddenly become an eel: slim, wet and slippery.

"Aha!" She lunged for him, but he managed to side-step and catch her off-balance. In a fast turn, she was stuck between him and the wall, and, holding her still by pressing her into the wall with his body, he could maneuver more easily. With a lucky grab, he got one and then both of her hands in one of his, even though she tried to twist away. He trapped her hands between them, removed the piggy bank gently, placed it on a nearby curio table and let the irrevocability of her situation sink in.

It was his turn to say "Aha" in a soft, meaningful tone. Against the wall, the pale ivory curtain of her hair kept her prisoner. He disengaged it from its trap, shifting it to spill over her shoulder in a long shower of gold. Still holding both her wrists, he used his other hand to carefully tuck a strand behind her ear.

Only inches separated them; she could feel the warm puffs of his breath ruffling her bangs, and the slick, wet cotton of his shirt pressing up against her.

"May I say 'uncle' now?" she asked, looking up into the deep blue of his eyes.

When he spoke, his voice was low and husky, rubbing her nerve endings sensuously. His dark eyebrows dipped in the center, revealing an intensity that made her shiver. "No 'uncles' allowed. I thought maybe I'd tickle you until you begged for mercy."

Tickling? That was something reserved for children. Kit didn't feel much like a child at the moment. "Please, Riley, don't," she pleaded in an uneven voice, which had never before appeared in her repertoire.

But it was too late. The long, strong fingers of his free hand were already brushing her ribs. She screwed her eyes shut and held herself tightly, not breathing, preparing herself for an onslaught that never came. Reopening her eyes, she found his in confusion. What she saw there made her stand absolutely still for a long moment. Maybe Riley didn't feel like her brother after all. She felt a small surprise and a great pleasure. It was real. He wanted her. And, in that split second, she admitted that she wanted him, too, and there was no earthly reason to deny it.

He saw what he wanted to see, what he was waiting for. Not fear this time, but knowledge, pleasure, and expectation. She looked as if she knew exactly what was happening, and she couldn't wait. Instead of tickling her as he'd threatened, his fingers stroked the soaked fabric of her T-shirt tenderly, sketching the outline of each rib. He could feel his hand trembling against her, and he found her eyes once more, just to be sure.

She swallowed and then swallowed again, staring into his eyes and wondering why this felt so awful and so wonderful and why her breath wouldn't seem to come. She became suddenly and excruciatingly aware that she was wearing little clothing and that the material between them was soggy and cold.

Riley dropped her wrists, and lost in the power of his gaze, she didn't notice for a second or two. Then she lifted her hands, still between them, to smooth back the damp waves at his temples. One dark gold lock fell onto his forehead, and meticulously she edged it back into place.

Shutting his eyes, he savored the feel of her cool fingers on his forehead. He had wondered for so long what it would feel like to have her touch him that way, and he had feared that the moment would never come or that it would fall short of his hopes. But the reality was incredibly more potent than the fantasy. Even that mere brush at his temple had inflamed him, destroyed him, and he fought with himself to hold on.

As she continued to study him, Kit's thoughts moved farther and farther away from the silly mood of only a few moments ago. Now the thought of putting anything in his pants made her fingers pulse and her temples pound. How could she have been so naive as to start something like this? When he had touched her that way, everything had changed. Everything. The Kit and Riley she knew from the past didn't exist anymore. Two strangers, who shared no past and worried about no future, had taken their places.

She heard herself sigh, the sound far away and indistinct, and then she moved one hand to barely brush the gold dust of stubble on his jaw. It was rough, but soft, ruffling against the backs of her fingers, rubbing against her nerve endings, etching its image irrevocably on her picture of Riley.

"I wondered what it felt like," she murmured.

"Did you?" he inquired in a voice that was as slurred and low as hers, thinking, *If I kiss her, I won't be able to stop.*

"Uh-huh," she agreed, thinking, *Why doesn't he kiss me?*

Instead, he flexed the hand at her side, spreading his fingers and rolling his thumb to the underside of her breast. What had been happening in slow motion suddenly began to pick up speed. As his thumb moved, her pulse accelerated, and a jolt of electricity sparked down her spine. His hand closed over her breast, and she moaned, leaning into him and reveling in the heightened sensation. Her nipple peaked and hardened, feeling as if it might burn a hole right through the chilled fabric of her shirt.

She shifted in his arms to find his lips, but he eluded her, not ready to give in. Nipping her earlobe with his teeth, he wanted to shock her and excite her. He could feel her trembling under his lips, and he was victorious. But that wasn't enough to satisfy his own desires, rising within him, making it impossible to stand back from the kiss she was desperately seeking. Now it was what he sought, too. He needed to taste her.

Every devil that had been smoldering in Riley came flaming to the surface. Kit could see those devils in the hot sparks in his eyes, in the long groove of his dimple, in the upward curve of the corner of his mouth. He looked irresistible and insatiable, all at once.

She rubbed her hands back and forth over his shoulders, and he felt warm and pulsing to the touch even through his T-shirt. He was intense, obsessed, ardent. Playful, casual Riley? This fire-breathing dragon must be someone else.

The power of her own imagination and anticipation sent her reeling when he finally lowered his lips to hers. Wrapping her arms tightly around his neck, she met him with an open, ready mouth. Without warning she had turned into a wanton, and it was such a departure she couldn't begin to stop it. At first his lips were hard and demanding, but the kiss soon deepened and grew liquid. Her tongue spiraled and spun with his, trying desperately to satisfy the need that she only now realized had been building for years. On and on she met his kiss, drugged with need, afraid to breathe or break the spell, until she was forced to back away to gasp for air.

As he dropped small kisses down the slope of her neck, she pressed her cheek to his, ruffling her fingers through the silky, sandy hair at the base of his neck. It was wet, too, like everything else, but thick and soft between her fingers.

"Oh, Riley." The sound came from deep inside her, denoting surprise, pleasure and a certain dizziness all together. "I feel on fire. This can't be."

He pulled back, framing her face with his hands, and gazed into her gray eyes, clouded now as they focused on desire. "It can be. It is. Don't deny it now, Kit. I couldn't stand it."

"Me, neither." She shivered again and folded her arms around him.

Still bracketing her cheeks, he eased her face closer, finding her lips again with searing intensity. His passion was becoming uncontrollable, and he groaned into the kiss. He was coming perilously close to suggesting that they make love right there in the hallway. His breath ragged, he demanded, "Where can we go?"

"Upstairs?"

He nodded, catching her hand, and cut across to the stairs without hesitation. At the landing, though, he paused. He ran his free hand over the rough surface of his jaw and looked back at Kit. "In your mother's house?"

"I don't care."

"I do." Grimly he expelled a stream of air. "It just wouldn't be right."

"Don't do this to me, Riley." She heard her voice take on an edge that she didn't like, and she knew that she was speaking too quickly, without taking time to sift or censor her words. When she acted impulsively, she didn't always make the right choices. "Don't turn me away again."

"Kit," he said softly, elongating her name into a caress, "this isn't the right place. Your mother or any of your sisters could be home any minute." Raising his hand to her cheek, he brushed his knuckles carefully sensuously, along the pale peach curve. "It has to be special for us—the perfect time and place."

She wheeled abruptly, abandoning him to pace off a few steps. "This is really your way of turning me down again, of sending me away under cover of pretty words and phony sentiment, isn't it?"

Riley stepped back. Raking his fingers through the hair that Kit had so recently touched, he turned and looked out over the railing into the front hall. "Turn you down?" He shook his head with disbelief. "I want you so badly my knees are shaking. Why would I turn you down?"

Kit pressed her lips together. She lifted her chin defiantly. "You did before, didn't you?"

She was talking about the night before she'd left town four years ago, and he knew immediately. Although that night had been a nightmare for both of them, and central to her flight from St. Paul, neither had cared to discuss it. Until now. He had thought he was sparing her—or both of them—embarrassment, unhappiness perhaps. But it looked as if it was time to put it behind them once and for all.

"That was a long time ago, Kit. We were different people then. I said no because you didn't mean it anyway."

"How could you possibly have come to the conclusion that I didn't mean it?" she demanded.

He held his jaw very tightly, giving it a hard line even under the softening layer of stubble. "You made it pretty damn clear."

"That's nonsense! I came right out and said, 'Riley, will you please make love to me,' and you find some room for doubt as to my meaning?" she asked, incredulous.

"Yeah, well, you also told me you were in love with some other guy who preferred your sisters." He stuffed his hands in his pockets, even now steeling himself against the hurt and helplessness he had felt then. "No matter what I thought, the situation was wrong. Very wrong."

Kit blew her bangs off her forehead. She knew that he was right. She had acted like a child, asking him for something he couldn't give. "Riley, I'm sorry. I would give anything to make it so that it had never happened." How could she explain what she'd been thinking then or how it had come about? "I should never have asked you. It was so dumb. But I was hurting so badly that night, and I came to you to make it all right for me, just like you always had."

"Only I screwed up and made it worse," he said softly.

"I thought you of all people would understand why it meant so much to me. But you were like everyone else, and I guess you just didn't find me attractive." Saying her fear aloud made it seem childish and petty, but it had been so real four years ago. She had put her vanity on the line and asked him to prove to her that she was a woman, but he had refused. A woman? She had been an idiot. Her emotions were running very close to the surface, and tears began to well behind her eyes. Just what she didn't need. "The irony is that I didn't really care about that guy, no matter what I said at the time. I blew our friendship to bits because of some jerk whose name I can't even remember. He was the straw that broke the camel's back, that's all. It had happened one too many times."

"With your sisters, you mean?"

She nodded and started to pace again, taking a diversion in the painstaking precision of each step. "Ever since first grade, the boys I knew—except you—wanted introductions to my sisters. 'Kit, does Alex have a boyfriend?' 'Kit, will you ask Jo if she'd like me if I like her?' 'Kit, do you think Maggie would go to the football game with me?'" she mimicked. She continued, more to herself than to Riley, "I was so sick of it that I stayed clear of any man I thought had even heard of my sisters. But the guy in my marketing class was different, or so I thought. What a joke! He took me to dinner and then asked if I thought any of my sisters would date him. Not one in particular, mind you—he would have settled for any of the fabulous Wentworth redheads."

"Kit, you don't have to put yourself through this. I remember," he said gently.

"Well, so do I." Her voice turned bitter. "I couldn't stay here anymore. I couldn't face the competition. Even you didn't think I was attractive."

"I thought you were a knockout."

She shook her head sadly. "No, you didn't. You said no." Twisting her hands into fists, she let words spill out that should have been stopped. "I've tried to block it out. Do you know that? But I can't. I still remember it down to the last detail, even to what you were wearing. Or maybe I should say what you weren't wearing," she added dryly. "You didn't have much on that night when I came to your house. It was very late, and you were studying for an exam. Isn't that right?"

He nodded. "My last engineering final. I almost flunked it, you know."

"No, I didn't." Her fingers clenched tighter. "Even more guilt to lay at my door, I guess. I remember you were angry with me for interrupting your studying like that."

"I was tired. It was very late. And you scared the hell out of me, barging in like that and asking me to—"

"Go ahead—say it." Her gaze held him steadily. "I asked you to make love to me."

"I know very well what you asked." He was trying to understand and deal with it all better than he had the first time. If anything, it was tougher now that years had gone by.

"And you said no because you didn't find me attractive. Don't worry. I understand completely."

Crossing to her, he put both hands on her shoulders, forcing her to face him. Frustration was pushing him to say things he'd never shared with anyone. How could Kit have so misunderstood the reasons behind his refusal? "I could never have slept with you as a substitute for someone else," he said tersely. "You didn't want me. You wanted him, whoever he was." He stopped for a moment and then cautiously slid one finger under her chin to tilt her face up so that he could find her eyes. "When you asked me to make love to you, I wanted to say yes more than I've ever wanted anything in my life. But I couldn't. Can you understand that? Not when you wanted me as a stand-in for another man."

"What?" It had never occurred to her that he might see things that way. She understood only too well how low it made a person feel to know they weren't someone's first choice. Wasn't that exactly why she'd run to Riley's apartment that night? But that would seem to indicate he would have preferred being first choice. She drew away from him, confused. "Are you sure about this?"

"Positive."

"But that implies that..." She broke off, unsure of how to phrase it.

"That I was in love with you back then?" His voice dropped a notch. "I was."

Kit's eyes widened. "You were? Why didn't you tell me?"

"Because we were friends, and the timing wasn't right. You were all mixed up about your mother and your career, and I was trying to graduate after fooling around for four years." Shaking his head, Riley continued. "Besides, you didn't feel the same way. I knew that."

She didn't know what to think anymore. He had loved her then. He had wanted her then. And she had made all the wrong assumptions.

"What are you thinking?"

She looked up, amused. "That you should have said yes and saved us both a lot of trouble."

Holding her gently in his arms, skimming his jaw on the smoothness of her hair, he said, "I came so close. But I was afraid I'd make love to you and you'd whisper someone else's name. I would have died."

"So instead you said no, and I threw an engineering book at you and took the next flight to New York City."

"I never thought you'd leave me because of it."

"If I'd known you cared," she offered softly, "I would never have gone."

"I guess it really doesn't matter anymore, does it?" He held her back so that he could look at her, then ran his hands lightly down the edge of her hair, tracing a line from her bangs down her cheek to the sleek tendrils curving over her breast. He couldn't get used to the idea that she was there and that he could have his fill of touching her without fear that she might evaporate. "What is important is now, Kit. I need to know what you feel for me."

Looking into those familiar blue eyes, her skin felt flushed and warm. She wanted to feel him against her, to explore all the possibilities. Yes, passion was certainly there, pulsing strongly throughout her body. But what else? Anger at her own foolishness, for refusing to face what was glaringly obvious, filled her. She knew this man as well as she knew herself. She had loved this man forever. There was nothing to be ashamed of. "I love you and I want you," she said clearly. "I want it all."

He let out the breath he had been holding, but kept watching her, silent and subdued.

"Well?" she demanded, feeling naked with confession. "Aren't you going to say anything?"

"I'm damned if I know what to say." A smile lifted the left side of his lips, deepening his dimple, and even white teeth gleamed within his tan.

"How about that you love me, too?"

"You already know that."

"Do I?" As she recalled, Riley had loved a lot of women in his time, at least in the physical sense. He had probably dated thirty girls just in his junior year of college. He might have felt that he "loved" each one of them. "I'm not as practiced at this sort of thing as you are."

She looked up at him, watching him stand there all golden and careless in her mother's front hall. "And I'm afraid," she said quietly.

"Afraid of me?"

She nodded.

He seemed surprised, but not angry. "How could you ever be afraid of me?"

Shaking her head, she ran a hand through the long expanse of her hair. "I'm afraid to turn into one more in your discard pile. You forget that I know you too well. I know your record with women. Now I'm special, I'm different, because I'm your friend. But what if . . ." She faltered, unwilling even now to put it into words.

Riley wasn't so shy. "What if we sleep together and it changes everything and we lose the friendship, too. Isn't that what you're asking?"

"Yes." Her voice was soft; she continued to gaze at him as if expecting answers to appear out of nowhere.

"Kit," he protested, "how could you think you wouldn't be special to me, no matter what happens?"

"I don't know. It's just . . ." She turned sarcastic as a defense. "I don't want to be number 733 on the hit parade, even with a bullet."

"Kit," he said again, with a disapproving tone. "If I didn't see you for ten years, it wouldn't make any difference. We would still be connected somehow, someway. There are too many old times between us." He paused, and his eyes were so sincere it took her breath away. "If you want to hear it, I'll spell it out for you. Kit, I like you. I love you. I want all of you, not just the friend part but the lover part, too. Because you are the other half of me." Gaining steam, he continued, "I want you with me. I want to have kids with you. I want to grow old with you. I want it all."

"Whoa! Aren't you jumping the gun here?"

"Yes." He had spilled the entire story, the one he had been holding back out of fear of pressuring her. Had he blown the whole thing? She didn't appear to be running for the exit. His lips compressed to a narrow line. "But I don't care. It's the truth."

"One step at a time, Riley." She smiled and put her arms around him slowly, gently, laying her cheek on the cool, damp cotton of his white T-shirt. "Let's take it one step at a time."

Sighing, he enfolded her carefully, as if she were a very rare and precious treasure. When he bent his head to kiss her this time, it was soft and slow. Their lips met with only a slight brush of a caress. It was like drops of dew compared to the torrential downpour of the first kiss.

Breath mingling, touching along the complete length of their bodies, they stood there, wrapped in each other's arms, pressed together so tightly it was difficult to draw breath. It was as if they were afraid to let up even the smallest bit, for fear a malignant fate would intrude and force them apart.

One step at a time, she'd said. Could he be that patient? He'd have to be, wouldn't he? Riley smiled gloomily, tightening what was already close to a stranglehold. He had come this far, and it was a damn good start.

"Kit," he whispered in her ear, breaking the silence, "I still want to make love to you. But not here." He took her earlobe in his teeth and bit down ever so slightly.

"Yes," she murmured, "I suppose I see your point." It took them back to square one of their discussion, but her head was a bit cooler now. Now his compunction to find a different locale seemed like a sensitive, considerate gesture rather than a rejection. "Where?"

"My place?"

She regarded him as if he'd lost his mind. "The dust pit? Surely you jest."

"There's the new house," he said hopefully.

"Does it have plumbing?"

"Uh, no, not yet."

"Forget it." She cast him a cynical glance. "And if you suggest your car, this discussion is over."

"What about a hotel?"

"Oh, come on, Riley, this is so...so icky, like teenagers. Besides," she said, sighing extravagantly, "we have lots of time to figure out the perfect time and place."

Lots of time, he thought dismally. *Fourteen whole days before Christmas in July.* His mood brightened. Unless he changed her mind about her departure date and got her to postpone leaving indefinitely. A sly smile curved his lips. Once they made love, she'd never be able to leave him. In his mind it was as simple as that.

Kit noticed the mysterious smile and almost asked him why he looked so smug, when she heard voices from outside. Her heart sank. The high-pitched, excited tones were easy to identify.

Riley placed a tiny kiss on Kit's cheek and set her from him regretfully as they were swept up in a tide of incoming Wentworths.

Alexandra and Eliza tripped in first, talking and laughing gaily and skipping around Kit and Riley with a hello and a remark or two about the couple's bedraggled appearance. The sisters themselves were cool and lovely in pastel silk dresses with large-brimmed hats. Kit felt immediately self-conscious of her own bare legs and mud-streaked clothes.

"Afternoon weddings are so wonderful," Eliza offered with wide, misty eyes. She was pretty in peach, while Alex had a bit more sophistication in a lavender version of the same dress.

Maggie and their mother followed immediately, arm in arm, conferring over details on the job they had done that day. Their dresses and big hats completed this set of fabulous Wentworths, adding Maggie's elegant blue and Lilah's sea foam green to the mix. Framed together, a French Impressionist would surely have painted them. All creamy skin and muted tones, they made as lovely a picture as any water lilies.

Amid the swishing skirts and animated chatter, no one seemed inclined to get past the now-crowded hallway. Eliza cornered Riley without delay to pour out all of the fun happenings at that afternoon's wedding, and Kit realized their idyllic moment was officially over. She regarded her sister peevishly, wishing Eliza would find somewhere else to roost.

"Eliza," she began ominously, "don't you have anything you need to do?"

"No," Eliza responded airily. "Not a thing."

"Yes, you do," Maggie interjected so vigorously that the others turned to look at her in surprise. "In fact," she sped on, ignoring the strange looks she was getting, "I need to see everyone in the dining room immediately for..." She bit her lip. "For debriefing on today's wedding."

"A debriefing?" Alex returned, sounding horrified. "Maggie, darling, I haven't a clue as to what you're talking about."

"A debriefing," Maggie repeated forcefully. "I'll explain later. Just come on, will you?" She managed an abbreviated smile for Kit and Riley as she bodily pushed her mother and sisters into the living room. Eliza was glaring and fussing at being separated from her beloved Riley, but Maggie wasn't taking no for an answer.

Kit heard the questions from her unconvinced family as Maggie dragged them all to the dining room and shut the door behind them.

"She knew we wanted to be alone," she whispered to Riley.

"Remind me that I owe Maggie one."

"You owe me one first."

He raised an eyebrow, affecting surprise at the implication of her words. "One what?"

Kit winked in a manner she hoped was seductive. "You figure it out."

"Okay." He bent and dotted a quick kiss on her lips. "How about tonight?"

"No, not tonight."

"Headache?" His tone was the definition of cynicism.

"No," she retorted, "no headache. I'm exhausted, that's all. This has been a very weird day. Besides, you need time to find the perfect place for our little tryst, and I need time, too." She softened, staring into his eyes. "I need time to think about all of this. Remember, we agreed," she said playfully, pointing a finger at his chest as if to propel him out the front door, "one step at a time."

"One step at a time," he echoed morosely. But then he winked at her, grabbed her, kissed her hard and spun out the door.

Chapter Eight

She watched him skip down the front walk to his car, and a wide, unrestrained smile broke over her features. Kit began to sing the Pepe's Popcorn jingle at the top of her lungs, hitting, "Pop it up, Hot Stuff," with special gusto.

In her general delirium she almost collided with her mother, who hung back, radiating enough curiosity to unhinge Mata Hari. Lilah did not, however, ask any of the questions that were fairly bursting behind her lips. Instead, she said, in a rather strained voice, "You have a phone call, Katharine. You may take it in the kitchen."

"Oh, okay." Kit danced a few steps in that direction before whirling back around. "Who is it, anyway?"

"Someone in New York. Mimi? Fifi? Something like that."

Didi. A call from Didi could only mean one thing. Trouble in the office. And Kit had neither the wits nor the desire to deal with trouble right now. In fact, she was having a great deal of difficulty remembering she even had an office. With a reluctant smile, she went for the telephone.

"Kit, is that you?" Didi's frantic voice came leaping over the wire.

"Hi, Didi. How are you?"

"Thank goodness I got you!" Not stopping for idle chitchat or how-do-you-dos, Didi rushed on. "Sloan's on a rampage, and I've been trying to call you for three days! Doesn't anyone in that place ever answer the phone?"

The fact that John Peterson Sloan, Kit's immediate boss and the senior partner in McCafferty and Sloan, was in a dither, was nothing new. As Didi was wont to characterize it, he often had his undies in a bundle. But usually Kit was there to smooth things over and calm him down. On her own with the big boss's tantrums, Didi was liable to have a nervous breakdown.

"It's been pretty hectic here," Kit responded lamely.

"It doesn't matter. I've got you now. What did you do with the Lush Plush toilet paper storyboards? We can't find them anywhere, and the Lush Plush people flew in from Toledo yesterday expressly to see them. Sloan is furious that I can't find them."

Her office mind-set returned in a rush. "Didi, there are no Lush Plush storyboards," she said carefully. "Sloan turned down my last set of ideas, and I haven't come up with anything to replace them."

There was a short silence on the other end of the phone line. "You know what they say about people who bear bad tidings. Sloan's going to kill me, Kit, literally. He already told the Lush Plush guys that you were a genius and they'd love your ideas. With no storyboards, I'm dead meat, Kit."

"No, you're not." It was easy for Kit to be so sure when she was a thousand miles away from Sloan's wrath. "I'll tell you what, why don't you pull out the ones he rejected? The chances are he won't remember, and at least he'll have something to show the people from Toledo. I thought the original storyboards were pretty good anyway, to tell you the truth."

Didi released an extended sigh. "I guess it's better than facing him and telling him he has to send those nerds back to Toledo empty-handed."

"I agree," Kit returned decisively. "The storyboards are filed under Rejects. You shouldn't have any trouble finding them. Now that that's out of the way, is there anything else?"

"Yes! There are a million things. When are you coming back?"

"Two more weeks, that's all. You can handle it for two more weeks, Didi."

"That's what you say." Didi paused. "By the way, how's our friend Fu Manchu? Has he got you under his thumb yet?"

"Of course not," Kit answered, laughing. She broke off when she realized she was lying through her teeth. It would have been tough to be any more under his thumb if she'd tried.

"What a relief!" Didi returned, unaware of the choking on the other end of the line. "I was afraid I'd have to come and rescue you from old Fu's lair. Hurry and get back here, will you?"

"I will, I promise. And, Didi, don't worry about Sloan. I'll take care of him when I get back."

As she replaced the receiver in its cradle, Kit was thinking of how easily she had slipped back into her "professional woman" mode. Home for two weeks, she counted blowing up beach balls and paddling a canoe as her most significant professional achievements. But, put her into her chosen milieu for a few minutes, and she single-handedly fixed a crisis, even from a thousand miles away. It was a real boost to feel the wheels turning again, to feel smart and capable and in charge.

She had set New York so far from her mind that she'd almost forgotten the person she was when she was there. Was that the same person Riley thought he loved? Or was he only enamored of some childhood Kit who didn't exist anymore?

She honestly didn't know.

Kit found a chair at the kitchen table and sat down slowly, staring unseeingly at the fussy wallpaper. She was going back to New York in two weeks, and she knew it and Riley knew it, and yet they had actually given in to the idea of falling in love with each other.

She felt like Dr. Jekyll and Ms. Hyde. Dr. Jekyll said, "I love you" to Riley and listened to him talk about children, for goodness' sake, while Ms. Hyde blithely assured her secretary she would be back in two weeks without fail.

She groaned, remembering her instructions to Riley to find the perfect place. She had as good as dared him to jump into a wild and passionate fling. How could she even have considered such a thing? Once they made love, she'd never be able to leave him. In her mind it was as simple as that.

HER MIND WAS MADE UP. She had to leave in two weeks; there was no way she'd consider staying in such close proximity to her family indefinitely. And if she wanted to leave, she'd have to keep Riley at arm's length. She was on pins and needles. The next two days passed agonizingly slowly, with more weak smiles and vague answers than she had ever used in her life. She pretended to be caught up in her sisters' activities, because at least that was a diversion. He couldn't very well come on to her while she was with Jo, bundling newspapers at the recycling center on Sunday or trampolining for traffic safety on Monday.

After less than forty-eight hours, she was sick of it. Even while she was bouncing up and down on the trampoline, smiling and pretending she was having a good time for a good cause, she wanted to be with Riley. And he was there, waiting for her, watching her, tantalizing her. She could tell he was mystified by her friendly yet noncommittal behavior, and she was confused and frustrated herself.

Her sisters were vivacious enough and entertaining enough to be good company to a tree stump, but most of their efforts went over Kit's head. She was thinking about the way Riley's smile lit up a room, and the way his eyes crinkled at the corners when he smiled. Her mind and her heart kept reminding her of just how much she wanted him.

There was no room left for opinions on whether Alex looked better in the gold lamé or the electric-blue evening gown, or whether Eliza ought to punch a few more holes in her ears. Kit felt jumpy and restless. She ran from the room each time the doorbell rang.

But Riley caught up with her on Monday night. Her sisters were collected in the living room, shouting and arguing about something or other, and her mother was off playing bridge with the governor's wife. Kit was rocking gently on the front porch swing, listening to the sounds of summer wafting up from the lake and the park. She was miserable.

When she saw Riley's Ferrari pull up, Kit stood up, ready to bolt, but he jumped out of the car and raced to the porch before she had a chance.

Blocking the door into the house, he announced, "I want to know what's going on."

"I'm sure I don't know what you mean."

"Oh, yes, you do." He narrowed his eyes, trying to discern some reason for Kit's stalling tactics. She'd been perfect—wonderful, in fact—on Saturday, and yet yesterday and today she'd acted like a scared rabbit every time he had appeared. Setting his hand carefully on her arm, he pulled her back to the swing and sat her down. "Tell me what this is all about."

"But, Riley, there's nothing to tell!"

"Kit, don't play games with me," he warned. "You're putting me off on purpose. I try to see you or talk to you and you go bounce on a trampoline! It doesn't make sense. Just tell me why."

She stood up, rubbing her arms, and pushing past him. "Our timing's been off, that's all. You're the one who said things should be perfect when we got together."

He recognized a defensive posture when he saw it. Coming up behind her, he draped his arms around her and eased her back to rest against him. Inside the embrace, she was stiff and unyielding. He spoke softly, trying to reassure her, to melt the tension. "I'm not talking about our sex life, Kit. If that bothers you, we can let it go for now. I know you don't like dealing with pressure, and I don't want to put you in that position." Tilting around her, he brushed her neck and cheek with tiny kisses. "But I thought we had all this settled. I thought we both wanted to be together. Let's not waste the time we have fooling around playing games."

Kit was torn. She wanted to give in, and it seemed so silly to hold back when she did want to be with him. But she also knew he was harboring dreams of happily-ever-after, which she had no way of fulfilling. It would break both their hearts to let this go any farther. She tried to be honest. "Riley, I'm sorry, but I'm not so sure of things anymore. I'm not sure I can be the person you want me to be."

"I want you to be who you are!" Riley tightened his arms around her and shook his head impatiently, amazed. She could be so mercurial and impulsive that it made him crazy. But damn it—he meant to have his two weeks if it killed him. She couldn't deny him his last-ditch efforts to find a future for them. He took a deep breath and counseled himself to be patient and calm, settling on, "Don't be afraid of me, or of us, Kit. I love you."

"I know." She tried not to, but her body began to relax a little in his arms. The love she felt was very tough to stop from seeping out around the edges. "I'm sorry," she said uncharitably. She hated apologizing. "I don't mean to make things so complicated."

"You're overthinking this," he soothed. "Let's just play it by ear."

"That's not like you." She shifted so that she could see his face. "You're the one with plans laid out for the next zillion years."

He bent his head to kiss her and stop the nonsense once and for all, when a long screech of wood on wood interrupted him. Still holding Kit, he turned to see Jo's head emerging from the window next to the swing.

"Kit, Kit, we need your help!" Jo shouted from the living room. "We have to do a skit for the hunger benefit show on Wednesday night, and we haven't got any ideas. Come on in now, will you?"

"No," Riley said flatly, "she's not going anywhere."

"Oh, come on!" Jo exclaimed. "Don't be selfish, Riley. This is an emergency. And a good cause."

Riley set his jaw in a severe line. "It's always a good cause with you, Jo. And usually an emergency. But Kit's busy and can't help you this time."

"Wait just a second," Kit said vehemently. "I don't need you two fighting over me. I can decide for myself."

Three other faces peered out the window from behind Jo, and Kit grimaced, not thrilled to be the center of attention. There was Alex, enjoying every minute of the spectacle, Maggie, embarrassed and grim, and Eliza, staring daggers at the place where Riley's hand lay protectively on Kit's shoulder.

Riley swore and bent over to slide down the window from the outside, threatening to slam it on Jo's fingers if she didn't butt out.

Kit yanked on him from the back. "Stop it this minute! I'm going to help them." At the black look on his face, she said, "We were finished anyway."

"Not as far as I'm concerned."

"I'll see you tomorrow, Riley."

The finality of her words convinced him there would be no dealing with her tonight. He would go home, replenish his forces and come back tomorrow stronger and more persuasive. "All right," he said abruptly, "but we are not finished. As far as I'm concerned, we've only begun."

His car spun gravel on its way out of the driveway, and Kit flinched at the rough, menacing sound of it. She didn't want Riley to be angry with her, but she didn't want to be in over her head, either. Inside the house, Kit barely heard Jo fill her in on some of the other acts expected at the hunger benefit.

"What fun!" Jo said excitedly. "The trial attorney who gets all the murderers off is doing one of Hamlet's soliloquies, and the anchorman from Channel 4 is going to wear a Twins uniform and recite 'Casey at the Bat.' And the mayors of Minneapolis and St. Paul are planning a soft-shoe routine to the tune of 'Me and My Shadow.'"

"This sounds worse than the Miss America pageant. I don't want to be a party to this," Alex groaned.

Jo glared at her. "You're going to be in it whether you like it or not."

"No one's going to be in anything if we don't think of something to do," Maggie contributed dryly.

Eliza chimed in with, "Let's do a fashion show. We could wear gorgeous dresses, and Mother could play 'A Pretty Girl Is Like a Melody' on the piano."

"I hardly think gorgeous clothes are a great idea at a benefit for hunger," Jo responded heatedly. "Talk about rubbing it in!"

Alex regarded her younger sister with horror. "Well, I'm certainly not going to wear ugly clothes in front of all those people."

"Me, neither." Eliza crossed her arms over her pink knit top.

"Ladies, ladies," Kit remarked disapprovingly. "I'm sure we can think of something." Figuratively rolling up her sleeves, she prepared to get to work. After all, coming up with ideas to knock people's socks off was what she did for a living. It also gave her an opportunity to rest her brain from worrying about Riley. Her lips tilted upward as she looked around the room at her sisters' expectant faces. They were at her mercy, and she sort of liked the idea.

By the time she let them go to bed at five o'clock in the morning, they were calling her "Your Imperial Majesty" and "Herr Reichmaster," but they also had the makings of a halfway decent song and dance number. Shrewdly playing against their images as clean-cut, all-American girls, Kit convinced them to stuff themselves into their sexiest outfits and vamp "Hey, Big Spender" to a crowd of would-be big spenders at the hunger benefit.

"I feel like I ought to stand at attention and salute with all the orders around here," Eliza grumbled, plopping down on the sofa and putting her feet up. "You're worse than Maggie."

Meeting Maggie's eyes over the heads of her sisters, Kit smiled. It was weird but strangely satisfying to have something in common with one of her sisters. "Maggie and I know what it takes to get things done, don't we?"

Maggie nodded. "I guess we're just two of a kind."

"Just what we needed," Alex moaned. Dramatically casting her hands over her eyes, she added, "Another slave driver in the family."

At that remark, Eliza and Jo began to boo and hiss and throw paper wads at Kit and Maggie. It was obvious to Kit that they'd all stayed up too late and had lost their marbles, and she told them they were excused for the time being.

Under the skylight, which was already bringing in streaks of dawn, Kit fell into bed still wearing her clothes. She was gratified to have exhausted herself playing director so that she could now lose her worries in sleep.

She woke up to the bright heat of a noon sun and a patient voice calling her from the hallway.

"Kit, are you in there? It's Jo. Riley's downstairs and he wants to see you."

"Tell him to go away," Kit mumbled. "Come back later."

"This is his second visit," Jo explained dutifully. "And he called twice, too. I don't think he'll go away."

"Oh, brother." Kit sat up reluctantly. "Okay, okay. Tell him I'll be down as soon as I can, but it may take a minute."

She swung herself out of the bed and took stock of her appearance in the mirror above the dresser. "Bleah" was the only appropriate reaction. She muttered to herself and headed for the bathroom. It ought to be easy to get rid of

Riley when she was this grumpy. Who in his right mind would want to talk to her when she was in a mood like this?

Riley, of course.

He spun around as she entered the living room. "How are you? Are you okay?"

"Of course I'm okay. I'm just tired. We were up half the night working on our skit for the hunger benefit."

"*Our* skit?"

She shrugged. "So I got involved. I won't die."

Standing there with his hands in his pockets, Riley felt ridiculous. Why had he rushed over here, insisting on seeing her, when he suddenly had nothing to say?

"Kit," he began cautiously, "about last night..."

"Oh, no," she groaned, "I don't think I can deal with this right now. I'm tired and cranky and I told my sisters we could rehearse again in a little while. Can't we talk about this later?"

"No, we can't. We've already wasted valuable time."

She took one look at the stubborn cast to his features and knew she wasn't going to get out of it so easily. "Okay," she said with a sigh. She tossed herself casually on the sofa. "What's on your mind?"

"You know very well what's on my mind." Preferring to remain on his feet, he tapped his fists against his sides restlessly. "What goony idea has dropped into your brain and convinced you that you don't care about me after all?"

"I *do* care about you!" she protested, sitting up.

"Then what's the problem?"

"I wasn't aware there was one," she responded stiffly.

His gaze was steady, unflinching. "Saturday you told me to find the perfect place for a rendezvous, Sunday you avoided me, last night you were weird, and today you're even weirder. Does that make sense to you?"

"Yes!" She relented. "No, I suppose not." She pulled her legs up onto the sofa and hugged her knees. "It's just that everything is so rushed, and I'm so confused, and..." She paused. "And I got a call from my office Saturday night."

Well, at least she's talking. That's a start. "Okay, so you got a call from your office," he prompted. "What then?"

"And they needed me back, and I promised I'd be there in two weeks."

"Okay." He took a short breath, telling himself he already knew that. "Why is that a problem?"

"Because..." She glanced up with vulnerable, unsure eyes. "Because I felt like a traitor to you saying I'd be back there as scheduled, and like a traitor to myself if I said I wasn't coming. I felt so hassled and pressured and guilty, and I hate that!"

He nodded. "You feel that if you give in and love me, you won't be able to leave."

"Maybe," she said softly. "Oh, Riley, I don't want either of us to be hurt any more than we already have been. But a two-week sizzle of an affair just isn't us!"

He lowered his brows, confused. "Why does it have to be that?"

"Come on, think seriously for a moment. What future do we honestly have?" she asked gloomily.

"I take it we've eliminated the idea of you moving back here?"

She sighed. "I've considered it, which is a monumental achievement by itself. But how could I? We have no idea whether we'll last a month or a year or a lifetime together, and it would be like burning all my bridges to give up my job and look for a new one here. I'd have to start from the bottom and prove myself all over again. Not to mention the fact that my mother would take a move as a de facto invitation to run my life.''

"What if I moved there?'' he offered, coming and kneeling next to the sofa so that he could see her more closely.

"To New York?'' She responded with a curt laugh. "Even if I let you, it would be a disaster. No,'' she continued, "in New York, there wouldn't be any high school buddies to play softball with, or any kids of high school buddies to coach. I couldn't give you noisy family dinners at the Wentworth house, or lilacs in the backyard, or any of the other things that are important to you.''

"But we would be together. That's something.''

She shook her head sadly. "I wish it were that easy. But I know you better than that. You've lived in the same lousy apartment since college, for goodness' sake. You're a creature of habit, of roots. You'd be miserable somewhere else.''

"I don't think that's true,'' he argued, but she put a finger to his lips.

"It doesn't matter anyway,'' she returned, "because it's too much and too soon and I don't even want to think about it.''

"So your solution is to forget the whole thing? What kind of an answer is that?''

"I don't know,'' she answered, distress underlining her voice. "But at least this way I don't have to go back knowing what I've lost.''

"So you'll let us both wonder instead?'' He broke off and stood up, cursing to himself violently before concluding, "That makes no sense to me whatsoever.''

"I said I was confused!''

"Well, I'll agree with you on that one.'' Shaking his head, he sighed and studied Kit where she sat on the sofa.

He knew her too well to get caught up in her objections to a future in St. Paul or in New York or anywhere in between. That discussion was really a smoke screen, anyway. He figured the real problem here was pressure. Pressure to get back to the office, pressure to be with him, pressure to decide what she felt for him. What an idiot he'd been to put his cards on the table and mention growing old together or children or whatever else he'd blurted out, even in passing.

And pushing her further or trying to show her the error in her logic did not seem destined for positive results. *Back off. Let her decide,* he told himself, but it was damned hard advice to follow.

"I'll give you this much," he decided. "You're all wound up with your sisters' skit right now, and I don't think you're seeing things clearly. So I'll give you until after it's done. But you think, Kit, and you think hard. At least give us a chance to see what we could be together."

"For two weeks?" she asked with a voice of a skeptic. "How would we know in two weeks, anyway?"

"I'd take twenty minutes if that's all I could get. But we deserve a chance, Kit. At least a chance."

EVERY TIME SHE THOUGHT about it, she got more confused, so she threw herself into cracking the whip over her sisters.

When it came time to perform, she had her hands full. Jo and Eliza were feuding with each other over who'd tripped whom in the last practice of their number, and Alex was stopping people she didn't even know to show off her strapless gold lamé gown. Maggie seemed cool enough, but when she put her top on backward, Kit knew she, too, was riddled with nerves. Their mother was as jittery as anyone, even though she would be done after a few words of introduction. Lilah looked glorious, but that didn't stop her from fussing over her appearance, and everyone else's.

She thought, for one thing, that all of her daughters looked like ladies of the evening. "We're supposed to," they protested, but nonetheless she wasn't pleased. And she accused Kit of putting her makeup on with a shovel, which was actually not far from the truth. But Kit was bound and determined not to be cast into the shadows by her sisters. She let her hair hang down over her shoulders, parted on the side and partially veiling one eye. She slid into a silky magenta dress that resembled lingerie more than a dress, and she wondered what had possessed her to wear it. She felt naked. But very sexy. And she would not fade into any backgrounds tonight.

There were lots of reasons to enjoy this night, even if her entire family did look like rejects from the Tina Turner school of fashion design. No one had ever seen the Wentworth sisters quite like this.

They were a smash. After approximately two-and-a-half minutes of lipsynching, bumping, and even grinding a bit to "Hey, Big Spender," they bowed, smiled and then hooted with triumph as they hugged one another in the wings. It was over, and they had done just fine!

Kit was surprised when she stepped back and looked at herself. She was as excited and happy as anyone, joining right in with the jokes about Eliza's overdone dancing and Maggie's painfully shy attempts to look seductive. Somehow Kit had found camaraderie with her sisters, and it felt good.

It was like a thunderbolt from the heavens. She liked her sisters, and they liked her. She hadn't felt threatened or unattractive or sulky, even once. What was the world coming to?

Riley surprised her by showing up outside the communal dressing room, carrying a bunch of roses wrapped in green tissue paper and standing tentatively in the doorway like the backstage suitor of a chorus girl.

"Hi!" Her enthusiasm for the performance spilled over into happiness at seeing him. Still wearing her slippery magenta dress, she hugged him quickly. "Did you like the skit?"

"You were...something," he said lamely, handing her the roses. Good grief, she didn't look like Kit at all. After seeing her play the role of temptress on stage, wearing that clinging dress, flashing long, black-stockinged legs and strutting on spike heels, he had had about enough shocks for one evening. "Where did you get that outfit?"

She sniffed the roses, comparing the deep garnet color to her dress. Not a bad match. "Alex took me to a store called The Naughty Closet. Do you like it?"

"Yeah, sure," he managed, and muttered, "More than you can possibly imagine," under his breath. He had never known Kit to be so blatantly provocative, and it made him sweat under the collar of his formal shirt just thinking about it. It was a steamy, humid day, and yet his own heat was largely unconnected to the weather. Here he was, feeling her slinky body undulate next to him, on the verge of exploding with pent-up passion, and forced to be patient yet again. If only he could be sure that tonight would end this impossible waiting game. He had to end it tonight, or die trying. He ventured, "Have you thought about our situation yet?"

"No," she returned softly. "I haven't had a chance." She cast her eyes down at his tuxedoed pant legs. "Sorry."

He put his hands on her bare shoulders and felt her shiver under his touch. He had to fight hard to hold on to the shreds of his self-control. "I've done enough thinking for both of us," he said curtly. He refused to let himself get sidetracked, even if he was feeling very unsure of his game plan or her reaction. All he knew was that he couldn't be patient anymore. "I've come to some conclusions about what has to come next for us."

"All right," she said hesitantly. "Why don't you tell me?"

He said, "Well, the thing is...I mean, you have to agree that this has gone on long enough. I want what's best, but dammit, Kit, this isn't it—"

He stopped as a muffled bump sounded from the other side of the dressing room floor, followed by Maggie's voice loudly telling Eliza to get her ear away from the keyhole before someone affixed it there permanently.

Heeding the timely warning, Riley raised an eyebrow, almost relieved by the interruption. It hadn't been going that well, anyway. He grabbed at the straw that it would be foolhardy to give Kit ultimatums in a hot, stuffy hallway full of intrusions and distractions. "Once again we need a more private place."

Kit nodded grimly. "I told you my family was a nuisance. You're the one who likes them."

"Not all of them." He inclined his thumb in the direction of the dressing room, where they could still hear Eliza's shrill, unhappy voice, instructing Maggie in no uncertain terms to mind her own business.

"I think someone should deal with my little sister before she goes any farther off the deep end."

"I'll talk to her," he responded sharply. "And then you and I will talk."

Again she nodded.

He wanted more from her than a nod, dammit. "Well? When? Where? Do you want me to wait here for you?"

The hallway was stifling, and she wouldn't have asked her worst enemy to wait out there. "No, I don't think so." He seemed so grim about whatever it was he wanted to tell her. How bad could it be? Was he planning to say he wanted her out of his life even as a friend? She couldn't imagine he'd go that far. Perhaps he'd tell her to move in with him or get out of town, or sleep with him or forget the whole thing. She searched his face for a clue, with her heart beating rapidly inside her breast. "I have to change my clothes and make an appearance at the ball that goes with this benefit," she said gingerly. "Were you planning on going?"

"Yeah. Maybe."

"Do you want to meet me there in an hour or so? We could talk there, or go somewhere else."

He raised a hand to tuck back the hair that was tipping over one side of her face. "An hour," he repeated. He leaned down, closed his eyes and kissed her as gently as he knew how. "I'll see you then."

Chapter Nine

Her hands were shaking as she changed into an evening gown borrowed from Alex to ensure presentability at the Hunger Benefit Ball. After trying in vain to put her hair up or back, she decided that tonight it would have to lie straight down her back, pale and plain, because her fingers wouldn't cooperate on any other style. As she scrutinized her ice-blue watered silk gown with its tight bodice and extremely full skirt, Kit complained nervously that all she needed was a tiara to look like Princess Di. That set Jo offering to run home for a tiara until Kit assured her she was only kidding.

Now if she could be sure her strapless dress would stay put on her modest bosom, she might be able to take a few calm breaths. But breathing was what endangered her dress's safety in the first place. Oh, well, surely a person could last a few hours without breathing. Anything for the sake of fashion, it seemed. At least she'd look like Her Serene Highness when she saw Riley, even if she didn't feel like it.

It had been such a fun and exhilarating evening that she was disappointed when she learned Jo and Maggie weren't coming along to the ball. She could have used their support in facing Riley and his mysterious discussion. Heaven knows Eliza and Alex were small comfort. But Jo shuddered at the very idea of fancy dress, so she was helping Maggie supervise the operation from behind the scenes. Kit hadn't been aware that Grand Affairs was doing the arrangements for the ball, but she had to admit, even as she chewed her lip and prayed her dress would stay up, it was a lovely party. There was no sand tonight, no ocean on slides, no beach balls. This evening was old-world elegance with fresh flowers in silver vases and sparkling crystal on white tablecloths.

Picking up and putting down bits of pretty little hors d'oeuvres from her untouched plate, Kit surveyed the crowd, wondering where in the world Riley was and why he didn't show up and put her out of her misery. He'd said he had important information to share, and she wanted to know what it was. Now.

When she finally caught sight of him across the crowd of Twin Cities society, he was engaged in a very earnest discussion with Eliza. From the looks of things, he was explaining the facts of unrequited love to Eliza as carefully as he'd covered the infield fly rule with his eight-year-olds. Kit smiled to herself. Eliza might be pouting and stamping her pretty little foot, but at least the effort was being made. She hoped it went well, that Eliza understood, and that it wasn't too difficult or sticky. No matter what happened later between them, she wanted Riley to disentangle himself from Eliza's fantasies.

"Excuse me, young lady," someone interrupted at her elbow. She turned to see a distinguished white-haired gentleman regarding her eagerly. "Aren't you one of Lilah Wentworth's girls?"

"Yes," Kit answered as politely as she could manage. "I'm Kit, well, really, Katharine, her middle daughter."

Her lips curved as he took her fingers in his hand and kissed the tips in a courtly gesture.

"I'm Ephraim Stone, my dear. Retired from Stone, Maxwell and LaCreevy, the best agency in the Cities. Your mother has been singing your praises to me, my dear. She has described you as an advertising genius."

"Oh, really?" Kit murmured, concentrating on her wineglass in order not to laugh. She knew what would come next. Charming old Mr. Stone would ask her to come and work at Stone, Maxwell, whatever-its-name-was. Trust her mother to go scrounging up job offers.

"Although I'm no longer officially with Stone, Maxwell, I like to think I entertain some measure of influence there," Ephraim Stone continued, oblivious to Kit's lack of interest. "The Stone currently in the title on the door is my son, Ephraim the third, you see. We're always on the lookout for outstanding young talent like you, my dear."

She demurred immediately, wanting an end to this awkwardness before Riley ventured out of her sight. "Thank you very much, Mr. Stone, but I don't think I'm interested right now. Thank you so much for your generous offer, however."

With that out of the way, she smiled weakly and swept back to the hors d'oeuvres table. As she feared, she'd lost sight of Riley in the crowd, and she didn't want to fiddle with any more of the results of her mother's misguided job search. No doubt every adman within fifty miles was here tonight to extol the virtues of his agency.

"Psst."

The sound was coming from a slightly open doorway behind the table. The crack widened, and Kit discerned Jo's frantic features.

"Psst, Kit. Can you help me out for a second?"

Kit put down the hors d'oeuvres plate she was holding and extended her hands in surrender. "Wait, don't tell me. It's for a good cause."

"The best!" Jo retorted. "Your family's livelihood."

Coming around to the doorway where Jo was hiding, Kit asked with resignation, "What is it?"

"The cookies got here late, and they need to be put on the dessert table. Maggie and I are the only ones back here, and we're both in jeans, so we can't go into the party. Can you just take a few trays over to the small table near the potted palm?"

"Won't I look pretty silly carrying a tray in this dress?"

"No one will even notice, and it will only take a second. Look, will you do it or not? I feel ridiculous whispering through a doorway like a spy or something."

"I suppose so," Kit responded dubiously. "But there seem to be a million little helper types in black uniforms running around here. Why can't they do it?"

Peering out her door, Jo expelled a long breath of air. "Because you're here and they're not. If you want to find someone to help you, I don't care. But get moving, will you? The desserts should have been put out an hour ago."

"Okay, okay," Kit murmured, and maneuvered the round silver tray around Jo and through the door. "Chocolate chip cookies?" she asked in surprise. Given the sophistication of the rest of the buffet, these were going to stand out like a sore, or at least very casual, thumb. "Why not mousse or a torte or something?"

"Look on your program," Jo returned testily. "Dessert courtesy of Grandma Cooper's Cookies. When we get donations, we don't turn them down."

"Did you say Grandma *Cooper*? It couldn't possibly be as in Riley Cooper?"

"Of course. What else would Riley's cookies be called?" Realization dawned on Jo, and she turned wide eyes up to Kit. "Oh, no—I forgot! It was supposed to be a secret, wasn't it?"

"Cookies!" Kit crowed, looking down at the tray and ignoring Jo completely. So these innocuous little gems were the key to Riley's mystery occupation. "Amazing," she whispered under her breath. She didn't care what dire messages he wanted to share; she was ecstatic. She'd figured out his job and won her bet! Quickly leaving Jo behind, Kit strode over to the proper table and dropped off Riley's cookies. After that, she corralled one of the black-uniformed servers and sent the man back to Jo to get the rest of the trays. With that duty satisfied, she couldn't wait to find Riley.

"Eliza, where's Riley? He was with you a minute ago."

"He went looking for you," Eliza answered woefully.

Wonderful. So where was he? She tapped her foot with anticipation and excitement. Kit saw a decidedly odd look come into Eliza's eyes as she gazed petulantly over Kit's shoulder. Before even turning, Kit knew who was standing there.

A tall, clean-shaven, golden-haired man in a dinner jacket demanded, "Where have you been?"

He'd been looking for her for what had felt like forever, and getting very impatient in the process. When a man bit back his desires for this long and then finally made up his mind to get the whole thing right out in the open once and for all, any extra delays tended to make him seethe and get testy.

"Cookies!" she declared, poking a finger at his pristine white shirt. "Cookies!"

"So?"

"So, Riley, or should I say, *Grandma* Cooper, you owe me a dinner."

"I owe you a lot more than that." So she'd figured it out. The funny thing was that he couldn't have cared less that he'd lost the bet. He had important issues on his mind, and he didn't want to fool around talking about cookies. He scowled at her, managing to look disreputable and dangerous even in his staid formal attire.

"But what about our bet? I figured out what you do for a living, Riley, with a week and a half to spare!"

"Congratulations, but I haven't got time for that right now."

She eyed him suspiciously. "Because of what you wanted to tell me before?"

"Exactly. I've been waiting far too long already. Far too long to give a damn about cookies or dinners or any asinine bet." He had concocted delicate ways to tell her this, to bring her around to admitting the inevitable, as he had. But he had lost the ability to stay calm and spin a nice story for her. The bare, unvarnished truth was going to have to suffice. "The truth is I want you. I have always wanted you. And I want to make love to you. Now."

Eliza gasped behind her as warmth suffused Kit's cheeks. "Riley," she whispered frantically, "not here!"

He didn't lower his voice. "Then where?"

"Anywhere but here! Why are you bringing this up now?"

He smiled then, and a sparkle flickered in his blue eyes. The lazy dimple reappeared; it was even more effective now, when he was clean-shaven for once. "I told you I came to a decision. That's it. I tried to be patient with you and let you come to your own conclusions, but I can't take my own noble attitude anymore. I've been stewing for the past forty-eight hours, and I swear I'm losing my mind. So

I decided to tell you that I don't care about the future, and neither should you. I'll take whatever it is you're willing to give. One week—one weekend—twenty minutes. But let's go for it. Now. Tonight. Before we change our minds."

Kit's eyes widened in shock. "You can't be serious. You're not the impulsive type."

"I've decided to change my style." One of his dark eyebrows curved upward at a rakish angle. "Remember, I caught your sister act tonight. Whatever control I had went out the window after that one. You sold me, Kit. I want you to 'pop your cork' for me, like in the song. What do you say?"

"Have you been drinking?" Kit was suspicious of this abrupt change in attitude. He had always been so patient with her, so careful of her feelings. What he was proposing was anything but careful.

"We've already lost so much time. Think what we could've done in that time." His eyes were very blue and very intense.

Kit swallowed. She *was* thinking about what they could have done in that time. They weren't comforting thoughts.

Riley continued in a hot, husky voice that penetrated to places she couldn't control. "You told me to find a perfect, special place. I did. I'm ready when you are."

His eyes held hers as if challenging her to say no.

As she looked at him now, splendid in his dinner jacket, she remembered thinking how disreputable he looked, even clothed so formally. Disreputable? Yes, he did look that. And reckless and dangerous, too. Standing in front of her, he was a vision of sharp, tanned features and blazing blue eyes. How could she have thought she could keep sexual attraction out of the picture where Riley was concerned? He was her golden boy, her fallen angel, and that streak of recklessness and danger, of erotic depths untapped, had been a part of him as long as she'd known him, which was a very long time. Where he was dangerous, she was stubborn and hotheaded and didn't back down from dares. They both knew that. "All right," she returned before she had time to think or care that she might be acting like a crazy person. "Let's do it."

Then she held out her hand, and he took it.

ENSCONCED RESTLESSLY in his Ferrari, she realized with a jolt where they were headed. "Downtown St. Paul?" she demanded, trying to make sensible thoughts come together in her fevered brain. "What perfect place is downtown? I thought we ruled out hotels."

"It's not a hotel. Just be patient a few more minutes. You'll see."

And she did see.

In the midst of a nondescript area of mostly run-down homes and business, not far from the hub of downtown, he turned a corner to go down to the river terrace on the St. Paul part of Mississippi. It was a departure into the past. Ahead of them, Kit saw a small square of green, surrounded by old-fashioned houses, most of which had been restored to their former elegance. It was a tiny, lovely park, boasting a dainty white gazebo, wrought-iron lampposts and a fountain spouting water from gargoyles' heads.

She was enchanted. "I've never been down here before," she murmured. "Where are we?"

"It's called Irvine Park. The house I'm fixing up is here."

Even in the heavy, humid summer air, it seemed a quiet, gracious place. The only sound she could hear through her window was the splashing and tinkling of the fountain as they drove past it.

He pulled his car into a garage tucked behind a large creamy yellow house. As they walked up to the house itself, Kit could only guess at the effort required to recreate its style so carefully. Not unlike her mother's house, it had a corner tower with a conical cap, and even in the dark she could make out intricate variations in gingerbread, white against the soft yellow of the house. But this one looked like real Victorian, with the delicate lines and graceful charm of another era.

She gazed fondly at Riley, not really surprised at his choice of a reclamation project. A one-of-a-kind house, eclectic and distinctive, where his own work could make a difference. His taste and energy would be stamped all over it.

"It's lovely," she whispered, and took his hand, linking his fingers with hers in a gesture of communion. "Simply lovely. I didn't expect that. Somehow I got the idea your restoration project was in pieces."

One corner of his mouth lifted. "Wait till you see the inside before making judgments."

With their hands still firmly connected, he led her around to the front of the house and swung open a dark heavy wood door with a glass oval cut into it.

"Here it is," he announced, and flicked on a light.

She saw bare, unpolished wood floors, and walls that still showed tape markings on the drywall. The overhead light was little more than a bulb on a long orange cord. What she could see of the downstairs looked like one big room, with a staircase rising out of one side. This was the raw framework for a house; it was nowhere near a finished project.

He saw her take in the spare surroundings and explained, "I have a lot left to do." Enfolding her in his arms from the back, he slid her hair aside and bent to drop a kiss on her neck. "I promise, however, that it does now have plumbing."

She smiled, even as his lips stirred up delicious sensations on the sensitive slope of her neck. "Oh, that's right," she said in a distant voice. "I made plumbing a requirement, didn't I? Good thinking on my part."

"Uh-huh." He whispered into her ear, "What you don't know is what I had to do to get the plumbing installed in three days. Have you ever heard of moving heaven and earth?"

"For me?" She was delighted. She swung around in his arms to see him face-to-face. Tilting up, she bestowed a fleeting kiss on his lips, and then on the tip of his nose. Feeling reckless, she asked bluntly, "Is there a bedroom in this place?"

He nodded and stared at her, his blood pounding in his veins. He was supposed to be the one pushing this relationship forward from the stalemate, wasn't he? Where did she get her nerve all of a sudden? But he knew. Once Kit decided something, it was damn the torpedoes, full speed ahead. Thank God she had decided. "Upstairs," he murmured. "But I need to get a few things ready before you go up. Will you be okay here by yourself for a second or two?"

She assented, and he kissed her again, briefly but fiercely, and then backed away regretfully, holding on to her hand until he simply had to let it drop. Then he slipped off his jacket, flipped it over one shoulder, grinned at her and raced up the stairs.

Above her, she heard his footfalls and a muffled scraping noise, followed by no sound at all. Whatever he was doing, he was doing it clear up inside the heart of the house. She hoped his errand would be quickly accomplished, because her thoughts weren't particularly good company at the moment.

Standing there without him, she began to feel rather nervous. In his presence, in the calm atmosphere of this eccentric neighborhood, she had felt alive and exhilarated, not afraid of anything. But by herself in this very strange and empty house, she wasn't so sure of anything. She shivered, cold even in the sultry summer heat, and ran her hands over her bare arms.

When he returned, he was minus his tie and jacket, and the sleeves of his crisp white shirt were rolled up at the elbows. He lingered a few steps up, watching her, and then slowly descended toward her.

"Ready," he said softly, and took her hand to pull her toward the stairs. "You can have the whole tour tomorrow, but tonight I have other plans." Pulling her, leading her, he strode up the increasingly dark stairs, turning at the top, and rapidly making his way to the middle of the hall. "Here," he announced, pointing to a huge hole in the wall. "This way."

"Through a hole?" She was careful not to sound too suspicious or disapproving in case he was telling the truth and he really did expect her to climb through this chasm in the plaster.

"That's right." He smiled anxiously, and she loved him for the anxiety. She heard him say something about the house being a duplex in the fifties, and him unmaking it into one whole house again. "If I'd had time," he said hurriedly, "I would've torn out the whole wall, but I was concentrating on the plumbing to comply with the specifications of a certain lady friend of mine."

"Right," she responded. "Good thinking."

"I hope you don't mind the unorthodox method of entry."

She smiled, trying to be brave. "Would I let a little thing like no doorway stand in my way?" In the dimness she peered at the hole, which seemed to glow from a source of light on the other side, and then back at him to make sure he was serious. Taking the unspoken dare, Kit bent to remove her shoes and handed them over to Riley without a word. She kept her silence as she gamely gathered up the yards of blue silk that created her skirt and somehow managed to ease it and herself slowly through the hole in the wall.

After taking a few steps into what she now saw was a bedroom, she glanced around her, catching the muted glow of a candle in a hurricane lamp and sniffing the fragrance of flowers, roses perhaps. Yes, there was an arrangement of dark red roses, like the one Riley had given her outside her dressing room, on a tallboy against the wall. As she turned her head the other way, she saw the light of the candle flicker as it was reflected and magnified on a shiny brass bedstead. There was a gentle patter against the window, telling her the humidity had broken and a summer shower had begun.

After crawling through the hole behind her, Riley swept her around to face him and took her hand in his, raising it to his lips. He kissed it gently, and Kit gazed from her hand to his face with a look of delight. The sweet gesture did more than send tingles from her hand down her arm. It also melted her heart. It made her feel special and treasured.

Even entering through a hole in the wall suddenly took on a new and favorable significance. It made the place seem completely private and uniquely their own. Who else could boast that kind of entrance to their bedroom? It was like an outside force had conspired to drop the two of them into a small, cozy and very special place.

She looped her arms around his neck and rubbed her cheek against his, instinctively needing to feel the comfort of skin against skin. Shutting her eyes, she leaned into him, and he pulled her closer, sliding his hands around and along her slick, tight bodice and the curve of her bottom through the full, gathered folds of her skirt.

It didn't seem to matter what he touched. When he reached it, it leaped into action as an erogenous zone, even if it had never dreamed of anything like that before. Her whole body was alive with dark, dangerous currents of longing, from the tips of her toes, curling into the hardwood floor, to the top of her head, tingling as it became the beneficiary of Riley's kisses and Riley's touch.

Kit moaned near his ear, sending vibrations of erotic sound to a portion of his body that responded immediately. Groaning, he slid one arm behind her and the other under her knees, attempting to lift her against him. Instead he found himself collecting an armload of dress in a series of awkward shifting motions. He heard her giggle as he finally succeeded in hoisting her and the damned dress up into his arms. He leaned down to drop a delicate kiss on the tip of her nose. And then he grinned.

"Trust you to conduct an affair wearing this crazy outfit. I've never in my life seen you in anything this complicated."

"I have to provide a few challenges, don't I? I don't want you to lose interest." She tightened her hold around his neck. "Besides, the dress is easily disposed of."

"Oh, yeah?" His eyes were hot and challenging.

"Yeah." She slipped out of his arms with a rustle of silk, captured his hands in hers and drew them around to the back of her dress. Keeping her gaze steadily on his, Kit led his finger to the catch at the top of her zipper and rubbed it back and forth across the small tab. "There," she murmured. "Do you feel it?"

"Oh, yes." His voice was rough and smoky. "I feel it."

"All you have to do is pull down," she whispered, "and the whole thing will be gone."

His fingers hesitated at the back of the dress, sensuously testing the skin around the edge of the fabric. "Gone?"

"Gone." Capturing and holding his gaze, she spoke with only the merest attempt to make a sound. "It's been threatening to fall down all night."

"I wish it had." He shook his head, and one corner of his mouth lifted as he tugged the zipper he couldn't see down the tiniest bit, and then he slid his finger in and around the opening he had created. "Oh, God, I wish it had. That would have been something to see." He paused, then asking gruffly, "Are you wearing anything under this?"

She raised an eyebrow. "Only one way to find out."

"My sentiments exactly."

With a swift, soft whisper, the zipper was undone, and the dress slipped away. He picked her up again, and his hands on her skin felt hot against cold. Which were his hands and which her body? She couldn't tell, and she didn't care. He lay her gently in the soft depth of the brass bed, and then joined her, pulling her into his embrace and biting her gently on the neck.

Dracula, she thought. Good heavens, that meant Didi had been right after all. She giggled into his shoulder, but the laugh lengthened into a soft moan as his fingers trailed over her. She tipped her mouth up to be kissed, and when he obliged, she opened to him immediately. She was wild and free again, the way she felt only when Riley kissed her that way and held her that way. Suddenly she wanted all of

him. Her body seemed to flow around him of its own accord, meeting him and molding to him, as liquid and as
golden as the thrust of their kiss.

Pressing forward, she searched for the secret of his tantalizing kiss. She delved into him, found him ruthless, seductive, addictive, but it didn't seem to end her need to
search. Tongue met tongue, curling and colliding with a
ferocity she wouldn't have believed possible.

The deep kiss was only the beginning, as its impact
echoed throughout her body. Every place his hands
skimmed, they left a path of shivers and licks of flame.
Her body was alive with it, wondrously alive. She laughed
softly, wickedly, into the kiss, bringing her hands up to
smooth back the tawny hair above his ears and to gaze into
his blue, blue eyes. With her fingers resting on his temple,
she could feel his pulse, erratic and strong and definitely
real under her fingertips—real and hot and vivid.

The gentle, mocking echo of her laugh only served to
further inflame him. He broke the bond of the kiss, moving instead to the slope of her neck and shoulder, to grace
them with a series of tiny brushes of his lips. He found
each inch of velvety skin begging to be included.

Instead of giving in to the spell of his lips against her
body, he held back, just to look at her. He could tell she
was on fire; he could feel it in every response she made and
read it in the dull flame in her eyes. Oh, yes, she wanted
him. But some devil inside him made him need to be sure
she was operating on more than impulse. He tucked a
strand of fine hair out of the way and then stroked her
cheek, gently tracing a line between her lips and her ear.

"What is it?" she inquired. "What's wrong?"

His eyes blazed a path of blue fire straight to her heart.
"I'm worrying about my own ethics," he admitted softly.
"I dared you to come with me tonight. But I don't want

you here on a dare. It has to be willingly, because you want me as much as I want you."

"I want you more."

Closing her eyes, she concentrated on the sweet, gentle pressure of his fingers on her face. It felt to her like the first drops of rain after a long drought. The raindrops of sensation cascaded from her face, where he was still slowly, painstakingly, touching her cheek, and ran merrily through her body, pooling at the very core of her being. Underneath him, molding herself to meet him, she telegraphed exactly what she wanted. "Now," she said simply.

He grinned again. "You're too impatient." His voice was low and unhurried, but the huskiness gave him away. "We've barely begun. You forget that I've had four years to dream up all the possible variations on this theme. I want to make it last. I want to make it count."

"No matter what," she whispered, "it will count."

Still holding her gaze fast, he leaned down to brush her lips gently with his in the most casual, careful of kisses.

His hand edged the lacy top of her underwear, dancing across her stomach before it slid across her ribs. He traced each rib as if it were precious to him, until finally, inexorably, he reached the curve of her breast.

She moaned in frustration as his clever hands, those hands that created beautiful skylights and rooms out of nowhere, teased her unmercifully. As his thumb brushed across her nipple, it peaked eagerly, begging for attention.

With his mouth and hands, he was making her come alive with feeling. From the hard, rosy tips of her breasts to the sensitive curve just under her ear, she tingled and ached. But he moved slowly, so slowly she thought she would expire from too much sensation.

If his hands moved at a measured, deliberate pace, hers could not. Boldly she found the top of his trousers and slid his shirttails out, running her hands up and under the crisp, cool fabric. His skin was warm and golden, and velvety soft beneath her fingers, much softer than she'd expected. Anxiously she pushed his shirt out of the way, unbuttoning and unfastening as fast she could manage. From his smooth torso to the top of his pants, he was all sleek muscle. It was wonderful.

He had been the soul of patience thus far, but when her hand slipped to the waistband of his trousers, he groaned, knowing he could keep up the pretense of self-control no longer. Quickly he shed his clothing and gathered her closer so that it was only body against body, with no impediments of clothing or anything else.

It only took a moment before they were naked and smooth and tangled together in the four-poster bed. Kit ran her hands down his strong flanks, urging him to come even closer. Her hands couldn't get enough of the lean golden lines of his body, and she ran them up and down his back with a certain sense of proprietary interest. *Mine,* the gesture said.

It seemed impossible that the very thing he had imagined for so long was now at hand. The enormity of the situation hit him, but he gazed into her eyes one last time and saw such love and trust that he knew they were right to take this step. As gently and as slowly as he could, he slipped inside.

She gasped, not prepared to feel such incredible pressure mounting inside her, but there it was. Slow, even delicate at first, it leaped into prominence and sped up in a rhythm she couldn't control. She held on to him, trusting him to hold her and guide her and bring her with him to a sweet, fascinating place of their own. Beauty, love, security and her most deeply buried desires—they were all there, just beyond her grasp, and she was trying so hard to reach them. Beyond her grasp, but reaching. Reaching once, twice, until yes, there it was, within reach now. The secret resolution of her search wafted over her in waves, giving her comfort, triumph and the marvelous sensation of coming home.

Her gaze widened as she stared into Riley's beautiful, lazy-lidded blue eyes. "Oh, Riley," she murmured, drawing out the syllables. "I love you."

Afterward, they lay wrapped in each other's arms, and Riley kissed the top of her head and smoothed the long mass of her hair out of the way. For Kit there was a sense of completeness, love, reality and fantasy in a crazy mix. She had never thought she'd know another person as well as she knew Riley, but this put the relationship on a wholly new plane. This wasn't just knowing; this was sharing. Sharing herself and her wants and needs as she experienced his, too. Kit felt joy and justice in her discovery, and she hugged him tight.

Kit and Riley. She smiled to herself and nestled closer against his chest. They were pals, lovers, roommates, best friends. And it was the best of all possible worlds.

For her at least. Did Riley feel the same way?

She sneaked a peek at his handsome features. He looked relaxed and happy, but that wasn't enough.

"Was it what you expected?" she asked meekly.

He shifted so he could look straight into her eyes. "How can you even ask something like that?"

"Well, I don't know," she mumbled. She knew she was behaving like an idiot. As usual that only made it worse. She plowed ahead. "I mean, you've had this in mind for so long. I just wasn't sure the reality of plain old me would measure up."

He sighed and leaned his head on pillows propped up against the brass headboard. "You're being ridiculous," he chided gently. "Believe me, where you're concerned, the real Kit is a thousand times better than any fantasy." Tightening his arms, he bent and kissed her small, pretty nose.

She remained unconvinced. "But I know you've imagined this scene so many different ways. You're sure it was okay?"

"In the first place, it wasn't just okay." He shook his head, wondering what in the world had gotten into confident, impulsive Kit. Probably just bullheadedness. Whatever the problem, he felt sure he could fix it. "I thought it was wonderful and spectacular and I love you. And in the second place, we don't have to act out the entire *Kama Sutra* in one night." A cocky grin lit his face. "We've got lots of time for the rest of it."

"Lots of time, hmm?" Trust Riley to tease her and make it all okay. She relaxed, letting her doubts slip away into someone else's world. This was an enchanted evening, with the faint smell of roses, a gentle summer rain and the radiance of a candle shining on the brass bed and in the eyes of the man she loved. She ought to savor every morsel of it. She sighed with contentment.

"Yeah," he said, with a definite edge of smugness. "We have plenty of time." Still smiling, he wrestled her to her side and then pinned her underneath him. "Practice makes perfect, you know."

Chapter Ten

Waking, she saw that the room was much prettier than she'd noticed last night. It was done in French blue and white, with tasteful striped wallpaper and simple white curtains. Except for the hole in the wall, it was finished completely, even to details like the wax on the hardwood floor, and a small print of yellow-and-blue sailboat over the dresser. She liked it. It was uncomplicated and bright, and she felt comfortable there. She even liked the big brass bed they were sleeping in, with its small white porcelain knobs on the bars of the headboard.

Spinning a funny little knob, she gazed down at Riley with overwhelming affection and tenderness. This morning, with tousled hair and pronounced stubble, he looked soft and vulnerable.

She smiled. Even with several days' worth of beard, he seemed very young, as if he were still the boy she had collected lilacs with. Slipping back down inside the covers, she snuggled up next to him and listened to his heartbeat.

"What's this?" he grumbled, sitting up a bit and blinking at her sleepily. "You weren't supposed to be up first. I had a surprise planned to wake you up."

"I'll just bet you did," she returned slyly. Under the covers, her hand traveled to his knee. Pointedly, she walked her hand, finger by finger, up his thigh.

He caught her hand swiftly, "Insatiable." He gave a mock disapproving shake of his head. "I was talking about breakfast in bed."

"Oh, is that all?"

He lifted a rakish eyebrow. "Is that all? Forget the romantic little gestures, then. You can get your own breakfast."

"Don't be sulky, Riley. It ruins your pretty face."

"Funny, but uncontrollable lust seems to suit you just fine." He grinned, returning his face to "pretty" status. "It puts a sparkle in your eyes and color in your cheeks."

"The color in my cheeks is embarrassment, turkey," she returned, retreating farther under the covers. "Polite people don't discuss lust before breakfast."

"Why not?" he asked innocently. "Besides, whoever said I was polite?" At the concertedly nasty look she gave him, he relented. "I promise to avoid the topic of your uncontrollable lust until after breakfast. And since breakfast has been referred to," he added tactfully, "I think I'll revert to my original plan. Will you pretend to be asleep so I can surprise you?"

"Certainly."

As he tossed back the covers and neatly exited the bed, Kit couldn't help watching. He seemed unconcerned by his nakedness, and she was too curious not to cast a few surreptitious glances. Funny that she had known him most of her life and seen him in a bathing suit or other abbreviated attire hundreds of times and yet never noticed how finely he was put together. Her cheeks flushed with warmth as she realized that, after last night, she would never fail to notice again.

He shrugged into jeans and a work shirt, covering up all those nice bronzed angles before she had a chance to look her fill, and then he winked before escaping out the hole in the far wall.

Once he was safely gone, she jumped from the bed, realizing with a sense of panic that all she had to wear was last night's outrageously inappropriate blue ball gown. After a moment, she decided to wear whatever she could find in his drawers. Luck was with her, and she found a long T-shirt that reached to midthigh when she put it on. It was in mint condition, unlike the rest of Riley's wardrobe, so she figured he probably didn't like this shirt much anyway. Even though he wanted to surprise her with breakfast in bed, she planned to be somewhat clothed under the covers. She didn't feel as confident about her charms in broad daylight as Riley apparently did. And she planned to make a quick exit for a new supply of clothes as soon as possible.

She lingered at the window, fingering the edge of a crisp white curtain and gazing outside into a cool, rainy, summer day. Drops spattered the window, giving the trees and sky outside a soft, romantic haze. It was just the sort of day to curl up inside a big cozy bed with the man she loved.

It was difficult to be quick about anything on such a lazy day, but Kit managed to run a brush through her hair hastily and splash water on her face before she heard scuffling that she recognized as the sound of Riley's entry through the hole in the wall. She leaped for the bed, successfully sliding in and under the fluffy eiderdown before Riley reentered. Fanning her hair out to shield the side of her face that was exposed, she pretended to be asleep. After a pause, her hair was carefully set to the side and a small kiss placed sweetly on her cheek.

Slowly she opened her eyes, and with feigned surprise she turned over to meet Riley's gaze. "Good morning," she murmured, yawning delicately and sitting up slightly.

"Good morning," he returned, and laid a pretty wicker bed tray across her lap.

She looked down, and her lips curved upward. There was toast with strawberry jam, orange juice and coffee, placed neatly on cool white linens and accompanied by a rose in a crystal vase.

"Oh, it's lovely!" she exclaimed, and, careful not to disturb the balance on her lap, dragged Riley down far enough to give him a kiss. "You romantic little devil you."

"Thanks." His returning smile was almost shy as it lifted one side of his mouth and formed the long dimple in his cheek.

Fluttering pale eyelashes, Kit said sweetly, "And such a surprise, too. Why, I had no idea."

"I have ways of making you show the proper respect for my sentimental impulses, my dear."

She smiled serenely. "Oh, yeah?"

"Yeah."

"Prove it."

Without another word, he grabbed for the bed tray. She managed to snare a piece of toast from the threat of sloshing orange juice before the tray was whisked away and dumped unceremoniously on top of the dresser, next to the hurricane lamp.

She hadn't missed the meaningful gleam in Riley's blue eyes, or the amusement that hung around his tense jaw. In the bed she held herself ready for whatever his next move might be. Tickling? She would roll to the side and off the bed. Seduction? She'd tickle him.

But he fooled her. He advanced on her, one step at a time, like a cat ready to pounce, and she wondered what she'd started. She couldn't stand the suspense, and she put out her hands—one of them still clutching a soggy triangle of toast—in supplication, saying, "Come on, Riley. I didn't mean it. Let's be pals, okay?"

"No way."

His smile had become dangerous, and she thought suddenly that she didn't know where the piggy bank was and could he possibly be planning to stick it into her pants? She looked up at him with outrage in her eyes and then changed tactics, squeezing them shut, deciding to become a coward at this late date.

She barely felt anything as he reached over, first to dispose of her toast and then to snatch the nearest pillow, but she was knocked about a foot to the right when the pillow slammed her shoulder with considerable force.

Then, whoosh, there it was again, bopping her squarely on the other shoulder and begging for retribution.

"You, you..." No expletive rotten enough came to mind as she tried not to laugh, and she groped around for a weapon of her own. "A pillow fight?" she gasped as she lashed out and landed a good blow on the top of his head. "How juvenile are you, anyway?"

"I notice you're not too mature to fight back."

"Creep!" she shouted, and got to her knees through the tangle of bedding, trying to find a stronger base for swinging her pillow.

He only laughed and bonked her in the midsection, now that she'd opened up that new target. She responded in kind as he knew she would, and the pillow fight raged on.

They were both breathless and exhausted from thrashing about when they collapsed into the covers and laughed until they cried.

"Much more effective, and a whole lot more fun than an alarm clock," Kit commented wryly, wiping tears from her face. A lone feather fluttered down to light delicately on her nose.

"Would you like to do this every morning?" Riley inquired softly. "I think it could be arranged."

"Odd Job Cooper takes on a new one, hmm? Human alarm clock and pillow fluffer all in one." Trying to pull herself together from halfway underneath him was no easy task, and, giving up for the moment, Kit sank farther into the comfortable bed. She reached over and pinched his cheek affectionately. "Sorry, cutie, but I prefer not to add myself to your ever-increasing list of employers."

"That's all right," he returned easily. "I'm not crazy enough to want to be your lackey, anyway."

He propped himself up on one elbow, leaning over her, and traced a line down the middle of her forehead to the tip of her nose. His comment about waking her up every morning had been intended as an oblique reference to marriage, but he let it drop without explaining that. Just last night he'd told her they wouldn't think about the future, yet here he was, bringing it up at the earliest opportunity. It was hard to bite it back when he wanted to bind her to him irrevocably, but he knew he didn't have a choice. He had a week and a half to take it slow and easy, which was pretty much of a contradiction in terms. But he'd damn well better pull it off.

Tapping her nose to accentuate the words, he said, "So, Katherine Emily, are you going to behave yourself and eat the breakfast I toiled over, or do I have to win a few more rounds of pillow fighting to convince you?"

"Win a few more rounds?" she challenged. "Who says you won this one?"

"I do."

"Big deal." She sat up, brushing his hand away from her. "Even if you did win the pillow fight—which I'm not admitting for a minute—you still owe me a dinner for finding out about your cookie racket. Riley Cooper—Cookie King. I love it!"

"My cookies are terrific. And don't worry. You'll have your dinner." He rolled over her to get to the edge of the bed, where he stood and extended a hand. "But first you have to eat breakfast."

"Breakfast immediately followed by dinner?" She tried to pull him back into bed but rose from the bed when that didn't succeed in the least. "At this rate, I'll be as round and plump as the piggy bank."

"But a whole lot softer." He pinched her bottom as he gathered her into his arms. "Anyway, I have some other diversions planned to keep you exercised." His goofy leer made it clear what kind of diversion he had in mind.

"Let's see—this is Thursday, isn't it? Are we playing on Bob Powers's softball team?"

"Not on your life."

"Why not?" She gazed into his eyes and feigned innocence. "You said you'd arrange it so I could play."

"Oh, no, I didn't. I said I'd defend your right to play if we went and if Bob said no. I didn't say I was enough of a fool to show up in the first place."

"Some hero," she complained, but she kissed him anyway, messing his hair with her fingers and pretending to box his ears.

He laughed into her kiss, propelling her backward with him to the dresser where he'd stashed the breakfast tray. After making sure she drank her juice, he took care of the toast and now-tepid coffee himself and then took her out through the hole for a guided tour of his whole house.

There were a few places where they had to duck through similar holes and around stacks of two-by-fours or other obstacles, but Kit told herself that only added to the adventure. The house was in bits and pieces, with only the one bedroom and the kitchen downstairs completely re-done. Conditions ranged from the upstairs bathroom, which had fixtures and plumbing but bare walls and floors, to one of the bedrooms, which had a gaping chasm cut into the floor. Riley explained that the previous owners had tried to put in a fireman's pole for their children. Like-wise, most of the downstairs needed plaster and paint and demarcation into definite rooms. All in all, it was a big shell of a house, and a big project.

Nonetheless, Kit was impressed with the gargantuan ef-fort required to get the house this far, and how much more would be necessary before it approached being finished.

It wasn't until after she'd had a quick bath in the new claw-footed tub and redressed in a pair of Riley's gym shorts and a work shirt that she discovered she was to play a role in the restoration of the house. Riley had her pegged as a wallpaper person and refused to take her objections seriously.

"Come on, Kit," he maintained. "You have to help out. I got the tub and everything in here so fast because you asked for them. All that's left to do in this bathroom is the wallpaper, and I want to get it over with." He gave her a confident smile. "You know I hate leaving things half done."

"So I'm to work for my keep, is that it?" she asked dryly.

"Exactly." He grabbed for her, trying to tickle her and make her give in. "I wouldn't want you to feel like you hadn't done anything to deserve the fine accommodations I'm providing."

"Jolly." But she really didn't mind. She had never got-ten near wallpaper before, and she was actually somewhat intrigued by the whole process of Riley's house renovation. It was a mystery why he liked this fix-up business so much, a mystery she wanted to delve into a bit. She even liked the paper he had chosen; it was mostly white, with a scattering of tiny green shapes, which could have been clouds or free-form flowers. A modicum of enthusiasm came over her as she pondered how much better the bathroom was going to look when they were done.

Her enthusiasm faded fast when the reality of the situation sank in. It wasn't difficult, she discovered, but neither was it creative, nor was it very much fun. Just sloppy. Riley cut the pieces of paper in the hallway, whistling and singing things like, "Jeremiah Was a Bullfrog," while she grumbled and carefully dipped the wallpaper strips in the partially filled tub. At first she tried to be neat and not slosh water around when she folded the paper strips, but it didn't seem to matter to cheerful old Riley if she approximated Noah's flood. But her hair kept tipping into the sticky water when she leaned forward too far, and she was getting cranky that Riley didn't seem to notice if she was neat or not, so she gave in and let the gummy water run in rivulets around the tiny bathroom.

Together they set the pieces on the wall, and then she smoothed out the air bubbles and tried, often in vain, to match the little green blobs in the pattern. Meanwhile, he teased, cajoled and generally made a nuisance of himself while supposedly cutting around plumbing fixtures and other obstructions and hanging the paper straight.

She tried to hold on to her grumpy mood; after all, she had often stated how much she hated doing things she felt inadequate at. But the bathroom was so small they couldn't help bonking into each other every time they turned around, and Riley was so cheerful it was hard to resist. And even though she wasn't enjoying the wallpapering itself, Kit couldn't help joining in on the chorus of

"Do You Think I'm Sexy?" in her best Rod Stewart imitation. Soon she was singing along with most of Riley's choices and even bumping her bottom against his in time to the music.

As Riley smoothed the next to last piece into place, he began to warble "Billie Jean" in falsetto, and Kit laughed so hard she dropped the final sheet of paper in the tub with a giant splash. But Riley was undaunted, singing on even more loudly. He added an incredibly bad—and cramped—"moonwalk" to the song, sliding himself backward a few steps and looking completely ridiculous.

"That's terrible," she said, shaking her head and pushing her hair behind her ears with sticky hands. "Singing that bad should be outlawed under the noise pollution statutes."

"Oh, yeah?"

"Yeah!"

"Who says?" he challenged, advancing toward her with his hands on his hips.

With her hands on her own hips, she whirled to face him and discovered that they were now toe to toe. "Get away from me!" she said with mock menace, but she laughed a little as she pretended to push him back. "I'm sure it must be dangerous to my health to be near any man who sings that off-key."

"Oh, yeah?"

"Yeah."

"We'll see about that." Reaching around behind her, he retrieved the soaked strip of paper still floating in the tub. Before she could do so much more than ineffectually protest, he had brought it up and wound it around and around her, all sticky and clinging, succeeding in binding her arms at her sides and immobilizing her completely. To add insult to injury, he managed to grab the seam roller and then slid it up and down the overlapping end of the paper, humming as he pretended to finish her edge.

She was trapped in a wallpaper strait jacket. Attempting to keep her mouth from curving into a smile at Riley's nonsensical attitude, she raised an eyebrow and asked, "Well? What are you going to do for an encore?"

"I'm just guaranteeing myself a captive audience," he replied with a mischievous twinkle in his eye.

Wrapping his arms tightly over her and the paper, he burst into, "Billie Jeannnnn..." in an even higher and more obnoxious voice, paying no attention to her weak laughter or struggles to free her arms.

"You are certifiably bananas!" she shouted over the din. "Quit torturing me with that wretched excuse for singing."

Her words didn't seem to faze him, but at least he took a breather, settling her even nearer in the circle of his arms. "You make such a pretty package, Kit," he said judiciously, peering at her with his head tipped to one side. "What you need is a great big bow."

"What you need now is a great big sock in the kisser."

"Tsk, tsk, Kit. Don't be so feisty, or I'll add another coat of paper, only higher up this time." Bending down, he brought his lips very close to hers. "You talk too much," he murmured, and then he kissed her wallpaper-paste-flavored mouth as though it contained nectar of the gods.

Kissing her, he loosened his hold enough for her to wiggle her arms free of the paper, and she sighed happily as she slid her arms around his neck and ran her gummy fingers through his hair. The length of paper peeled away slowly, until it finally fell off and sank to the floor, where Kit kicked it out of the way. He became as untidy as she was; she made sure of that, rubbing every pasty, sticky inch of herself up against him.

When they pried themselves apart, they heard a long, smacking noise as the paste on their bodies separated. They both laughed out loud and looked down at the mess they'd made of themselves.

Kit asked, "Do you think we've done enough wallpapering for one day?"

"We've done enough damage for one day, that's for sure." Riley shook his head as he cleaned up the room in a flash, pitching scraps into a big barrel in the hall and draining the tub. Then he took Kit's hand and led her out into the hall.

With their arms draped around each other, they stood back and admired their handiwork. Luckily the unfinished portion was over the door they were looking through and didn't mar the view from this angle.

"Nice job," Riley decided.

"Not just nice!" Kit protested, squeezing him around the middle. "Why, this may be the best wallpapering job in the history of mankind."

"I don't think I'd go that far."

"Pooh. I would."

"It's easy to tell you're in advertising," he said, dropping a kiss on her nose. "You have a real talent for overstatement."

"It's not overstatement—it's blarney. And it's a gift, don't you know? I get it from my mother's side of the family," she informed him loftily. "Besides, even if it isn't the greatest wallpapering in the history of mankind, it's the best wallpapering I've ever done."

"And the first, no doubt."

"Well, that, too. So you see it's a double accomplishment. And the bathroom looks brighter and nicer, and we had fun."

"You weren't having fun at the beginning."

"'Billie Jean' put me right over the top." She grinned and hugged him quickly. "Now when do I get to wrap you up in wallpaper and return the favor?"

"Maybe when we finish up this room. Or maybe when we do the other bathrooms or the living room or the four bedrooms..." He trailed off, watching her with unconcealed amusement. "Now that you're a full-fledged wallpaperer, I can keep you in work till the cows come home."

"Ha! I'm not sharing my house with cows." She pulled the door to the bathroom shut firmly. "Where are you taking me for dinner, anyway? Since I worked my buns off for you, I think you owe me another one. Better take me out quick before the bill gets even higher."

"Looking like that," he said, pointing at a wide white smear of paste on her cheek, "I can't take you anywhere fancier than a bowling alley. Anyway, you're supposed to pick, remember? The bet was whoever won got the restaurant of his or her choice, and you won."

"I love hearing those words. 'You won.' You can say that to me anytime. Let's see." She ducked under some low-hanging wires and maneuvered around a sawhorse on her way to the back stairs. "First I have to clean up again, and then I have to get more clothes from my mother's house. I can't go to the most expensive restaurant in town in the remnants of your wardrobe."

Following her, Riley skillfully avoided a collision with a table saw and edged on to the stairway behind her. "Oh, so we're going to the most expensive restaurant in town, are we?"

"As soon as I figure out what it is." Kit smiled up at him from a lower step. "But I'm sure Alex or my mother will know. It's their stock-in-trade to keep tabs on that sort of thing."

He caught her hand and intertwined their fingers. "If you're picking up clothes, does that mean you're planning on staying with me for a while, instead of going back to your mother's?"

She blinked. "That is okay, isn't it?"

He released the breath he'd been holding. "You bet that's okay. That's better than okay." Still holding her hand, he jogged down the rest of the stairs ahead of her, humming "Billie Jean" with a newly happy rhythm. He was developing a real fondness for that song.

THE WENTWORTH HOUSE was bustling, with each of its occupants running a different direction at the same time.

Nonetheless, they heralded Kit's arrival after a night away with avid interest and all the subtlety of Sherman's march through Georgia. Kit was intensely relieved she had convinced Riley not to come in with her, but instead to meet her later in the park across the street. The Wentworth inquisition was bad enough when faced solo, but unbearably embarrassing with one's lover present.

"All right," Alex said, pinning her to the couch. "Spill it."

"Alex! Do you mind?" Just when she thought she was beginning to like these people, or at least tolerate them, they made her feel pushed and pressured again, and the desire to escape leaped in her breast. She looked up for exit routes, but Eliza was blocking the door to the hall, and her mother was standing squarely in front of the one to the dining room. Jo was fluttering in between their mother and Alex, looking terribly curious and ashamed of herself for it. Kit wished in vain for Maggie, the one person strong enough and sensible enough to get the inquisitors off Kit's back.

Left to her own devices this way, Kit realized she was going to have to keep a cool head. "How can I discuss this when Eliza's here?" she asked Alex in a rushed whisper. "That's awfully tacky, don't you think, considering her feelings?"

"Oh, heavens," Alex replied, waving an arm in the air carelessly. "Eliza doesn't like Riley anymore. That's yesterday's news, Kit, old girl."

Kit glanced up at her youngest sister, whose pink cheeks and pink pinafore graced the far door. "Is this true, Eliza? Are you really over Riley?"

"Well . . . yes." Eliza blushed furiously and offered defensively, "I'm dating someone new, too, someone who likes me for a change. I mean, why waste my time on a lost cause?"

"Why indeed?" Whatever Riley said to Eliza last night had done wonders. Kit could only guess that Eliza had found her new beau at the benefit, but in any event, her little sister certainly did fast work. However it had come about, Kit was relieved to hear that Eliza's hot and cold heart was running cold for Riley and hot for someone else. "I'm glad that's settled."

Alex leaned forward. "Nothing's settled, Kit, dear, until you clue us in on the scoop between you and Riley. Are we talking marriage here, or just a torrid affair?"

"Alexandra!" Lilah countered, leaving her post at the door. "I am shocked, horrified and appalled at the way your mind works. Of course they're discussing marriage. Aren't you, Katharine?"

Her first inclination was to deny everything and run from the room screaming. Her second was to shout at

them that she and Riley were having a wild, passionate
fling and marriage was out of the question because neither of them would ever stoop that low. She did neither,
remembering Maggie's counsel to expend energy when it
really counted. Now that she considered it, what difference did it make if they were trying to pump her for information? She didn't have to tell them anything if she didn't
want to. And she didn't want to.

Kit's expression was serene as she rose from the sofa. "I
don't believe I want to discuss this right now, if you don't
mind." Her sisters and her mother stood like statues, staring at a calm, even-tempered Kit they'd never met. "I
know you're curious, but you'll simply have to restrain
yourselves. When and if I have any announcements to
make, you'll be the first to know. Until that time," she said
sweetly, "my love life is off-limits." And then she made a
graceful exit, heading for the stairs with her head held
high.

"Oh, by the way," she commented, turning back
slightly. "I dropped the blue ball dress off at the cleaners,
and I'll have it back some time next week. I hope that's
okay."

"Oh, sure," Alex mumbled.

Kit dashed upstairs in a wonderful frame of mind. For
the first time in her life, she had dealt rationally and un-
apologetically with her family. And the weirdest part was
that it hadn't been that hard.

"My, my," she said to herself as she shed Riley's clothes
and looked around for something to wear to dinner.
"Maybe I've finally grown up after all."

She grabbed a red knit T-shirt dress and linked a belt
around her waist. With red flats and big plastic earrings,
she was all set except for packing a bag to take to Riley's
house. As her eyes swept the room, they lit on an out-of-

place object standing on the dresser next to Alex's Homecoming Queen tiara. A small, clear glass object with its stomach full of pennies.

"Good grief," she said aloud to the empty room. "It's that lousy pig again."

She knew she would have to come up with something diabolical to do with it. She decided she'd even the score if it was the last thing she did, and she stuffed the pig in with the other things she was taking to Riley's place.

A few moments later she was all packed, but not quite ready to go for some reason she hadn't fathomed yet. Hauling her bag, she wandered down a floor, finding herself in the new office, the one that used to be her room. The project was finished now, with a rocking chair and a rag rug and bookshelves on one side and a big rolltop desk set up next to the window.

She ran a hand over the smooth wood of the rolltop, gazing out the window into the branches of the maple in the front yard. It was tempting to yank open the window and climb out into the maple tree just for old times' sake. She was surprised at how nostalgic she felt, and how sad in a way.

It was as if leaving her mother's house this time would be irrevocable. When she had bolted from this place four years ago, she hadn't looked back. But now, with much less luggage and a much more temporary residence in mind, it felt like such a final exit.

Her reverie was interrupted by her sister Jo.

"I thought I heard you in here," Jo said quietly. "Can I talk to you for a second?"

"Sure," Kit returned, tearing herself away from the window to attend Jo's words. "What can I do for you?"

"Well, it's about the clean water campaign I'm working on." Jo hesitated. "I don't know if you want to get involved, but we could certainly use you."

Although she wasn't totally paying attention, Kit nodded.

"Taking petitions around or something? Sure, I can do that."

"Oh, no, nothing like that. I meant advertising." Jo's eyes sparkled as she began to get into her persuasive mode. "We need a really exciting marketing campaign to raise funds and get ourselves noticed. It's so important that we do this right!"

"Advertising?" Kit took a step in Jo's direction, surprised. "You really want me to come up with a campaign for you?"

"Oh, yes, if you don't mind. If it's not fair to ask you to donate your service, we can probably pay you," Jo offered.

"No, no, that's okay. I'm really flattered that you asked." Laughing excitedly, Kit put an arm around her small sister's shoulders. "It's a good cause, right?"

"Of course," Jo returned. "The best!"

Discussing the issue with a great deal of enthusiasm, they headed out into the hall and down the front stairs.

"Thanks so much," Jo said as they hit the landing. "The things you're suggesting sound just great. With TV ads and a mail campaign, I can start counting the donations already."

Kit shook her head. "Don't get too excited, Jo. We haven't gotten into costs yet, and some of the ideas you like best are very expensive."

"Oh, pooh. We'll figure it out."

"Hey, you guys," Eliza stage-whispered from the living room doorway. "My new boyfriend is here. Do you want to meet him?"

Kit and Jo exchanged doubtful glances. If they hated this new boy, Eliza was sure to pout for days. On the other hand, if they liked him, Eliza might be jealous and out of sorts.

"I don't know," Jo began, but Eliza cut her off.

"Oh, come on. I want to know what you think."

She reached out and caught Kit's hand, dragging her into the living room against her will. Jo followed slowly, pleating and unpleating her full peasant skirt with her hands.

"Well, Jo, Kit, this is Steve," Eliza proclaimed proudly. "Steve, my sisters Jo and Kit. Kit's the blonde."

"Pleased to meet you," the nice-looking young man on the couch said nervously.

They talked for a few moments about nothing in particular until Kit elbowed Jo meaningfully, and they both got up to leave.

"No, no, don't get up," Kit told Steve as she backed out of the room in front of Jo.

Eliza scrambled after them. "Well?" she demanded.

"He's very nice," Kit offered.

"Very sweet," Jo added.

"And good-looking."

"Oh, yes. Good-looking, too."

They both regarded Eliza hopefully, praying that would be sufficient. Eliza seemed to be considering whether to let them off the hook so easily, when Kit spun her youngest sister around rapidly and pushed her in the direction of the living room.

"You'd better get back in there before Steve gets restless."

Eliza obliged, and Kit was astonished. She and Jo had almost reached the landing to the stairs, where she'd left her bag, when Steve's loud whisper caught her ears.

He said in a voice full of awe and admiration, "Your sisters are so beautiful."

Kit grinned at Jo with wry amusement. It wasn't that looks meant that much to her, but it certainly was nice to be in the same room with two of the fabulous Wentworth redheads and come out classified "beautiful." Kit had never thought she'd see the day.

As she packed up her bag and said a quick goodbye to Jo, Kit wondered what she had once found so distasteful here. The house was overdecorated, to be sure, and her sisters and mother were the same exasperating people they had always been, but she was forced to admit to herself that it really didn't bother her that much anymore. If dealing with them had at first been touch and go, now it was a lot of fun.

She actually felt like one of them. The odd thing was now that she was leaving, she couldn't think of any reason not to stay one of them.

Pushing open the front door into the full brunt of an afternoon sun, she thought about Jo's advertising campaign and the fact that she had no intention of bringing McCafferty and Sloan into the project. If she could do one campaign by herself, why not others? Why not take the good facets of her job in New York—autonomy, creative control—and bring them here to St. Paul? It hadn't even occurred to her before, and she couldn't think why not. Probably because she wouldn't let herself consider the possibility.

After all, she was a risk taker. Why not take a big one and start her own agency in St. Paul? There were drawbacks, to be sure, but with some business guidance she just might be able to pull it off, and pull it off with style.

If it really could be possible to live here as a whole, secure person... She just might be able to stay.

Bounding down the porch steps, she rushed to meet Riley in the park at the appointed place. She couldn't wait to hear what he would say.

Chapter Eleven

No one else she knew would have started off a dinner date by running through the park in a red dress, but it was a glorious, sunny summer evening, and Kit was happy beyond belief. The breezy, spunky attitude of her outfit and her surroundings captured her mood perfectly.

She raced the short distance from her mother's house, over the grass and past the trees, to the part of the lake where rowboats and paddleboats could be rented. The sun was still high in the sky, casting golden circles in the water, where bright orange paddleboats bobbed, begging someone to take them out for a ride.

Looking around frantically, Kit saw no sign of Riley. A quick glance at her wrist told her she was early, and she tried to get herself to relax. She found a wrought-iron bench under a tall black lamppost, and she sat down for a second, until pent-up energy sent her scrambling back to her feet to pace on the grass near the edge of the water.

Ducks and geese took that as their invitation to fly over to her side of the lake, assuming she had bread to share. With a great show of calling and cawing and flapping of wings, they jostled for position around her.

Although she wished she had thought of bringing food for them, Kit was delighted at the friendly birds' company. She held out her hands to show them she had no bread, but they were unconvinced and cackled and squawked more vociferously than ever.

"Hey, guys, come on, lighten up," she protested. "You can yell all you want, but I forgot, okay? I promise next time I'll buy a whole loaf."

One big white goose eyed her suspiciously. It let out a long, drawn-out honk, and ruffled its feathers, still fixing her with the evil eye. She felt sure it must be bad-mouthing her to all of its friends.

"Don't give the lady a hard time," Riley's familiar lazy voice instructed the goose. "She's only visiting."

Kit turned, fully cognizant that her heart would be in her eyes. Riley knew her too well, and he might guess what she had to say before she even framed the words. "Maybe not," she said casually.

"Maybe not what?" He must have had an inkling, because his voice became soft and slow, and his jaunty stroll toward her lagged immediately. "What do you mean?"

"Well, I've been doing some thinking. I haven't worked out the details yet, but maybe, just maybe…" She tried to keep her voice light. "Maybe I won't be leaving after all."

He asked quickly, "How definite is this?"

"Pretty definite."

He let out the sigh he'd been holding. "Now I know I'm hearing things." He shook his head and ran a hand over his face, from the tawny strands of hair threatening to fall down over his forehead to the gold-tinged stubble on his jaw. He widened and then narrowed his eyes, as if to focus more clearly. "Did you just say you might be home to stay?"

"Yes, that's what I said." She watched him doubtfully. "What do you think?"

"How? What will you do? Will you stay for good from now on? What exactly do you mean?"

She laughed at the rush of questions. "Hold on for a second—I don't even know yet!"

"Okay, okay." He jammed his hands into his pockets and shook his head, grinning. Was it possible to hold back the triumphant hallelujahs pushing at his throat? "But you must have some idea?"

"Well, I won't be working at Grand Affairs, that's for sure. And I won't be living at my mother's house." A look of stubbornness and decision flashed across Kit's features. "I truly believe I can tolerate them well enough to live in the same town, but not in the same house. Heaven forbid!"

Choosing his words carefully, Riley ventured softly, "You could move in with me."

Kit bridged the distance between them, winding her arms around his neck and hugging him fiercely. "I was hoping you'd suggest that."

Bringing his hands to rest on hers, he disentangled her arms but maintained a gentle hold. He searched for acceptance and trust in her eyes, not wanting to offend her, but willing to offer her a job if she needed one. "You could come to work at Grandma Cooper's, you know. We could use a PR director."

Her expression was cynical. "Just like Krystle on *Dynasty*, hmm? Thanks, but I have other plans."

He shifted his arm so he could drape it across her back, guiding her toward the pedestrian path around the lake. "Okay. Let's hear these plans."

She hesitated for only a moment before launching into her brand-new idea. "What would you say if I started my own ad agency? It would be small at first, and a lot of hard work for very little return. But I know the business. I'm smart. And I have good connections." She grinned then and winked at him. "I can think of at least two major Twin Cities businesses who'd give me their accounts."

"Meaning Grand Affairs and Grandma Cooper's Cookies?"

"Well, I'd certainly hope so."

"I don't know." He shook his head, assuming a skeptical facade. "You can't leave something as important as Grandma Cooper's image up to just anybody, you know. I'd have to see your ideas first. And what do you call those things with the ideas written out? Storyboards, isn't it?" The look he gave her was hot and steady and brought to mind little to do with advertising or storyboards. "Yeah," he murmured, leaning down close to whisper in her ear. "I think I'll have to check you out completely, top to bottom, before I can make any decision."

Pausing in midstride, Kit raised an eyebrow and inclined her head to the side to contemplate him. "So you want to see my—" she paused and touched the tip of her tongue to her lip "—storyboards, hmm? I think that can be arranged."

"I think I'm dreaming," he said slowly with evident disbelief. "I mean, it just hit me. You. Here. The two of us discussing your future in the Twin Cities. And I didn't have to kidnap you or browbeat you or anything." Shaking his head again, he laughed out loud and then swooped around her and hoisted her into the air.

"Riley!" she screamed. "Put me down!"

Holding her dangling a foot off the ground, he gazed up into her face and grinned at her, impudent and unapologetic. "I'm not ever putting you down. You might run away from me again."

"I told you, I'm not going anywhere." She wiggled, but his arms held fast around her waist. "Come on, I feel silly up here."

"Kiss me first."

"Okay," she said matter-of-factly. She tilted down to meet his lips, merely brushing them with hers. "If you want more, you'll have to put me down. That's my final offer."

"Tease," he scoffed.

"No way," she retorted. "I'll kiss you anytime you want. But not in the middle of the park, and not when you're tossing me around like a sack of potatoes. In case you've forgotten, I don't like being manhandled, manipulated or pushed. Speaking of which, what's all this about kidnapping me and browbeating me into staying?"

His smile held the mischief of a first-grader knee-deep in mud pies. "Who knows what I would've tried if you didn't come around? I was getting desperate."

"Right." She tried to be annoyed with him, but he was too adorable. She didn't believe he ever would have done it anyway. Playing along, she tipped her head down and gave him a big, sloppy kiss near the corner of his mouth.

"Bleah," he said, but she only laughed and fastened her lips to his cheek. Blowing out air rapidly, right next to the skin, she made an obnoxious noise, what she and Riley used to call a raspberry.

"Kit!" he protested, but he loosened his hold, and she twisted free. The ducks and geese honked and scattered, protesting the disturbance in their midst.

Kit's bright, delighted laughter reverberated in the sunshine as she issued a challenge. "Catch me if you can." Long legs flashing, she blasted off to the running path with a healthy head start.

She heard her name called out in an ominous tone, but she ignored Riley and continued to run as fast as she could. A stitch caught her side very quickly, making her realize what lousy shape she was in. And she had chosen the wrong outfit for footraces. Even she didn't do well in skirts and flats when shorts and tennies were required. It didn't matter. Riley caught up with her quickly, and, holding her side and trying not to laugh, she ambled over to the side of the path, practically collapsing onto a black iron park bench.

"What took you so long?" she demanded in between gulps of air. "If it had taken you any longer to catch up with me, I might've died."

"Come on, Kit. You've lost your fighting edge, that's all."

"I have not!" To prove it, she made a muscle with her scrawny left arm.

He didn't seem to say anything. He just lifted his left eyebrow and looked at her.

"I suppose you're right," she admitted, sighing as she surveyed her meager muscle. "I need to get back into training. Pretty soon, I'll be back to lapping you when we run around the lake."

Now both eyebrows rose. "Back to lapping me? When could you ever beat me running around the lake, let alone lap me? Get serious."

"Ha! You wait and see."

"Naah." He shook his head. "The day you lap me is the day I skinny-dip in Lake Harriet in full view of a hundred people."

"Bet?"

"Bet."

She grinned at him, reflecting on the image of Riley skinny-dipping in front of all those people. She was going to have to work hard to pull that one off. Reaching over to poke his lean torso through his shirt, she taunted, "You're not so great yourself, old pal. Look how long it took you to catch up with me."

"I was going easy on you."

"Sure you were."

Shaking his head, he got to his feet and tried to pull her after. "Come on, let's get going. We're supposed to be enjoying our romantic interlude, and all we've done so far is run around."

"And hang wallpaper," she reminded him.

"Right. And hang wallpaper. But don't you think," he began, hauling her up next to him, "it's time for a heavy dose of romantic interlude?"

She licked her lips. "I suppose. What did you have in mind?"

He didn't say anything, but his eyes locked on hers. His finger crept to his top button, negligently sliding the button through its hole. She stared, fascinated, as the soft blue cloth gapped, revealing smooth, tanned flesh dusted with golden hair. Then he moved his fingers to the next hole and ever so slowly pulled that one open, too.

"Stop that!" she said heatedly, examining nearby trees to see if anyone was watching.

"Don't worry." He rebuttoned his shirt and draped an arm around her, but his voice remained low and seductive. "I wasn't planning on stripping in the middle of the park, but I wanted to let you know what I had in mind."

She swallowed. "I get the idea."

"Do you?" What had begun as a joke changed tempo when he caught the warmth of her gaze on his chest and the breathless way she spoke to him. Absently he slid his hand down the length of her fine white-blond hair, trailing a few strands through his fingers. "Did I ever tell you how much I like your hair down like this?'' The words weren't sufficient to communicate that it dazzled him, maddened him, just by swinging free like that, or that she dazzled him, maddened him, merely by existing in his presence. He closed his eyes and drew her nearer, trying to tell her how he felt with the strength of his arms and the pressure of his body against hers. "I'm so glad you're staying,'' he murmured.

Leaning back inside his embrace, Kit met his eyes with confusion. Why was he holding her so tightly when this was the moment for joy, for trust, for celebration? Instead, he looked more vulnerable than she had ever seen him. "I'm glad I'm staying, too,'' she said slowly. She shook her head and slipped out of his arms, still firmly holding his hand. Looking around her, she saw again the gold of the evening sun shining on the lake and the flash of the white wings of the gulls that soared and dipped overhead. She could hear the gulls calling and crying and the rustle of leaves on the trees. It was so lovely she shivered, and Riley drew her close again. "I have so many memories of this place—so many bike rides and so much laughter and so many smiles and such good feelings. Do you?''

"Yes.'' He spoke simply, not wanting to disturb the serenity. "Why?''

As she stared at the lake and the park and at Riley, a hundred snapshots of their shared past flipped through her mind, one after the other, in a crazy rush of images. Those were the days when there was time and love enough to relax in the security of having a best friend. "I was wondering if we could, for old times' sake, postpone dinner or your romantic interlude or whatever for a little while longer.'' Under his rapt gaze, she faltered and slid forward to rub her cheek against his rough jaw. "It doesn't have to take long. I just want to savor this gorgeous day for a little while, like we used to. I want to feel the grass and the water and the sun. Not just see it, but feel it. Do you understand?''

''No. But I don't need to. If it's what you want, it's okay with me.'' He dropped a tiny kiss on the sleek crown of her head. A wry smile curved his lips. ''And you called me a sentimental fool.''

''Don't worry,'' she offered with a stagy wink, ''You'll get your romantic interlude, and it will be worth the wait.''

His eyes threatened to singe her with their reckless disregard for propriety. ''Really?'' His voice dipped provocatively. ''Then we'd better get going right away. With that kind of incentive, it's going to be the fastest trip around the lake on record.''

Arm in arm, they strolled off, content to relax in each other's company. Every once in a while they stopped to watch a duck swim by with its mate, or to toss pebbles into the lake. Riley's promises notwithstanding, it turned into a leisurely trip.

To Kit, it was as if the best memories of her childhood had been dusted off and recreated, changed from two-dimensional black-and-white images in her mind to three-dimensional living, breathing color in front of her.

It was simply a perfect day.

At one point they came across a small stone bridge spanning a stream running away from the lake. Kit paused, contemplating the still blue water and thinking how lucky she was to share this day with Riley. A slight breeze blew her bangs off her forehead, and the sun smiled down, warming her as it made the water below her sparkle and shimmer. Not far off a bird called to its buddies with a pure, sweet trill of sound. When Riley folded his arms around her from the back, sending shoots and sparks and tingles of pleasure down her spine, she realized how wonderful she felt. Her world was, at that moment, perfect.

"Riley," she mused as she relaxed in his arms, "I finally get it. Your 'small moments' theory, with the lilacs and all. I'm having one of those special moments right now."

"You sound like it's a seizure."

She resented his mocking smile. "No, really! With the sun and the breeze off the water and the birds singing—life is perfect for this one moment. That's what you were saying about the lilacs, wasn't it?"

Nodding, he closed his eyes and slid his cheek along the smooth hair at her temple. "You make it perfect for me."

His simple words took her breath away. "Thank you," she said softly, meaningfully. "And you for me." With a small smile, Kit watched him for a moment. They were very near a large beech tree by the park pavilion, and she remembered that tree's significance to the Kit and Riley who had played in this park. She announced, "There's only one thing that could make this day even more perfect."

"What's that?" he asked indulgently.

"I want to ask you for something, and I want you to promise me to answer seriously."

Serious questions? His head came up abruptly. The only thing he could think of was that she was going to ask him to marry her. He said quickly, "The answer is yes."

"Really?" A look of delight spread across her features. "I think it's such a nice idea!" Grabbing his arm, she pulled them in the direction of the beech tree. "I knew you'd remember, too. I'm not so sure of the words, though. Wasn't it, 'Blood brothers forever,' mixed together with 'May lightning strike us if we lie,' or something like that?"

He stopped short, refusing to be dragged any farther. "What in hell are you talking about?"

"Blood brothers. Under the beech tree. I thought we could do the blood brothers thing again for old times' sake." She searched his face for clues as to the misunderstanding here. "What did you think I was asking?"

"I thought ... Oh, never mind." He shook his head, irritated beyond belief. "Blood brothers, for crying out loud."

"No," she said defiantly. "I want to know what you thought I was asking you."

He looked into her eyes and knew she wouldn't budge without an answer. And he didn't lie to Kit; that was against his personal set of rules. "I thought you were suggesting we get married."

"Married?" she echoed. "Oh, my, that does put a different light on things, doesn't it?"

"I suppose you'd prefer to be blood brothers the rest of our lives?" he asked dryly.

"No, of course not. I just hadn't thought that far ahead, as far as ... marriage, I mean." Her brain was in a state of chaos. "Marriage is permanent, irrevocable, forever. I mean, you have to be absolutely sure you won't have second thoughts."

"Are you saying you think you will have second thoughts about me?"

"No, no, no!" Truthfully she didn't know what she believed. "Second thoughts about you? I love you! I've loved you for twenty-one years and never regretted it. Why should I start now?"

"I don't know." His voice acquired an edge he didn't like much. "You're the one with the doubts. I've known I wanted to marry you since second grade."

"No, you haven't. Come on, be serious for a minute."

"I am being serious!" He stuffed his hands in his pockets again and wheeled away from her. "Damn," he muttered. "Trust her not to believe me."

She persisted. "But, Riley, second grade? You've dated hundreds of women—or girls at least—over the years!"

"So what? I always thought you and I would end up together. Didn't you?"

"I don't know. I never really thought about it." Sighing heavily, Kit swung her hair out of the way and absently rearranged her bangs with two fingers. "I loved you for so long—as a friend—that I never took the time to consider what it would be like if the friendship matured along with the rest of us. I can't imagine how I would've handled it if you'd married someone else, or what you would've done if I'd married someone else. Would you still have been my friend?"

"How could any other man have put up with you having me as a best friend?" he demanded. "I never would've stood for it if it had been vice versa."

She considered the issue. "You know, you're exactly right. I always hated your girlfriends, and they always hated me, because they were jealous of our friendship. You and I were like a married couple almost, without the sexual angle, of course." She felt her face suffuse with warmth, and she began to admit to herself that the sexual side of their relationship had always been there, under the surface. They had hidden it very well, but, given the depth of their feelings for each other, it had to come out sooner or later. "It's so bizarre," she said softly. "Deep inside we both knew we were meant to be together. Looking back now, I see that so clearly. I mean, my friends in New York gave me such a hard time for refusing to go out with men they suggested. I thought they were all too tall or too short or not intelligent enough—"

"Thank God," Riley mumbled.

"No, really! I came up with these dumb excuses for every single guy." Kit's gaze fell to her red leather shoe, and she saw that she had been rubbing the toe back and forth over a small section of grass without paying attention, as if her flurry of thoughts could find an outlet there. "I see now," she admitted slowly, "that I was comparing them all to you." She looked up swiftly. "Maybe you're right. Maybe we have been destined for each other since second grade."

He took a few breaths and then folded his arms loosely around her waist. "Does that mean you'll marry me?"

"You know," she returned faintly, "I think I will." A sense of wonder filled her at how inevitable and yet how right this all seemed to be.

It occurred to him that she was accepting this awfully easily. "Kit," he offered gingerly, "if you think I'm pushing you or pressuring you into this, I'm willing to wait. You only decided to stay in town a little while ago, and this is all pretty sudden. I don't want you to look back later and feel that it happened too fast, or that I pushed you into saying yes."

"I don't think that and I won't think that." She gave him a smile of reassurance and reached up to pinch his cheek saucily. "Don't think you're going to back out so easily, old pal. I have a lot of geese and ducks I can call as witnesses if you try to get out of marrying me."

He only shook his head. "You're nuts, Kit."

"Yep," she said cheerfully, "you're probably right. I hooked up with you, didn't I?"

Laughing, she tugged on his arm and tried to hustle him away from the pavilion and toward the parking lot. "We've got places to go," she drawled in what she hoped was a seductive voice. "I'm starving, pal, and I want my dinner. And then I want my romantic interlude."

"Oh, you're going to get it all right." The corner of his mouth curved upward in a sardonic smile. "You're going to get everything you deserve."

Later, much later, full of rich food and exotic plans for her agency, Kit slipped between the cool sheets of Riley's brass bed. "Riley, I hate to ask this, but, I'm awfully thirsty. Do you think you could sneak downstairs and get me a glass of water?" She phrased the question in her prettiest, sweetest tone, just the way she imagined Alex would do it.

Riley gave her an odd look, but he did it anyway. As soon as she heard his footfalls on the back stairs, she whipped the piggy bank out of her bag and slid it under his pillow. Then she settled back onto her own pillow with a smile of satisfaction. As far as she was concerned, the battle of wits was only beginning.

THEIR PLANS FOR THE FUTURE seemed to fuel Riley's house restoration fire even higher, and he conned Kit into helping him with a vengeance. If they weren't painting the living room, they were hanging the new double doors that defined the dining room, or picking out light fixtures and furniture to fill in some of the bare spots.

"The sofa and chairs will be delivered on Tuesday," Kit announced, turning away from her mother's phone and tapping a pencil against her master list of house items still left to do. Until the telephone was hooked up at Riley's place, they were using the Wentworth house and the dusty apartment near campus to conduct business. "The dhurrie rug for the living room won't be in until Friday, but the bookshelves are ready now. Also, the antique store on West Seventh may have found the leaded glass you want for the dining room windows. Can we stop by there on our way to your place?''

"Sure." Riley dropped a kiss on top of Kit's head and pulled up a chair at the Wentworth kitchen table. "I love you when you're all brisk and efficient."

"Really?" What a funny thing to say, yet what a nice thing to hear.

"You bet. You aren't getting sick of this house business yet, are you?"

"Nope."

"Not even a little?"

"Nope," she repeated. "I like being in charge, and I like being busy."

"Good. Because I want the house finished in time to have a wedding there in a few weeks."

"A few weeks?" Her eyes were round with horror. "You can't be serious! Christmas in July is one week from to-day, and my mother won't even think about anything else until it's over. And I can't make plans without her. Heavens! The first Wentworth daughter to get married and my mother not consulted? Talk about taking your life in your hands!"

Riley sighed and pushed back from the table, balancing his chair on the back two legs. He couldn't for the life of him figure out why he was being so stubborn about this. It was as if his dream had come true too easily, after too long a wait, and he expected there to be a catch here somewhere. "I want to do it now," he said plainly, giving in to his gut feeling.

"Then by all means let's run down to the courthouse right this minute and get it over with."

"I didn't mean it like that," he returned, relenting a lit-tle and feeling ashamed of himself. "You know I want to do it right, too."

"And there is the small matter of a license and blood tests and a ring." She leaned over his chair and poked him playfully. "I do want my very own diamond ring and my very own, one hundred percent approved, A-one, bona fide proposal. The one in the park was mostly a mistake."

"You're just insulted I let you propose to me instead of vice versa."

"Pooh. You tricked me into it."

"I don't care." His eyes sparkled mysteriously. "But don't worry, because I have a plan for a real, A-one, bona fide proposal."

"You forgot one hundred percent approved, but I'll let it pass this time." She gasped, capturing his chin in her hands and pulling his head around sharply. "Wait—don't tell me! You're going to bake the ring into one of Grandma Cooper's chocolate chip cookies and let me break a tooth on it."

"If I was, I'm not now."

"No clues, no hints?" she lamented, coming around the chair and lumping herself heavily into his lap.

"Not even one."

"I have ways of making you talk, you know."

"Go ahead and try. I dare you."

Accepting his challenge, she slanted closer and blew hot breath in his ear. Judging him to have remained annoyingly unmoved, she slid a hand down his shirt front and then, slowly, meticulously, she sent the hand up under his shirt, moaning into his ear as her fingers skated across the flat, warm expanse of his stomach.

"No clues," he whispered, even as he groaned when her hand dipped lower. "You aren't going to weasel it out of me."

"Oh, no?" She laughed, low in her throat, and ran both hands inside his shirt, eagerly spanning the inches and flicking tiny kisses up and down his neck and face.

"This isn't the place for this," he managed. "For all we know Eliza has her ear pressed to the keyhole right now."

"Nope," Kit murmured between kisses. "Eliza doesn't like you anymore." She clicked her tongue. "Poor Riley, thrown out with yesterday's trash."

"As long as that's out of the way..." With a wicked chuckle, he stood up, still holding her against what had been his lap.

Kit's eyes widened as she felt the evidence of his reaction to her little erotic game press into her thigh. She hadn't planned on starting anything of that magnitude. My, but his switch was easy to trip.

He put her down on the kitchen table, tilting over her, rubbing against her shamelessly. It was his turn to leave a trail of hot, moist kisses and to slide his fingers up and under her top.

"I can see you've upped the ante," she said breathlessly, shivering as his fingers crept to the sensitive, soft underside of her breast. She tried to bat his hands away, but they felt so delicious under there. Steeling herself, she cleared her throat and announced, "A horizontal kitchen table rumba is not what I thought I was starting."

He leaned to the side immediately, releasing her. "I didn't think so," he contended smugly.

"So let's get out of here." Her voice and manner returned to normal quickly as she stood and straightened her bright yellow crop top and shorts. Then she gazed at him with warm, avid eyes. "I want you back at our house, where I can be more... persuasive, shall we say?"

"That's fine with me," he whispered, meeting her gaze degree for degree.

He wrapped an arm around her, steering her out of the Wentworth house as fast as their feet would carry them.

Later, much later, with fires banked and both of them in a more receptive mood for conversation, he mused aloud, "Do you realize you called this our house?"

She retorted, "Hey, after all the work I've put in, I deserve part ownership."

"And you also deserve an afternoon off." He rose from the bed and started to dress. "I think we should let the house go for the rest of the day and have a picnic together. We can eat in the gazebo across the street. How does that sound? I'll pick up some wine and some fried chicken, and you can see what you can rustle up downstairs."

They haggled over food and who'd do what, but by the time Riley kissed her goodbye at the front door, responsibilities had been equitably divided.

Kit turned to go back inside, already organizing the picnic basket in her mind. Absently she stooped to pick up the newspaper on the front steps. She glanced over the headlines, humming to herself as she walked to the back of the house to see what was in the refrigerator.

The newspaper contained the usual Minnesota stuff—farm foreclosures, another Twins loss, next week's weather forecast—but a small item near the bottom of the page caught her eye: ARKANSAS HOUSEWIFE ACCUSES POPCORN KING OF RECIPE THEFT

As far as Kit knew, there was only one Popcorn King. Pepe Swanson. Her first client. Charming, obtuse old Pepe, who had been so sure his flavors would revolutionize the popcorn industry, who had adopted Kit as the only member of McCafferty and Sloan's staff with enough smarts to advertise his beloved popcorn. And now, reading on, she discovered that Pepe Swanson was accused of stealing the formula for his Tutti-Frutti Tahitian flavor of popcorn. An Arkansas woman claimed she'd tried to sell Pepe the exact recipe years before Tutti-Fruitti Tahitian hit the grocery stores.

Kit read and reread the story with a growing sense of righteous indignation. Poor Pepe! He was a sweet old man, honest to a fault, and fiercely protective of his popcorn. This kind of accusation would send him into a tailspin. Without the right guidance, Pepe would be granting interviews to anyone who would listen, including the worst of the gossip rags. He would feel it was his duty to proclaim his innocence in the loudest possible and most injudicious voice, blowing the story all out of proportion and probably convincing the American public that he was as guilty as sin. Pepe was as smart as a whip when it came to popcorn, but he didn't understand the first thing about public image or strategy. He needed her counsel to prepare him to handle this explosive situation, to mobilize an appropriate response.

With a sinking heart, she realized she had no idea when this disaster had begun. Whenever it had started, she hadn't been there to deal with it. No one knew the Pepe's Popcorn account the way she did, no one knew the right buttons to push to get Pepe on the right track, and no one but Kit Wentworth should be manning McCafferty and Sloan at this moment, shepherding Pepe's defense.

She was into the living room to look for a phone before she had a chance to fully think things over. But as she ran from room to room in the largely empty house, she groaned and stopped in her tracks. Of course, there was no phone in this place!

Damn her luck anyway, to be stuck in a house with no phone when a crisis with her biggest account blew up in New York. She would bet poor Didi had been ringing the

Wentworth phone off the hook since whenever the Arkansas woman's accusations had hit the newsstands. And no one had been home to pass on messages when she'd been at her mother's house this morning.

On the spur of the moment she decided to get back to the Wentworth house as soon as humanly possible. If anyone was trying to locate her, at least she'd be accessible there.

She grabbed her tote bag, scribbled a note to Riley and raced out of the house. It was only a few blocks to West Seventh Street, where there were enough businesses to guarantee a phone. From there it was an agonizing wait for a cab until she was finally picked up and delivered across town to her mother's house.

She ran in the door, breathing hard, and spotted Maggie in the living room. Thank goodness.

"Maggie," she practically shouted, "has anyone called for me within the past day or so?"

"Yes!" Maggie began hurriedly, jumping to her feet. "Your office called three or four times yesterday. Jo even tried dropping by Riley's apartment, but you weren't home. She left a note on the door. Did you get it?"

"No, I didn't. Oh, good grief—we haven't been at the apartment! We were staying at his new place, near downtown." She shook her head, wondering why the fates were conspiring against her. "Forget that now—it's not important. Did anyone get a name or number, so I know who to call back?"

Maggie, being Maggie, had indeed gotten all the important information, and Kit recognized the private office number for John Peterson Sloan, the senior partner at McCafferty and Sloan. If he was handling this personally, it could only mean trouble with a capital *T*.

Kit swallowed and thanked her sister before making a beeline for the kitchen and a phone. Pausing for a second with the receiver in her hand, she tried to figure out what she was going to say.

As it turned out, she didn't have a chance anyway. From the second he found out who was on the other end, Sloan did enough talking for both of them. Or perhaps, Kit mused, as she held the receiver away from her ear, what he did could be better characterized as enough screaming for both of them.

Sloan was upset. Pepe Swanson was upset. Pepe paid them big bucks for advertising so that Kit would personally handle his account. Now Pepe's stock was plummeting, people were picketing the Popcorn Palace headquarters, and Pepe hadn't a clue how to proceed. Should he yank his commercials off the air, do new ones, talk to the press, maintain media silence or what? Sloan himself had attempted to formulate plans for Pepe, but the Popcorn King didn't trust anyone but Kit to tell him what to do.

Kit realized right away that this was not the time to initiate the subject of her possible resignation from McCafferty and Sloan.

Sloan thundered that Kit had been gone for over three weeks, and when the hell was she going to get her tail back to New York and get the ball rolling on the campaign to counter Pepe's bad publicity?

As he railed, she thought of Riley and the picnic he had set for this afternoon, of the furniture arriving next week, of the surprise proposal he was supposedly planning. Damn, damn, damn. She was going to have to turn her back on him for who knows how long, and Riley wasn't going to like it a bit. She told herself he would have to understand. She owed Pepe that much, and she couldn't begin a new life in St. Paul, knowing she hadn't done her best for the job she was leaving behind. That job had been too important for too long, and she couldn't just dismiss it. Even now the wheels were turning on schemes for Pepe's Popcorn. Some of her old enthusiasm for her profession arose, and a distracted smile played around her lips.

Riley arrived at the Wentworth house shortly after she did, clutching her note and looking as if the devil himself had been whipping him along.

"What is it?" he demanded. "Are you okay?"

She sighed. "I'm fine. Unfortunately Pepe Swanson isn't." She showed him the newspaper article.

After quickly perusing the story, he met her eyes. "Thank God that's all it is. I didn't know what was going on."

"All it is?" she asked, raising an eyebrow. "This is a very serious matter."

"Of course it is, but you've called New York and taken care of it, right? So now we can take our picnic as planned."

"Of course not!" She slapped the folded newspaper on the table and began to pace. "I can't go on any picnic at a time like this." Gears shifted into place as she ticked off what she needed to do. "Let's see, I'll have to get back to your home long enough to pack and then see about the first flight to New York. Can you call a travel agent while I pack the things I left here?"

"Travel agents and flights to New York?" He was aghast. Surely a minor problem with an account she was ready to write off when she left McCafferty and Sloan didn't command that sort of attention. "You are kidding, right?"

"Kidding?" She wheeled and caught his amazed expression. "This is no joke, Riley. I'm needed there."

Coming over to him, she softened a little, putting her arms around him gently as she tried to explain. "I'm sorry about the picnic and things. And I'm sorry about Christmas in July. But I have to take care of this personally."

"You're sorry about Christmas in July?" he echoed, not believing his own ears. "You mean to tell me that you're going to be gone that long and that you're going to miss your family's most important celebration?"

She swallowed. "Well, yes. At least I'm not sure yet. I'll have to stay as long as it takes, and I can't guarantee how long that might be."

He tried to damp down the fury and frustration he could feel rising inside him. It wasn't just that he didn't want her to go; it was how easily she abandoned him when New York beckoned. It didn't help matters that a certain glass pig was burning a hole in his jacket pocket. Talk about rotten timing. He had tied a ring to the pig's nose with a piece of gold cord, and he was going to sneak it into the tub of fried chicken. The picnic was more important to him than Kit knew, because it was to have been the site of his formal proposal. Was. Definitely past tense.

Drawing his lips into a grim, narrow line, he asked, "So that's it? You're all set to light out without even talking to me about it?"

Her mouth dropped in surprise. "But this has nothing to do with you."

"Right. You leave me high and dry with my plans for the future, and it has nothing to do with me." He jammed his hands into his pockets, feeling the cool, hard surface of the piggy bank with his left hand. His frown became more pronounced.

"I'll come back as soon as I can," she protested.

"Sure you will. If Pepe Swanson doesn't develop any other problems, and if none of your other accounts need your expert assistance."

She knew his feelings were hurt, but this was ridiculous. Her own temper was threatening to ignite, and that wouldn't do them any good. "You'll have to trust me to handle things as I see best and to come back here as soon as it's feasible."

"Fine," he said angrily. "You do that. And you can call your own damn travel agent."

He despised this feeling of utter helplessness and lack of control over her and over himself. He wanted her to drop everything and behave the way he thought was right, and he knew that was as stupid and wrongheaded as anything Kit had ever done.

His hand closed around the pig in his pocket, and he fingered the ring in its nose as if he were prodding a sore tooth. "I need some air," he muttered. "You have keys, so you can get your things at the house. Can one of your sisters drive you to the airport?"

"I suppose so," she said softly, coolly. Her eyes were large and unhappy. "If you don't want to take me."

"I don't want to take you." Actually he couldn't face taking her, or seeing her walk off onto a plane. Because no matter what she said about coming back, he had lost every trace of confidence that she would.

He knew he was being a fool, that she was more likely to come back if he was calm and supportive. But damn it all to hell, how could he do that? How could he calmly watch her walk out of his life, when it was as if his greatest fear had come true? He was scared, so damned scared, that she was using this as an excuse to rethink her decision and commitments and to wrap herself up in the old commitments, the ones that didn't involve him.

It seemed only too possible that she wanted to resume her life in New York where she had been in control. Just looking at the sparkle in her eyes and the energy in her step since she'd talked to her office told him that much. It was obvious how exciting she found this Pepe Swanson thing.

"I wish you wouldn't go," he tried as a last-ditch effort, but she put up a hand to forestall him.

"My mind is made up. I have to go."

Nodding, he turned on his heel to leave, then sighed when he felt the pig settle into the palm of his hand. "I guess I'll see you . . . whenever," he said flatly.

She bit her lip, trying not to be impatient with his obvious disapproval of her decision. "Be good," she offered without enthusiasm.

"Yeah." He laughed harshly, shaking his head.

And then he left.

Kit pretended not to notice his attitude as she let herself get caught up in solving Pepe's dilemma. She decided swiftly that she would deal with Riley later. He might be miffed now, but there was nothing she could do about it.

Across town, Riley screeched to a stop in the driveway of his ugly brown house near the university campus. Inside the apartment, he surveyed the dusty, unsightly furnishings, and he was filled with anger at his own insecurities and at Kit for not understanding. Hell, she didn't have telepathy. What did he expect?

What he expected was for her to realize that she had left him behind once, and it made him feel as if he was dying inside. How could he face that again?

Frustration, rage, resentment and a host of other unfamiliar emotions swelled within him, choking him and making small spots of light dance on the periphery of his vision.

The uncontrollable desire to destroy something flared inside him. He withdrew his hand from his pocket and looked down at the piggy bank desperately clutched there. And then, as hard as he could, with every ounce of fury within him flowing through his arm, he threw it against the blank, unaffected wall opposite him.

The pig smashed into a million pieces, with the awful noise of shattering glass and scattering pennies reverberating in his small living room. Amid that mass of sounds he picked out the mocking sound of one small ring, rolling and bouncing across the wood floor to rest a few inches from his left foot.

Chapter Twelve

"I never thought I'd see the day that Riley wouldn't be welcome in this house," Jo said passionately, her hands planted on her slim hips. She glared at her sisters, arrayed prettily on the front porch, all three enjoying the sultry breeze of a July morning before the household was caught in the deluge of Christmas guests. Jo fixed them with what she hoped was a guilt-inducing stare. "It's terrible to treat Riley this way. Why, he's been like a brother to us for the past four years!"

"Brother?" Alex scoffed, sweeping titian waves over one shoulder as she perched herself grandly on the porch railing. "He hasn't acted like anything remotely human since Kit left, and you know it."

"Okay, so he yelled at Mother. Okay, so he yelled at all of us. He's been upset." Jo crossed her arms over her chest and paced back and forth outside the front door, creaking the worn boards of the porch.

"Yelled at?" Maggie asked dryly. "He practically took our heads off, all because we asked him if Kit would be back in time for Christmas in July. How were we supposed to know he was as much up in the air as anyone?"

"It's understandable that he's upset," Jo maintained. "He told me that he's been calling Kit like crazy all week, and he's gotten to talk to her a total of about thirty seconds. If she's not in a meeting, she's practically a zombie from lack of sleep." She sighed. "Poor man. He's just sure she's so caught up in the agency again that she'll never come back. We should be compassionate, not barring the door."

"Oh, fiddle-faddle," Eliza tossed in. "He was cranky and uncooperative and unlivable, and Mother didn't have any choice but to boot him out for the duration. She told him he could come back as soon as he could behave himself. I think that's fair." She reclined in the swing that took up one end of the porch, swinging occasionally and looking as if she hadn't a care in the world.

Alex said lazily, "Maybe Riley will shape up in the Christmas spirit and act like his old self today. It's only the growling beast routine that Mother objected to."

Edging Eliza's legs aside, Maggie made room for herself in a corner of the porch swing. She rested her chin in her hands and gazed thoughtfully at Jo. "Don't worry, Jo. As soon as Kit's back, Riley will be okay. If there's any way in the world, she'll be here in time for Christmas in July. I trust Kit to do what's right. I know she'll be here today."

"I wish I had your faith," Jo said miserably, causing the three other redheads to turn and stare immediately. The day Jo lost faith was indeed a day to prepare for disaster. Jo pressed her hands together and shook her head. "She's just got to make it. For Riley's sake."

"But Jo," Eliza stated reasonably, "I don't see what you're so perturbed about. Even if she doesn't come today, she'll be back soon. And then Riley will be so happy to see her, he'll forget he was ever angry, swoop her up in his arms and kiss her just madly. Can't you just see it? And then we can plan the wedding, with simply gorgeous dresses and absolute heaps of flowers... And, of course, they'll live happily ever after..." She sighed and gave Maggie, who had the misfortune of sitting next to her on the porch swing, a contented hug. "It will work out so wonderfully, that we'll all just expire of happiness."

"You don't understand." Jo's face descended one step farther into total misery. "I meddled."

Alex leaned forward on her railing and hooted with delight. "It's about time, I say. Come on, Josie, spill it. What grand scheme did you pull, and why didn't you include the rest of us?"

Jo sighed loudly and put her hands up to her face. "I was truly rotten, you guys, truly rotten. But Riley was so upset, and I wanted to cheer him up. He's been so unhappy."

"It's his own fault," Eliza contended with a pout. Since she'd given up her crush on Riley, she didn't feel she had to be particularly charitable where he was concerned. "Kit shouldn't have to explain every little action. He should trust her. That's what love means."

Maggie laughed. "I thought it meant never having to say you're sorry."

Ignoring Maggie, Jo addressed the issue Eliza had raised. "It isn't every little action. It's being gone for a whole week at a critical time. Even if he should trust her in theory, you know how he feels about this. He thinks she took the excuse to run away rather than face a relationship with him. It's as if his worst fear has come true. And for all we know he's right."

"Stop being so gloomy, Jo," Maggie protested. "It isn't like you to look on the negative side."

Alex sighed deeply, indicating that she was bored with the conversation. "Who cares about that stuff? Jo still hasn't said what she did that she considers such awful meddling. Spare me the analysis, and let's get to the good part. What did you do, Jo?"

"I lied to Riley," Jo said in a small voice. "I told him that Kit had called us and asked us to make sure that he was here today for the Christmas in July celebration." Jo's voice dropped even lower. "He didn't want to come, because he said he's sure she's never coming back, but I talked him into giving her one last chance. I actually saw the hope leap back into his eyes. Oh, heavens, what have I done? If he comes, and she doesn't show, he'll never forgive her. And it's all my fault." She regarded her sisters plaintively. "What have I done?"

Eliza's eyes danced. "Isn't it romantic?"

"Is that all?" Alex demanded. "That's it? Good grief, Jo, I expected real Machiavelli here, not Rebecca of Sunnybrook Farm."

Jo responded quickly. "But it was a lie! Alex, I don't believe in lies!"

"You were only trying to help," Maggie said soothingly. "Besides, Kit will make it. I know she will. She won't let Riley down." She paused. "And if it helps any, Jo, I meddled, too."

"Oh, no!" Jo groaned. "What did you do?"

Maggie bit her fingernail. "I sent Kit a telegram and told her she had better get herself home today or forget the whole thing."

"There, you see?" Alex waved her arm grandly. "Now she knows he's expecting her, and he knows she's coming. It all worked out perfectly."

"Good grief! Kit never does things when people tell her she has to! Now she'll never come. This is what happens when a person meddles," Jo moaned. "Maggie, we've messed up everything."

With complete conviction, Eliza sat up straight and tall on the porch swing. "Really, Jo, you know how it's always been between the two of them. When people love each other like that, things always work out somehow. Kit will be here, Riley will gather her up in his arms and smother her with kisses, and that will be that. I can't imagine what you're worried about."

After one last shake of her head, Jo faced away from all of them. Holding on to the big white wooden post that flanked the front stairs, she cast her eyes out over the lawn, past the trees and even past the lake shimmering in the center of the park, as if gazing into the distance for signs of their wayward sister. When she spoke, her voice was only a murmur.

"Kit will make it in time. She just has to."

KIT'S FLIGHT WAS VERY LATE.

Damn, but she wished her watch had numbers. She had reset it to Minnesota time the moment she'd fastened her seat belt, and she had been watching the second hand tick around for hours, but she still felt unsure of the time. It was so late already, past three in the afternoon, or so she thought. What if she'd put it back two or three hours instead of only one, and it was already five or six in the evening? She might have already missed Christmas in July completely!

All the presents would have been opened, all the wrapping paper neatly stowed away till next year, and she would come dragging in the front door to be greeted by bored glances and a chorus of "So what?" from her entire family.

She reminded herself that it didn't matter what hour of the day it was. She couldn't force the plane to land, or get there any sooner anyway. Whatever time it was, she would be there when she got there, and that was the best she could do.

Sighing with frustration, she leaned her forehead against the small oval of the airplane window and spied the IDS Tower in downtown Minneapolis as she passed over it once again in the plane's eternal loop. Why did it seem that airports chose only the most important times to screw things up this way and not have gates when gates were needed?

And why did it seem as though life itself were determined to put her into the midst of such badly timed situations? If only Pepe's Popcorn campaign could have been initiated a little more quickly. But, good grief, getting all of that together in one short week had been hell on wheels as it was. She had eaten, drunk and slept Pepe's Popcorn, but now she would rather die than mention the stuff by name. Shuddering at the thought of the incredibly perky, incredibly trustworthy ads that would soon be filling the airwaves, she tried to think of something else.

Riley. Even though he didn't know it, and she hadn't had a spare moment to tell him, he had been her constant companion for the past six days. He had been there in the back of her mind, nagging at her, irritating her and downright tantalizing her throughout the steamy, nasty sessions with Sloan and Pepe and the PR people as they'd brainstormed and hollered their way through every possible choice for the publicity and advertising response to Pepe's disaster. In the wee hours of morning, drinking endless cups of coffee and racking her brain for ideas, she would suddenly think of Riley and lilacs and get all misty, or the image of a wallpaper strait jacket would pop into her brain and she'd giggle out loud.

Pepe was picky, and they'd been through reams of potentially wonderful ads before he'd finally decided he was satisfied. In the chosen version, Pepe himself would take center stage in the commercials. He wouldn't speak directly about the theft accusation. Instead, he would stress his humble beginnings, mention how folksy and down-home he and his popcorn were and act all-around trustworthy and lovable. He would stand behind a mountain of popcorn, reflecting every color of the rainbow, to show the good folks at home that Pepe had more than one flavor of popcorn and that he literally and figuratively stood behind every single flavor. They had choreographed it down to the last little tremble of sincerity in his voice, and Pepe's performance hadn't let them down. If they didn't have middle America eating popcorn out of Pepe's hand, Kit had volunteered to cheerfully eat the four-gallon "Happy Pack" of Tutti-Frutti Tahitian Popcorn all by herself.

After the marathon effort of creating something decent and then convincing Pepe, Kit had been exhausted. But she'd still had to snatch a few moments with her boss alone to turn in her resignation. If she'd thought the decibel level was high in the meetings with Pepe's people, she'd had to rethink that after she'd gotten through with Sloan. Finally he'd run out of bluster and had actually told her they would miss her at McCafferty and Sloan.

With the Pepe disaster safely behind her, Kit had become very sure she wouldn't miss McCafferty and Sloan. The place was a nightmare! She planned to conduct her own agency with a bit more decorum and a lot more style.

And so here she was ready to give Riley the biggest hug he'd ever felt and then sleep—preferably with him—for a week or two. Her nerves were frazzled beyond repair, and she just wanted to get this damn plane on the ground and get home before she exploded.

It was getting to the point where she might shove her way into the cabin and try to land the plane herself. She hated to be a pain, but she asked the stewardess one more time how long it would be before they were on the ground.

"Five minutes," she grumbled, echoing the flight attendant's polite response. "They've been saying five minutes for the past half hour."

It was another half hour before they finally jolted to a stop, and she hustled into the aisle with her carry-on baggage before the seat belt sign had even faded. It seemed an eternity before she could get around the slow people in the rows ahead of her and actually get out to the concourse. Then it was more interminable minutes down at the luggage carousel, until they posted a sign saying the baggage from her flight would be late because of a technical snafu with the carousel.

"Too bad," she muttered, hefting her shopping bag of presents in one hand while she tried to balance her tote bag and hang on to a large, unwieldy package at the same time.

If she had to exist for a week in the red T-shirt and bright green jeans with suspenders she'd worn in honor of Christmas in July, so be it. *This girl,* she said to herself, *is getting out of here, luggage or no.*

A taxi was remarkably easy to locate, given her luck thus far, but Kit could barely restrain herself from telling the man to speed recklessly. It was only a twenty-minute drive from the airport to her mother's house, but it seemed like eons as each second dragged after the last on her silly plastic watch.

Then finally, blessedly, she was there, and she burst from the cab with her packages, tossing an extravagant amount of money at the cabbie as she dashed away. "Sorry," she said, laughing and struggling to hold on to her various bundles, "but I'm awfully late. Merry Christmas!"

"Merry Christmas?" the man asked. He shook his head as he got back in his taxi and slammed the door. "Takes all kinds, I guess."

Kit barely heard him muttering behind her as she raced to the door. She breathed in deeply, inhaling the fragrant smell of evergreen from the huge wreath on the front door. Taking in a bit too much of the strong scent, she coughed. But mere choking couldn't dissuade her, and she leaned over to hit the doorbell with her elbow.

She remembered wondering what lay inside the door a few short weeks ago as she faced mending her fences and reweaving ties with her family. Funny, now that she was in front of the door once more, she wasn't frightened of her family in the least, and she felt very sure of handling them. But her heart was beating an erratic and painful rhythm over the idea of facing Riley. How odd. She was secure that he loved her, and that she loved him. But she hadn't had time to speak to him properly in a week, and she couldn't gauge whether he was still angry with her or not. In any mood, her hurried "I haven't eaten, I haven't slept, and can I talk to you later because I have to get back to the office ASAP?" was probably not what he wanted to hear. She hoped he would understand that she had needed to concentrate totally on Pepe to have any chance of getting back in time. She hadn't been sure until three o'clock this morning that she was actually going to make it. How reassuring could she have been?

What if he hadn't come to Christmas in July? What if he'd stayed away because he'd thought she wouldn't be here? All of a sudden her surprise seemed like a ridiculous and infantile idea. Why hadn't she called first?

Her breath was short in coming, and she felt very hot under the weight of all these packages and all these worries. Why didn't someone answer the door? If she didn't find out very soon whether Riley was in there or not, she was going to lose control completely and go stark raving bonkers.

"Open this door!" she shouted.

And, as if by magic, the door cracked open. "Hello," a tiny voice said. "Who are you?"

"I'm Kit." She kept a smile plastered to her face so that she wouldn't alarm the small child standing guard at the door. "I used to live here. I have lots of packages, and I'd like to come in and put them down. May I come in, please?"

"Okay," the child answered placidly.

The door swung open an inch at a time, revealing a crowd of people and a din of voices and music. Everywhere Kit looked there were evergreen wreaths and garlands decorated with red plaid bows, and enough red and green candles to create a fire hazard. The sound of "Silent Night" wafted into the hallway from the living room, and Kit could hear genial chatter and the clinking of glasses.

"Hi," the child said again. Kit could see now that she was very small, maybe five years old, and she had red pigtails tied with red-and-white-striped yarn. "I'm Terry," she said solemnly. "It was too loud and no one heard the door. But I did."

"Good for you, Terry." She paused. "Do you know a man here named Riley?"

"Maybe." She licked her lip studiously, twisting her mouth as she regarded Kit from round blue eyes. "Is he the one with the cookies?"

Kit smiled. "Yes."

Terry nodded up and down twice, briskly. "Yes, I know him." A bright little smile turned her mouth up into a funny U. "I like Riley. He made cookies, and he gave me one."

Riley giving cookies to a five-year-old with pigtails? He must be in a good mood at least. "When did you see Riley?"

The child considered. She brightened. "Today."

"Today. Good. Where is he?"

The little girl brought her shoulders up nearly to her ears and then dropped them back down again. "I dunno. He was with my brother."

"Where?"

"Making snow. Riley said you have to have snow or it isn't really Christmas."

"Lovely," Kit mumbled. "But where did you see him?"

"With my brother."

Could this child have received anti-interrogation training from the CIA? "Terry, where did you see Riley and your brother?" Kit began, but the living room erupted into an off-pitch, ear-shattering explosion of "Joy to the World," effectively blocking all conversation.

Good heavens. Was Aunt Maud still making everyone listen to her murderous version of that poor song? Kit peeked around the corner, and, yes, that was definitely Aunt Maud, deafening generations of her kin with her Christmas caroling.

As it happened, Kit's small glimpse around the corner was a bad move. Uncle Edgar, a very old and distinguished relative, looking dapper in his special red velvet Christmas vest, spied her immediately.

"Look, everyone!" he shouted above Aunt Maud's roar as she hit the chorus. "It's our little Kitty!" He scampered to Kit's side, as did another three or four aunts and cousins.

Before she knew it, she was surrounded by a crowd of eager relatives, all pinching her cheek, remarking how thin she was, squeezing into her personal space and chattering excitedly in her ear that she hadn't changed a bit.

She tried to be pleasant and mindlessly answer the barrage of questions as she scanned the room for Riley. There was no sign of him. Meanwhile, her arms were breaking under the weight of her burdens, and her eardrums were splitting under the weight of Aunt Maud's soprano.

"Nice to see you," she shouted, struggling to get away before she was stampeded. "We'll talk more later."

"What's that about chocolate eclairs?" Uncle Edgar shouted back, cupping his ear.

"I can't hear you, Uncle Edgar! We'll have to talk later!"

"Merry Christmas to you, too, Kitty." Edgar smiled broadly and enveloped her in a hug that squeezed the stuffing out of her.

"You're strong for your age," Kit muttered.

"What's that about a rage? The newest thing, eh?"

She managed to say, "Never mind," loudly and politely, and, smiling weakly, pushed away from Edgar and his crowd.

"Have you seen Riley Cooper?" she asked a few times, trying to smile and say hello as she maneuvered in between lumps of people and made her way to the stairs. Those who had seen him had no idea where he was, and most hadn't seen him. But everyone was anxious to see Kit and to say that they were most pleased that she was back in the family bosom.

"Fine, fine," she murmured, shaking hands, accepting pats on the head with good grace, keeping her smile in place. But where was Riley? Catching sight of Alex's lush red waves at the top of the stairs, Kit tried to get her oldest sister's attention above the confusion. "Alex!" she yelled. "I'm looking for Riley."

"You're here!" Alex mouthed back. "Glad you made it! Have you seen Riley yet?"

"No! Is he here?"

"You'd better find Riley! He may leave!"

"Where is he?" Kit shouted, but Alex only held up her hands helplessly.

By the time Kit pushed through the crowd on the stairs to where Alex had been, the eldest Wentworth sister was gone.

Frustrated, Kit looked out over the railing into the crowd below. There was plenty of joy to go around, even if Aunt Maud was still mangling the song. People were laughing and shouting, toasting one another with eggnog in mugs shaped like Santa Claus's head. Children dressed in red and green were racing in and out and around their elders, leaving half-eaten candy canes stuck to every conceivable surface and playing house with the figures from the nativity scene on the table at the bottom of the stairs. The odors of gingerbread and evergreen filled the air, mingling with the scent of turkey and mincemeat pie. It was like a Norman Rockwell painting with scratch-and-sniff. Kit felt like drooping in comparison. She hadn't eaten in heaven knows how long, she had lost the big shopping bag of presents somewhere on the way up the stairs, and she was feeling very bedraggled even behind her red suspenders with the little embroidered holly decorations on them.

Ah, well, at least her tote bag was firmly in place over her arm. More importantly, she was still clutching her precious brown-wrapped package to her chest. It would have taken an atom bomb to have dislodged Riley's flat, oversized Christmas present from her possession.

Of course, if she couldn't find Riley, it wouldn't matter in the slightest if she held on to the damned thing till doomsday. *Where could he be?* she wondered for the twentieth time. With renewed purpose, she left behind the sweet sights and smells of her resting place at the top of the stairs and pushed on in her search for Riley.

It was easy work to cover most of the first and second floors; she got pushed through the various rooms against her will by the undulating mass of relatives. After that bruising expedition, she realized that only the third floor was left, but what in the world would Riley be doing up there? And why hadn't he sought her out when the crowd had taken up the news that she'd arrived?

She was becoming more and more concerned that he wasn't there at all, and her pulse was pounding in her temples. Was it a result of nervousness, or just a headache from Aunt Maud's singing combined with the confusion and high spirits booming throughout the house?

As she cleared the back stairs to the third floor, the din muffled to a dull roar. Even if she didn't find Riley, she decided she would hide out up here for a while to get accustomed to the overwhelming mass of sounds and sights and smells.

It took a moment or two to filter out the high-pitched chatter from below and to clear her head. When she did, she heard a sound that didn't belong. There was a rush of water and a low, husky voice. Laughing. Her heart leaped in her breast. That was Riley's laugh. She would have recognized it anywhere. Not only that, but he was close.

But where? She raced through the rooms, opening one door after the other. Not the bedroom, not the linen closet, not the junk room with its innocent pile of cardboard boxes. That left only the...bathroom.

"Riley?" she shouted, and pounded on the door. "Are you in there?"

The door to the bathroom swung open neatly, and she looked up into familiar blue eyes.

"Finally," she said breathlessly. "I've been looking all over for you."

He grabbed her and pulled her into his arms quickly before he had a chance to think about it. Holding her, he could forget what an ass he'd been making of himself since she'd left. He tightened his hold.

"Riley," she said softly, "I can't breathe."

"Oh. Sorry." He dropped his arms and backed off a step, drinking in the sight of her. Raising a hand to her cheek, he brushed it gently. "You're a sight for sore eyes."

"You, too," she murmured, covering his hand with hers.

"Riley," a small voice piped up from the tub, "is it snow yet?"

As Riley moved slightly to the side, Kit saw the small red-haired boy standing in the bathtub. He was knee-deep in the ice cubes and brandishing a cardboard container of salt.

"Snow?" she asked. "You must be Terry's brother."

"Yep." He nodded happily. "I'm Patrick."

"I'm happy to meet you, Patrick. I'm Kit. Do you think you could leave your snow for just a second? I need to talk to Riley."

"Riley? Would that be all right? It won't melt while I'm gone, will it?"

"I don't think so, Patrick. I think it needs a few more minutes before it makes snow, anyway." He put a hand to the boy's head and casually ruffled his hair. "You go ahead now, and we'll check it in a little while."

After the child cleared the door, they were alone. It was what she'd been waiting for, but suddenly she didn't know what to say. "Whose is he, anyway?" was the first thing she thought of.

"He belongs to your cousin."

"Oh." She couldn't even remember which cousins were married. She had a lot of catching up to do. And Riley wasn't making this easy. She had expected everything to fall into place because she was back. But she was too tired and too emotionally drained to even begin to sort out where they were now and where they needed to be. *Start with something casual,* she told herself. "How have you been?" she asked quickly.

He shrugged, returning rapidly, "Okay, I guess. And you?"

"Tired," she admitted. "It was a long haul."

"How did the Pepe's Popcorn thing turn out?"

"Fine."

"Good." He shuffled his feet and rooted in his pocket, pulling out a cigarette.

"Have you started that again?" she asked.

"Not really."

"Good."

He rolled the cigarette between his fingers before throwing it into the wastebasket. "You said you'd been looking for me?" he asked nervously.

"Oh, that's right." Awkwardly she held out the brown-wrapped package. "It's your Christmas present."

"Thanks." It was his turn to be awkward as he undid the tape and peeled off the brown paper. "What the heck is it?" he asked with a laugh.

"You have it upside down," she offered politely, and spun it around in his hands.

"Oh." He surveyed the strange board, which looked lik
a big comic strip. He was having trouble focusing on i
and he couldn't figure out what was going on here. All da
long he'd been biding his time, waiting for Kit, because J
had said she'd be here. But the hours had slipped by, an
Kit hadn't shown up. Every time Kit's sisters had seen hin
they'd cast pitying looks at him and begged him to stay ju
a few more minutes. He had planned from the beginnin
that he would tough it out till five and then give up on Ki
making himself accept once and for all that they woul
never be together.

Well, it was almost five, and he hadn't made any mov
to leave. He might have logically decided he was going t
give up, but his subconscious had no intention of playin
along. His pride was shot to kingdom come, but he woul
have hung on at the Wentworth house till the last guest wa
gone.

But that wouldn't be necessary. Out of nowhere, whe
he'd least expected it, Kit had come pounding on th
bathroom door, hysterically asking if he was in there. I
wasn't exactly the way he'd envisioned their reunion, bu
he wasn't going to be picky at the present moment.

Now, whatever the surroundings, she was here. Her gra
eyes, tilted up at the outside edges, were soft and gentle a
they focused on his face. Her face was a mix of cream
white and pale pink, and it looked as if it would be cool t
touch. If he touched her. God, how he wanted to touc
her. He was supposed to be furious with her, for leavin
without discussing it first, for wrecking his romantic pro
posal scene, but he was so glad she was back he couldn'
stand still. Joy and nerves were leaping inside him in equa
doses, making him incapable of rational thought. And hi
hands were shaking as he tried to examine this ridiculou
piece of cardboard that was supposed to be his present.

"What is it?" he repeated.

She bounced on the balls of her feet, seething with impatience. "It's a storyboard. Will you stop turning it round and read it, please?"

Read it? Okay, he would try. He concentrated. The first block showed a stick figure, notable only for long strings of yellow attached to its head and a wide smile drawn on its face. "You?" he asked, incredulous.

"Of course!"

Under the picture, it said CHEERFUL in large block letters. The next block was labeled THRIFTY and pictured a lumpish piggy bank, stuffed with coins and bills. That was followed by CLEAN showing the blond stick figure's head above an oval thing with lots of tiny circles in it that he supposed could be construed to be a bubble bath once you knew the theme was CLEAN. The stick figure was either taking a bath or was immersed in a can of peas. After CLEAN came BRAVE, where the two-dimensional blond held off a funny-looking lion with a pointed spear.

"Brave?" he choked, trying not to laugh.

"I was only trying to elucidate my features and benefits in a clear and easily understandable fashion."

He glanced from Kit to the storyboard and back again. "I hope you use a better artist when you have your own agency."

"Well?" she prompted. "What do you say?"

He raised an eyebrow, one of those maddening darker eyebrows that gave him such a rakish look. "I don't understand. What do I say about what?"

"Didn't you read the end yet?"

He shook his head, unable to take his eyes off the real Kit. It still hadn't sunk in yet that she was back and was

expecting some reaction from him other than his presen
daze.

"Read it, you turkey!" she steamed.

And so he did as he was told. After the list of Kit
wonderful qualities, from cheerful to thrifty, clean, brav
and kind, he saw a larger block, without a picture at al
There were only words.

It said MARRY THIS WOMAN!

"Well?" she demanded again.

"Do you mean it?"

"Of course I mean it! I went to all this trouble to dra
it, didn't I?" She thought she'd been so clever, putting he
dreams into a storyboard, as if she were selling herself th
way she'd sell a product. She'd thought Riley would laug
and say yes immediately. But he was asking if she meant i
as if he were the densest person in three states. Why didn
he touch her, or hold her, or kiss her? They were on
inches apart, yet it felt like miles. "If you don't answer n
now, I'm going back to New York. I'm an emotiona
wreck, and I can't take much more of this."

"You know what my answer will be."

She took a deep breath. "Do I?"

"Oh, Lord," he whispered. "Of course you do.
Watching her, holding her soft, luminous gaze, he wante
her more than he'd ever wanted anything in his life. H
couldn't keep it back, even if it meant making love to he
in the third-floor bathroom during Christmas in Jul
Would anyone know? "How could I ever answer any
thing but yes?" he asked, mystified.

"I don't know," she answered truthfully.

Holding open his arms, he gathered her close and hel
her, pressing his cheek next to her hair. It was back in th
braid again, and he'd have to do something about tha
"But I'm never letting you get away from me again."

"What?" She laughed, but it was stifled against his chest. "I'm perfectly capable of taking trips by myself, of conducting business by myself, and returning like a homing pigeon every time. I want to be here. You don't ever have to worry that you'll lose me." She pulled back in his embrace, to gaze into his eyes. "You have to trust me, Riley."

"I know." He held her away from him slightly. "You are sure, aren't you? This is where you want to be?"

"In the third-floor bathroom? I can think of better places."

"No, of course I don't mean in the third-floor bathroom," he retorted indignantly. "I mean here in St. Paul, with me."

"I'm here, aren't I?"

"Yeah, but only under duress. I know about Maggie's telegram."

"Maggie's telegram had nothing to do with it. I didn't even get it till after I'd already made up mind anyway." She smiled. "What is all this, anyway? Did you really think I wouldn't come back?"

"Well, maybe." He paused, considered. "Yes, I did. I was scared to death you'd decide New York was more exciting and there was no one there to push you around." He ran a hand through his hair. "I don't mean to push you or manipulate you, but I know you think I do."

"I think you don't know any other way," she commented softly.

"So you're sure? This is really where you want to be?"

"I'm sure."

"No more trips to New York to cater to old accounts?"

She reflected. "That's how you get new accounts, you know. If I'm needed there, I'll probably want to go." She sighed and stretched up to plant a kiss on the corner of his mouth. "But I won't do it without discussing it first with you, okay? I suppose that wasn't the smartest way of operating."

He smiled and linked his arms behind her back. "Maybe I'll come with you next time."

"Now there's an idea."

"Does this mean the wedding is back on?"

"In spades," she said with feeling. "I've officially resigned from McCafferty and Sloan, and I've moved some of my things out of my apartment in New York."

"Merry Christmas, Kit," he murmured, bending down very close to her lips.

"Merry Christmas, Riley," she whispered, tilting her head up to be kissed.

As he lowered his lips to hers, meeting them finally with a soft, warm brush of sensation, she sighed with contentment.

"Hey," she said suddenly. "I had a present for you. Don't I get anything?"

"You've already got me, glutton." He raised a thumb to stroke her cheek lightly. "But I thought I might get you a new piggy bank. What do you think?"

Eyeing him suspiciously, she asked, "What's wrong with the old one?"

He hesitated. "I, uh, broke it."

"You broke it?" She arched an eyebrow. Her voice rose significantly. "You broke my pig? Riley, how could you?"

"Well, there's something I haven't explained yet," he said cautiously.

"About the pig?"

"Kind of."

"Will this unpleasant revelation send me flying back to New York?" She was mystified. "What did you do, break it over my mother's head?"

Avoiding her eyes, he answered, "Of course not. I, uh, I had a plan the day you left."

"Riley Cooper, you're positively embarrassed. I've never seen you blush before in my entire life. What gives? And what do you mean about having a plan when I left?"

"I was going to propose, you idiot," he said bluntly. "I tied the ring to the pig's nose."

She swallowed. "Oh." That explained a few things. Like why he was annoyed to miss the picnic and why he seemed so insecure that she had taken off without time for discussion. "You were going to propose, and I didn't let you."

"I know I reacted badly. But damn it, Kit, I had it all planned. It's not the easiest thing for a guy to do, you know, to put it all on the line and formally propose."

"Especially when the ring is tied to the nose of a pig." She tried hard to keep her lips from curving up at the corners. "And, yes, I know how tough proposals are. I made one today, remember?"

"Oh, yeah." He smiled and nipped her neck. "But you got to do yours as planned. I had to pretend mine never existed."

"So you smashed my pig."

"Yeah."

"Well, you darn well better replace it. You owe me a pig, as well as another proposal and a chance at that ring." She wrapped her arms around his waist and stared up at him. "What a rotten temper you have in there. We're going to have to work on that."

He didn't have a chance to answer because a small voice from the other side of the door asked plaintively, "Riley, is it snow yet?"

Riley peered over Kit and then leaned down to scoop up a handful of the icy mixture in the tub. "What do you know?" he asked, wonder filling his voice. "It really is snow!"

Patrick burst in through the door, his eyes round with surprise. "It is? It's snow?"

"It's snow, partner," Riley said with a grin.

"A miracle," Kit offered, tilting up to kiss him on the chin. "A Christmas miracle, of course."

Patrick skidded to the bathtub, hooting as he jumped right in and grabbed handfuls to toss in the air. From Patrick's chubby little hands, the snow arched gently into the bathroom, pitching and falling as if it had been manufactured the real way.

Flakes began to collect on the top of Kit's head, and she laughed out loud, holding her hands up to catch the snow. Riley licked a tiny sparkle of a snowflake off the tip of her nose, and he laughed, too, keeping her steady as she dipped and turned to capture their miniature snowfall.

"What in heaven's name is going on in here?" her mother's voice demanded in a tone of absolute horror.

Kit only smiled, dropping her wet, snowy head to Riley's chest.

Still firmly entangled, they turned to meet a jumble of incoming Wentworths.

"Congratulations, my dear children!" her mother intoned with a vibration of sentiment in her voice.

"Congratulations!" her sisters echoed, crowding around to hug them as they stood in the bathroom.

Around her, Kit heard Eliza cry, "Isn't it wonderful?" as Jo added, "She made it! Thank goodness!" but Kit ignored them all.

"Merry Christmas, Riley," she whispered again, and then she kissed him in front of her mother and her sisters and everyone as the special, magical Christmas in July snow danced in the air around them.

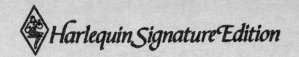

Harlequin Signature Edition

Carole Mortimer

Merlyn's Magic

She came to him from out of the storm and was drawn into his yearning arms—the tempestuous night held a magic all its own.

You've enjoyed Carole Mortimer's Harlequin Presents stories, and her previous bestseller, *Gypsy*.

Now, don't miss her latest, most exciting bestseller, *Merlyn's Magic*!

IN JULY

MERMG

Keeping the Faith

by
Judith Arnold

It renewed old friendships, kindled new relationships, but the fifteen-year reunion of *The Dream*'s college staff affected all six of the Columbia-Barnard graduates: Laura, Seth, Kimberly, Andrew, Julianne and Troy.

Follow the continuing story of these courageous, vital men and women who find themselves at a crossroads—as their idealism of the sixties clashes with the reality of life in the eighties.

You may laugh, you may cry, but you will find a piece of yourself in *Keeping the Faith*.

Don't miss American Romance #201 *Promises* in June, #205 *Commitments* in July and #209 *Dreams* in August.

KFaith-gen

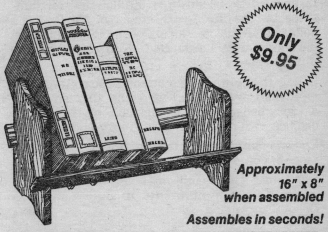